Fresh Air

CHARLOTTE VALE ALLEN

Fresh Air

MIRA®

MIRA

ISBN 1-55166-682-0

FRESH AIR

Visit us at www.mirabooks.com

Printed in U.S.A.

First Printing: April 2003
10 9 8 7 6 5 4 3 2 1

This book is for my "Texas Twin,"
Sandra Whitt.

1996

Chapter One

Lucinda didn't bother anyone, kept to herself as much as possible. It wasn't so much about privacy as it was about the effort required to speak. She felt as if she'd said everything she had to say at least a thousand times. There was nothing more to add. And, inevitably, talking—to anyone, about anything—either required elaboration on what had been said, or got you into trouble. She preferred to keep her thoughts to herself; it was safer that way.

Luckily, she had skills that allowed her to have something to do without ever having to leave her house; she rarely even had to talk to anyone in conjunction with the jobs she did. That was one of the beautiful aspects of the Internet. You could work in blissful solitude, responding to queries by e-mail or fax, and bill at an hourly wage that was well above that of most of the husbands of the yuppy-mummies whose newly built houses kept creeping ever closer to her secluded, intentionally overgrown piece of property. It wasn't that she needed the money, but she had to do some sort of work to keep herself sane.

She'd been inundated with offers for the land for the past decade; they'd started as sporadic feelers and had gradually grown to regular, insistent telephone calls. The instant she saw "anonymous" or the name of some now-familiar real estate agency on the Caller ID, she let the Auto Hang-Up field the call. She particularly enjoyed its message: "I'm sorry, we do not accept telemarketing calls. Please regard this message as your notification to remove this number from your list. Thank you." She did pity many of the people who worked these thankless, low-paying jobs; but a lot of them were con-artists who scammed people, particularly the elderly, out of millions of dollars every year. Besides, the calls were ceaseless and annoying. If you happened to pick up the receiver, you'd be saying, "Hello, hello," into dead space sometimes for as long as ten or fifteen seconds before the person on the other end realized that the auto-dialer had caught a live one. So Auto Hang-Up was her pal, keeping telephonic nuisances away from her. If it was a real estate agent, she said, "Sorry, not interested," and hung up.

She didn't want to sell her house or any part of her land; she didn't want something for nothing (she knew better and, anyway, she didn't have a greedy bone in her body); she had no interest in changing her Internet service provider, or her long-distance provider, or extending the credit line on any of her plastic cards. She knew categorically that she hadn't won a free trip, or a free anything. Those excited voices, prepped to make their pitch, merely made her tired. There wasn't a single service or convenience that she wanted that she didn't already have. So, unless it was work-related (and very occasionally, it was) there was no reason for her to answer the phone.

She had, some time ago, lost her skill in the art of conversation; lost the easy give-and-take rhythm she'd once had, and the ready humor that had been an integral part of her everyday interactions. With time and enough neglect, most of her friends gave up and quit calling. One or two had hung in, but she rarely took their calls. Along with the loss of her conversational skills, she'd mislaid her comprehension of friendship. Intellectually, she understood the reason for it, the need. But it had become like a dance she'd once known and had been able to perform automatically, effortlessly. Now she was awkward, uncertain in her movements; could no longer recall the steps or their sequence. And so, at her choosing, she lived in not unpleasant isolation. She wasn't out of touch, though, because everything she might conceivably need to know, or want, was available to her through the Web. Anything could be purchased online, from drugstore items to specialty foods, to books and music, and tools of every conceivable kind. There wasn't a thing she needed that she couldn't acquire in under half an hour on the Internet.

The arrival of a UPS or FedEx driver in the morning, and the mailman each afternoon were the focal points of her day. There was a small pleasure in opening packages to examine her purchases: computer accessories or software updaters, office supplies, bath products, even clothes. Diligently, she flattened the packaging and each week, tied with twine, she set the sizable bundle of cardboard out with the blue box of recyclables—the brown paper bags of newspaper and magazines, of hard copy, of junk mail.

She had routines and took something close to comfort in maintaining them. There were nights when she worked until two or three in the morning, then slept until nine-thirty, awakening with a guilty start. There was no one to know or care that she'd overslept, but guilt was a lifelong habit, unbreakable. Still, she liked the early-morning hours when CDs played quietly through the computer's speakers (oldies from the forties, fifties and sixties; tunes that each had a significance she didn't dare examine too closely) and she worked until her concentration began to flag. Then she'd close her connection, let whichever song was playing come to an end and, finally, shut down the computer.

Swiveling in her chair, she'd look around the living room from the vantage point of her L-shaped desk positioned in the corner against the outside wall by the broad window, studying the pictures on the walls, the arrangement of the furniture, the way the verticals defined the size of the windows. The place bore little resemblance to the way it had looked years before, when they'd first come to live here. Her mother had had terrible taste, just terrible. She'd been living proof that becoming rich and famous couldn't overcome what you inherited from a tainted gene pool. The few decent pieces of furniture in the house had been passed along to her mother from her sister Beattie (who'd had exquisite taste). And those pieces had stood out painfully—like new rich kids coming into a classroom filled with students whose parents worked in stores or factories—shockingly out of place, yet fascinating in their own right, with their expensive clothes and flawless teeth. A gorgeous teak sofa with nubby beige fabric; a wonderfully squat, sunny-yellow ceramic lamp with a generous, spreading shade; a wide wicker tray that had at Aunt Beattie's house held an array of glossy magazines but in which her mother had placed three African violet plants that leaked dirty water through the wicker onto the top of the coffee table so that the veneer eventually lifted and split. Given the extreme ugliness of the table, it had been no hardship for Lucinda to consign it to the trash.

In the years since her mother's death, the house had become entirely Lucinda's. Almost nothing of her mother's remained, except some old framed photographs on the mantelpiece, half a dozen carefully packed cartons of highly collectible memorabilia, and eight or nine photo albums that had been started in the early forties and covered nearly thirty years of a remarkable career, and random, almost incidental, family moments.

Now and then, when stricken by something like an esoteric form of amnesia, Lucinda would get one of the cartons down from the attic and sit on the living room floor while she examined the contents: souvenir playbills from special screenings, film scripts, head shots, publicity stills, lobby cards, old contracts, even props from some of the movies. It was weird. A black cigarette holder, cracked and brittle with age, could bring back to Lucinda an entire ninety-six-minute film, complete with dialogue and wardrobe. She'd study the holder and remember the first morning of the shoot and the makeup woman chattering away as she'd painted Lily's face, oblivious to Lily's mounting irritation. Lily had not only been unable to converse at five in the morning, she also hadn't wanted to hear a single word spoken—by anyone. What she'd wanted, always, every morning, was a lot of coffee, two or three cigarettes, and silence, while her system got itself ready for the heat of the lights and the possibility of repeating a scene twice or twenty times. To her professional credit, Lily had never been one to make a fuss; she'd just gone onto the set, and quietly told the assistant director, "She talks." The next day there had been a new makeup lady.

Every morning, Lucinda had sat on the floor, reading and glancing over every so often to see how the glamour was progressing—convinced at the age of five and a half that it got applied every morning by a woman with a big suitcase full of pots and jars and brushes and tubes. Lily's face got carried around by somebody else, until it was time to get put on.

The same was true of Lily's wardrobe and her personality, depending on who she'd been hired to pretend to be. When she was just Lily at home, Lucinda couldn't find any of the characteristics that appeared when she was Lily on a movie screen. Lily at home was a tiny, very thin woman, pale, with very fine naturally blond hair (her mother had been Finnish) and pretty enough; but not someone anybody ever noticed at the market or on the street or at any of the restaurants where they went to eat. The dichotomy always fascinated Lucinda: that plain Lily, with the terrible taste, was glamorous, sultry, smoky-voiced Lily with a shimmering curtain of gold hair that slid to conceal half her face when she turned or leaned just so; sexy Lily who got thousands of fan letters every week at the height of her career, some of them containing marriage proposals. Lily didn't even read them; six-, then seven-, then eight- and nine- and ten-year-old Lucinda did, picking out the ones she thought should get answers. The others were handled by the studio: Signed glossies were sent to every single person who wrote, regardless of what their letters said—unless Lucinda decided a specific reply was in order. Then one of the secretaries in the press office typed up whatever she and Lucinda concocted. People at the studio took Lucinda very seriously, even as a small child. And not because she was Lily's daughter, but because Lucinda was so clearly possessed of exceptional intelligence that most often what she said had actual weight and significance. She was observant, smart, and easy to have around. She didn't require entertaining, and was content to amuse herself—wherever she was.

Lily, too, deferred to Lucinda in this and other matters. Later, Lucinda realized it was because her mother was neither particularly astute (although certainly not dumb) nor particularly sensitive. She didn't suffer fools gladly and she hated explaining herself. Which led Lucinda to keep asking who her father might have been, because she had no doubt that whatever intelligence she possessed—and people were forever commenting on how smart she was (because she wasn't a particularly pretty little girl and they had to say *something*; she was Lily's daughter after all)—had not come from her mother.

The stories in the press at the time said that Lily had been on location in France and had adopted Lucinda there. Some silly story about having a baby left almost literally on the doorstep of her rented villa. It was ludicrous. For one thing, there never was a movie released. The press boys put out the word that there had been "artistic differences." Anyone with half a brain would have questioned the whole thing. Clearly, Lucinda was Lily's child; they had the same shape eyes (although Lily's were a clear blue and Lucinda's were a hazel that was almost green) and similar features. Lucinda's mouth was fuller and her chin a bit more prominent; she had darker, thicker hair, and a sturdier build, but their similarities—to Lucinda's mind—outweighed these differences. Evidently, the press back then was so hungry for material that it swallowed what it was fed, and there were spreads in the movie magazines showing Lily in the Beverly Hills house with her adopted baby; spreads of Lily at the pool with her splashing toddler; spreads of Lily overseeing her adopted five-year-old's birthday party.

When pressed, Lily finally said, "I've got no idea who your father was. Okay? It could've been a couple of different guys. What's it matter anyway? I did right by you, didn't I?"

That was true. In the privacy of their rented California homes (there were three of them over the years) Lily never pretended. "I'm your mother," she said often, "and this is a company town that doesn't go for mothers without husbands. You follow that?"

Lucinda followed that.

"So me and my press agent, we cooked up the story, and we stick to it. Forever, if we have to. Okay?"

"Okay."

"Lotta women would've given you away, afraid to take the heat here, but I didn't, Luce. You're my kid. I *wanted* you. So just stick to the script and things'll be hunky-dory. Okay?"

"Okay. But which couple of guys could've it have been?"

"Jeez Louise! You get your teeth into something, you just don't let go. I. Don't. Know. Okay? A couple, three guys it could've been."

"Actors?"

"Nah. Those guys are all feathers and no bird. There was a director, a writer. And a grip. I just don't know."

"How come there were so many guys?"

Lily had shrugged. "I liked 'em. That grip was a cute patootie, lemme tell ya."

"Why do you talk that way? Hunky-dory, cute patootie. Nobody says things like that."

"Lots of people say things like that. You're starting to give me a headache, Luce. Go read or something."

Lucinda had gone to read. Her mother's tolerance for questioning was never very high. Her tolerance for men, however, was fairly limitless. She always had a man or two, even three, on the string. Marriage was out of the question, though, a taboo subject never to be discussed. Lucinda didn't mind. Life was acceptable the way it was. Lily made few demands, except for silence in the morning, and Lucinda's presence for yet another photo session. For the most part, Lily let her go her own way. "You get in trouble, it means I get in trouble. So don't. Okay?"

"Okay, Lily."

"Good girl."

———

Lucinda was one of the very few kids in the classroom on the lot who wasn't under contract, so she could just be herself. Most of the other kids struck her as stiff and overly polite, as if they were perpetually auditioning—which, in fact, they were. Everything they said and did was noted. Usually the kids hated the whole thing, and complained together in fevered whispering sessions. It was their parents who called the shots, always pushing for their girl or boy to have a crack at this role or that one; showing up dressed to the nines, flashing big smiles and asking how their little Rose, or Jimmy, or Alice was coming along.

During the years she attended school on the lot (because Lily wanted her close by, refusing to leave Lucinda in the care of a housekeeper as most of her peers did), she only met maybe three kids who wanted to be there, who wanted a career in the movies and were prepared to do absolutely anything to have one. The rest of the kids disappeared after a few months or a year, or two, but not without having had some experiences that they were unlikely ever to forget.

There were moments, scenes, branded into Lucinda's brain and she could, effortlessly, shuffle through them like a deck of cards. With a shudder or a grimace she could recall eight-year-old Emily returning from a meeting with a director. She'd skipped out of the room happily, having been prepped by her father that she was up for a good supporting role. Pretty Emily with gleaming, carefully curled brown hair, in a fussy, full-skirted dress that would've been more appropriate at a party, white ankle socks and shiny Mary Janes. An hour later, she'd returned looking as if she'd been caught in a sudden windstorm. Her hair had somehow lost its gleam, the curls had wilted. The starch had gone out of her dress and out of Emily. She moved like a robot, her eyes unblinking, rubbing the back of her hand across her mouth over and over. It was the last time Lucinda ever saw her.

Then there was perky little Jimmy, with the startlingly low, raspy voice. He had unruly red hair and freckles, and an energy that was almost visible; he was constantly moving, couldn't stay still for longer than two minutes. His mother dressed him like a miniature farmer, in overalls and gingham shirts and lace-up work boots—a boy who'd spent the first nine years of his life playing stoopball in lower Manhattan, and the last year pretending to be a farmer. He laughed about it, saying, in his unmistakable New York twang, "She's got a screw loose, my old lady. But we're eating good, so I'm not gonna make a stink."

Jimmy got called in for a meeting with that same director a couple of months after Emily left. And when he came back, it was as if someone had unzipped Jimmy's skin and removed his spine. His energy was completely gone. He, too, walked like a robot; his eyes unblinking, hands hanging heavily at his sides. As he went past her, Lucinda saw a dark stain on the seat of his overalls and wondered if Jimmy had wet his pants. Later that night, in bed, hands tucked under her head, gazing at the ceiling, Lucinda decided that the stain had been blood. But how could it have got there?

Jimmy lasted another month on the lot, silent and still. And then one morning, he just wasn't there. Lucinda never saw him again, either.

Ginny Holder was one of the kids who'd pushed her mother to let her have a shot at the movies. Ginny wanted to be a movie star, and dressed and acted like one. Ten years old and she wore nylons and high heels and dresses that would have better suited someone twice her age. She blackened her eyelashes, rouged her cheeks, and wore Tangee lipstick. She sashayed and called people "Darling," and Lucinda thought she was hilarious: a miniature Mae West, with a tiny little body as shapeless as a lozenge. But she had brass and she could actually act, and already had four small parts under her belt by the time Lucinda started going to school on the lot.

"Say, kid," Ginny said that first day, "if you're lookin' to get anywhere, you're gonna have to drop some of those pounds and do somethin' with your hair." She said it without malice but matter-of-factly; passing along some helpful hints.

"That's okay," the then six-year-old Lucinda had told her. "I only like *watching* movies. I don't want to be *in* them."

"So how come you're here?"

"My mama works on the lot," Lucinda explained.

"Oh! Okay. So whaddya think of my dress?" She did a slow turn to show off the diagonally striped black and white, knee-length, form-fitting garment that had puffed sleeves to the elbow and a big white collar.

"It's ... " Lucinda searched for the right word. "It's amazing," she said.

"Yeah, isn't it?" Ginny beamed and stood, one hand on her hip, eyes alight with pleasure. "Saw it in an ad and had my mother make it for me. She sews."

"She's really good."

"Yeah. She's a dressmaker. When I'm rich, I'm gonna get her a brand new Singer machine."

Ginny got called to the director's office for a meeting one morning in Lucinda's third year on the lot. Ginny had made fourteen films by then and was getting featured roles, invariably playing girls well into their teens. At thirteen, she easily passed for seventeen with the help of her makeup and a wardrobe remarkable for its inappropriateness. She'd grown a couple of inches taller but still had the body of a child. The wardrobe department built curves into her costumes.

Concerned, Lucinda watched the girl hip-swing her way out of the classroom. At the door, as if she'd known Lucinda was watching, Ginny blew her a kiss, then sailed out.

Distracted, nervous, Lucinda kept glancing over at the door, waiting for Ginny to come back. By lunch time, the girl still hadn't returned. Sitting with Lily in her mother's trailer, Lucinda said, "Tell me about Lloyd Rankin."

"Why?" Lily asked, her fork poised over a plate of salad with no dressing.

"He's always having kids in for meetings and when they come back they don't look right."

Putting her fork down, Lily said, "What d'you mean, they don't look right?"

So Lucinda told her mother about Emily and Jimmy and a couple of the others.

"Son of a bitch!" Lily said in a deadly quiet, angry voice she only used when things were very, very bad. "That Ginny girl didn't come back?"

Lucinda shook her head.

"Sit tight, Luce. If I'm not back by the time you finish your lunch, go on back to the classroom." Clad in her wrapper, wearing scuffed mules, Lily marched out of the trailer. Through the window, Lucinda watched her out of sight. No longer hungry, she dumped her sandwich in the trash and tried to read while she waited for her mother to come back.

After half an hour, she got up and went back to the classroom where Ginny remained conspicuously absent.

That evening, while they were eating Chinese at a little restaurant in the middle of nowhere, Lily said, "Anybody ever try to touch you, Luce?"

"Touch me?"

"You know. In the wrong places."

"No. Is that what Lloyd did to the kids?"

"And then some," Lily said hotly. "But he won't be pulling any more of that shit any time soon. Caught him red-handed, the disgusting son of a bitch. He was off the lot inside an hour."

"What about Ginny?"

Her mother smiled suddenly. "I like that kid."

"You do?"

"Yup. She reminds me of myself."

"Unh-hunh." Now that she thought about it, Lucinda could see that it was true. "But she's okay?"

"She's gonna be fine, just fine." Lily's smile dissolved and she looked down at her plate as if seeing something ugly. After a few moments, she forked up some more chow mein, chewed, then said, "Anybody ever touches you, you tell me right away. Okay, Luce?"

"Okay."

"That son of a bitch," Lily murmured, then went on eating.

Ginny was back in the classroom the next morning. She looked fine, so far as Lucinda could tell.

"Say, how come you didn't tell me your mama's Lily Hunter?"

Lucinda shrugged, closely studying the girl, looking for signs that she was different, but finding none.

"Well, she's a peach. I'm gonna be in her next picture. Whaddya think of that?"

"That's great," Lucinda said with relief. "You're playing the younger sister?"

"You know the script?" Ginny looked surprised.

"I pick my mama's scripts," Lucinda confided. "But don't tell anybody. Okay?"

"Sure. So, yeah, I'm the sister."

"It's a good part," Lucinda said judiciously. "You'll get noticed."

"About time, too. Say, listen." Ginny lowered her voice. "I, uhm, just want to say thanks ... for saying something to your mother."

"Are you okay?"

For a second or two, Ginny's eyes went flat. Then she flashed one of her big smiles and said, "I'm hunky-dory, kiddo. Top of the world."

At that moment, Lucinda realized that Ginny should've been Lily's child; they were more alike than she and Lucinda. The thing was, Lucinda loved her mother more than anyone else in the world. But she hated being Lily Hunter's daughter.

Chapter Two

According to the story her mother told her any number of times through the years, Lily got to be in the movies entirely by accident. She was eighteen when she took the train into the city one afternoon to meet up with her girlfriend, Kay, who'd been her best friend in high school. Kay was working as a receptionist at the New York office of one of the Hollywood studios. While Lily was waiting for her to come back from the powder room before they headed off, a director (who just happened to be in the office to talk numbers for his next picture with the big money boys) emerged from his meeting and spotted Lily at the reception desk. He walked right over, introduced himself, and invited her to Delmonico's for dinner.

"I'm waiting for my girlfriend," Lily said. "I came into the city to spend the evening with her."

"Okay. I'll take you both out," he offered.

So the three of them laughed and drank martinis, had the club's famous steaks for dinner, and after seeing Kay into a cab, the director (as Lily loved to say in private ever afterward) had Lily for dessert. And after dessert, he offered her a part in his next movie.

She laughed and said, "You've got to be joking. I'm no actress. I just finished high school and I'm looking for a job."

"Well, I'm offering you one."

"Are you trying to be funny?"

"I couldn't be more serious. It's got nothing to do with this," he said, with a sweep of his hand indicating the hotel room. "Let me arrange for a screen test. I think the studio boys are going to feel the same way about you that I do."

"What way is that?" Lily asked.

"I'm willing to wager serious money that if you're on-screen no one's going to be able to take their eyes off you. You look like a sexy waif, and that husky come-over-here voice of yours is one in a million. You don't *look* like anyone else; you don't *sound* like anyone else. And you're sure not like any other girl I ever met. Give it a try. What've you got to lose? The studio'll pay your way to Hollywood; we'll put you up someplace nice for a couple of weeks. You'll do the test. They like you, they sign you, you do my picture. One, two, three, done."

"And if they don't like me?"

"Then you've had a paid two-week vacation."

"You married?"

"Does it matter?"

"No."

"I'm married."

"That's what I thought. When would I do it?" Lily asked, looking at the time.

"Soon as you can get away. I was planning to catch the train to the coast tomorrow. You could come with me."

"Okay. Let me phone my uncle and tell him I won't be home."

"What about your folks?" the director asked.

"Haven't got any, just an older sister who doesn't live with us."

Without further discussion—so the unvarying details of the story went—she made the call, saying into the receiver, "I've got a job offer in California, so I'm not coming home. But I might be back in a couple of weeks if it doesn't work out."

"You'd better not be fooling around," she then told the man sitting beside her in the bed at the Waldorf Astoria. "I just cut myself loose, don't even have a toothbrush."

"I'll buy you one. D'you always make decisions that fast?"

"Uh-hunh. I do. Why not?"

"That's something I haven't encountered in too many women."

"Well, if this works out, you'll have to get used to it. It's how I am. And you're not just going to drop me like a hot rock once we get there, are you?"

"Not a chance," he said with a smile.

He was thirty-three, his name was Lester Foxcroft and he'd already directed half a dozen not-bad movies, followed by five big box office hits in a row. By casting her as the be-spectacled, dowdy younger sister of the decent but boringly rigid heroine, he made Lily a movie star. Doing the first half of the film without makeup or hairstyling, in long shapeless dresses, so that she looked washed-out and sexless, she played a clever, intelligent career girl who reinvented herself and became glamorous. As a result, her sister's fiancé fell in love with her, and she with him. But, being as decent as she was clever, Lily's character rejected the man, even though it clearly grieved her. The final scene showed her in a medium shot, as her sister's maid of honor at their wedding—her glamour considerably toned down, her dress unflattering. Then the camera came in for a tight close-up of Lily smiling tremulously, with a glaze of tears in her eyes.

She took a clichéd role and invested it with such naked honesty and emotion that even though it was a supporting part, hers became the memorable role in what might otherwise have been merely a so-so picture. As Lester had suspected, Lily Hunter was a natural. During the filming, something about her elicited strong responses from the other cast members so that their performances had more depth, too. The camera loved her and so did the cast members, the crew and, most importantly, moviegoers.

Lester said in later interviews that the men in the audience looked flushed and agitated as they filed out of the theater after the sneak preview, avoiding their wives' or girlfriends' eyes. And almost every comment card asked about Lily. She was the sexiest woman the men had seen since Jean Harlow, and her transformation on screen was breathtaking. The women liked her because of that waiflike quality Lester had spotted right away, and because instead of casting to type and using Lily as a sexpot, he'd cleverly cast her in a sympathetic role that she made completely her own.

The publicity department wheels started turning in earnest, and by the time Lily's second movie was released less than six months later (this time cast by Lester against the type he'd established for her) in a starring role as a lovely but completely heartless manipulator who gets murdered, finally, by the hero), people flocked to see her. The bonus for everyone involved came in the form of good reviews. It turned out that the critics too liked Lily. "Here's a girl who can act!" raved the *Hollywood Reporter*. "And she pulls out all the stops as bad girl Marilyn." The *New York Times* said, "Lily Hunter not only holds the viewers' eyes, she also holds their hearts. She displays a rare blend of toughness and fragility that is captivating. Her portrayal of the cold-blooded Marilyn Maddox is a miracle of subtlety. That she can make you care about the fate of this woman is nothing short of remarkable."

Lily often told her daughter, "It's a hell of a lot more fun playing bad girls than it could ever be playing namby-pamby girls who take off their glasses, let down their hair and, suddenly, they're beautiful. Plus they keep paying me more and more money, thanks to Lester's getting Freddy to represent me. Boy, can that Freddy ever drive a hard bargain! All of which means I don't have to count on anyone else to look after me. I can look after myself—and you, of course, Luce. And I can help Beattie out from time to time."

When it came to money Lily was caution personified. She rented small houses, drove small cars, and wore nondescript clothes at home or if she wasn't going somewhere *impor-tant*—openings, arranged romantic dinners with actors she rarely liked, or studio business; in short, anything that had to do with her life as a movie star. If she was just being what she called a "civilian," Lily went about with limp hair and plain clothes and was almost never recognized.

When Lucinda asked about it, Lily would light a fresh cigarette and say, "I've always hated getting all dressed up. Slacks and a blouse are fine for me. Makeup's more trouble than it's worth. The people who get recognized are out there *wanting* to be noticed. I could give a care about that. As for cars, they make me nervous. And I've already got a house back in Connecticut, so what do I need with one here? Renting suits me fine, lets me hang on to my money."

"How come you've got a house there?" Lucinda, then ten, asked.

"I just do."

Well able to tell when an answer wasn't going to be given, Lucinda moved on. "Why do you say *when* it's over? What if it's *never* over?"

"Luce, you're a very smart girl, smarter in lots of ways than I'm ever going to be. So tell me this. How many old actresses have you seen around here? I mean stars, not character players. I'll tell you how many: none. You know why? Because the same way this town doesn't go for mothers without husbands, it doesn't like women over forty. And I'm already thirty-five. I'm still passing for being in my late twenties, 'cause I've kept my shape and I don't have much in the way of wrinkles yet. My mother was just a year older than I am now when she died, and she was still getting asked to show ID if she went out for a drink. Your Aunt Beattie's almost forty and doesn't look a day over thirty.

"But, see, in another five or six years, when my tits fall to my knees and I've got some sags here and there, a few lines around my eyes, they'll stop sending scripts. It'll happen, and I'm not about to get my face cut up by some quack so I can keep on looking younger than I am. None of those gals that've gone under the knife can do a thing about the other parts that show. Their arms and hands give them away—that loose skin and those big veins on the backs of their hands. You can't hide that stuff. I'll never be so desperate for a job that I'd let some guy take my face apart and put it back together so everything's all tight and shiny. Gives me the willies just thinking about it. So I plan to take a hike before they get a chance to turn me into an overnight has-been. One day you're a star, the next day you're nobody, and you're taking parts you would've spit on once upon a time, just so you can stay out there in the public eye. Not me. I'll quit while I'm ahead. This isn't *real*, Luce. It's just a big game.

Smart players know when to fold a losing hand and leave the table."

"But what if you get to be forty, or forty-five and they're still sending the scripts?"

"As long as they're sending me the good stuff, we'll hang around, keep socking money away for your education and my old age. But the minute it starts looking like I'm heading into B movies, we're going back east. I miss seeing the leaves turn, miss the first big snowfall of the winter. That's what I grew up with, what I know, what I like. Not goddam ratty coconut palms, and every season is summer all over again. It's *boring*. Sitting in the sun is my idea of torture; all I get for it is a headache. I never did learn to swim so I sure as hell don't need a pool and all you get at the beach is sand in your bum. Besides, I show up on the set one morning with a tan, somebody'll pitch a fit and say I violated some silly-ass clause in my contract, 'cause Lily Hunter's pale and interesting." She made a face, to show what she thought of that. "So, we'll be going home one of these days, Luce. You liked it when we were in New York last year on that publicity junket, didn't you?"

"It was okay."

"It wasn't great, I know. But you'll like Connecticut. I'm the first to admit that it's boring, too. But not the way this is. For one thing, there are honest-to-God trees, big old maples and oaks and chestnuts. And everything's nice and green, not all dry and dusty like here. The city's only an hour away. We want fun, we drive into town. Maybe you'll go to college back east and I'll come visit you. I always wanted to see if a real school was anything like those ivy-covered sets they're forever using. And you know something, Luce?"

"What?"

"You're too damned smart to waste your life in a fake place like this. I want more for you than this."

"You're smart, too," Lucinda argued.

"I'm smart enough to play the game," Lily disagreed. "But you're *smart*. You could have yourself a very interesting life."

"I might not want one."

Lily gave her one of the rare, unalloyed smiles that always made something inside Lucinda's chest lurch. "Luce, a girl like you can't *help* but have an interesting life. Bet you dollars to donuts it's gonna be a doozy."

Looking slowly around the living room so many years later, Lucinda said, "It's been a real doozy, mama. A lollapalooza."

All at once sad and a little angry but, primarily, confused, she saved her work, shut down the computer and walked across the room to flip on the TV.

"Goddamn," she whispered, her eyes suddenly filling. That *A & E* bio on her mother was being rerun. She held the remote, ready to change the channel, but instead muted the sound, then let her hand drop to her lap and kept watching. She knew all the words, but she wanted to see the faces again. Maybe this time she'd be able to spot what she'd missed for such a long time.

———

On a morning in July, some movement in her peripheral vision made her turn from the computer screen to look out the window. There on the grass, studying the chaos of the flower bed that ran the length of the driveway was a small black girl who, as if feeling Lucinda's eyes upon her, turned in her direction. The child was close enough that Lucinda could see her gaze moving across the front of the house; then the child's eyes connected with hers. And, incredibly, the girl smiled suddenly and waggled her fingers, beckoning Lucinda to come out.

"What the hell?" Lucinda said softly, for a moment wondering if she was seeing something real or imagined.

She blinked several times, the way she did when, tired or having a blood sugar dip, dancing spots floated across her eyes. But nothing changed. The child was real: small and dark; with long too-thin arms and legs emerging from the sleeves of her yellow T-shirt and the legs of her baggy blue shorts. Her bare feet were laced into sneakers that looked almost comically large. Her hair had been fashioned into a dozen or so short braids, each fastened with a bauble or small barrette, sticking out in all directions. The effect should've been comical but, actually, was charming. Those many small braids had a crownlike effect.

Lucinda sat unmoving, studying the child who waved again.

"This can't be real," Lucinda said, pushing her chair back from the desk to stand closer to the window.

In response, the girl took several steps across the lawn, so that the distance between them was now no more than twenty feet.

Yet again the child signaled, beckoning, and, unable to resist, Lucinda turned and walked to the front door. The heat that met her when she opened the door was shocking after the air-conditioned cool of the house. She stepped out onto the porch, closing the door to keep the heat out, and watched the child come across the grass to stand at the foot of the steps. Smiling all the while, the girl moved with innate grace, her spine impossibly straight, her teeth so white they seemed to glow.

She stared appraisingly at Lucinda for a long moment, then, with what looked like mixed surprise and satisfaction (as if something she'd suspected had been proved true), she said, "Hi! Whatchu name?"

"Lucinda."

"That a nice name, like music. Loo-sin-dah."

"You think so?"

"Unh-hunh. Ain't never heard it before. Nice," she repeated.

"I'm glad you think so. What's *your* name?" Lucinda asked. The girl had a sweet face, heart-shaped with enormous dark, almost black eyes with thick curly lashes, a wide mouth and delicately pointed chin; tidy little ears tucked tightly to her well-shaped skull, and a long, long neck. She would grow up to be a very beautiful woman.

"Katanya Taylor."

"*I've* never heard *that* name before. It's pretty."

"It okay." The girl shrugged her narrow shoulders, her eyes never leaving Lucinda's face.

"Are you lost?" Lucinda asked.

"Unh-unh." She shook her head. "I stayin' with them people"—she swiveled, surveying the houses behind her, then pointed—"over to that house."

"I see. You're visiting."

"S'posed to be," the girl said, shrugging again. "Two weeks I'ma stay here. The Fresh Air Fund. You know?"

"I've heard of it."

"So yeah. But Miz Crane be alla time busy with her l'il boy, Jason, what is spoiled so bad it a *sin*. Child have screamin' fits from time he gettin' up 'til time he get put to bed. She ain't got one *clue* what she suppose to do with that boy. An' Mister Crane, that man off to the city early every mornin' like he can't wait to get gone from her and that screamin' boy. I could set that child right in no time, give him a good shake"—she demonstrated holding an imaginary child by the shoulders— "like he want and need, give him some *rules,* show him *no* a couple time to put him right. But no *way* she gonna let me close to that boy, not even lemme touch him, like she afraid some color gonna rub off on him and next thing anybody knows, she's got her a Afro-'Merican child." Katanya shook her head in amusement. "Jason be angry, be lonely, he wanna play wit me. But unh-unh. She talkin' re-tarded nonsense to him 'bout how he gotta play nice wit his toys or whatever, an' control hisself. Hah! Not even three years old. Like he *know* how he gone control hisself! So, ain't a thing for me to do. Cuz I would. I be good at helpin'. But she always makin' out I'm inna way. She not sayin' it or nothin'. But I can tell. Don' know how come she even say she wanna take a child inna house for two weeks, she don' be wantin' one. So I come out for a look-see, just to be doin' somethin'. You know? This a *fine* house. Not like them oth-ers, all new, all the same." She swung her hand in a graceful arc that took in, by suggestion, the entire neighborhood. "You live here, huh?"

"Yes, I do."

"Yeah, I seen you on that 'puter yesterday. You was on there in the mornin', you was on there in the aft'noon, you was on there when it got to be dark and I hadda go inside. Whatchu doin' on that thing anyway?"

"I do Web content editing."

"What? Like you make all the words spell right and like that?"

"That's about it," Lucinda said.

"You like doin' that?"

It was Lucinda's turn to shrug. "It's something to do."

Katanya studied her thoughtfully for a moment, then said, "House be really old, right?"

"About a hundred years."

"Yeah, that old, awright. You do them flowers?"

Lucinda sat down on the top step of the porch, saying, "Once upon a time I did. Now they pretty much do themselves."

"How's that?"

"They just grow every year. They're called perennials."

"Oh! I know what they be."

"Do you?"

"They be flowers what come every year, forever."

"That's right," Lucinda said, pleased. "Will Mrs. Crane be looking for you?"

"Don't think so," Katanya said astutely. "They don't see me if I there, not there. Be like as if I invisible. You know? 'Cept when it time to eat. Then she be callin' after me. 'Katanya,'" she mimicked. "'Come right now. Dinner's ready.' Her food ain't no good," she confided, lowering her voice slightly. "So far, mostly she buy stuff from the market what be already cooked. Got no taste to it. Ain't no way near good as my gramma's. My gramma's cookin' be *fine*. Okay I come sit down?"

"Okay."

The girl climbed five of the six wide steps then turned and sat down near Lucinda on the top step. Looking at the view from this new perspective, she said, "This a big place, lottsa grass 'n' stuff, even got you a barn."

"It's two acres. Do you know what an acre is?"

"Four thousan' eight hundred an' forty square yards."

"That's right! Very good. How old are you?"

"Nine an' a half. I be ten in December. How old're you?"

"Forty-six."

"That how old my gramma be. My moms, she twenny-six. You real, real pretty. An' *tall*. I wanna be tall when I get grown."

"Is your mother tall?"

"Not so very. Not like you."

"I'm only five-eight. Nowadays, that's not so tall."

"You suppose-a say thank you when somebody say you pretty."

Caught, Lucinda said, "Thank you. Do you have brothers and sisters?"

"Unh-unh. Moms, she says she ain't havin' no more kids. She satisfy wit me."

"I can certainly see why she would be. May I ask you a question?"

"Go on. Ax me anythin'. This *way* better'n sittin' watchin' the TV all day. Nothin' good on, 'cept dumb 'toons or talkin' shows with sorry-ass people wantin' everybody should pity 'em cuz they fat, or they got husbands what wanna sleep with their mamas, or some other dumb stuff."

Lucinda laughed. "You're absolutely right."

"So whatchu wanna ax me?" Katanya placed her long-fingered hands on her bony knees and looked expectantly up at Lucinda.

Lucinda admired the girl's flawless complexion, its rich brown color, the deep pink tone to her high-boned cheeks. "What grade are you in?"

"You gone disbelieve me."

"No, I won't."

"School starts September, I be in the sixth." Katanya's eyes challenged her to dispute this.

"I'm not surprised. You're very intelligent."

"Yeah, ever'body say it."

"So," Lucinda said, "given that we agree you're intelligent, why do you talk street talk?"

The girl stared into her eyes, searching, then, as if satisfied with what she saw, she slapped her knees all at once and laughed delightedly. "That," she declared, "is what I call We-bonics."

Her eyebrows raised, starting to smile, Lucinda waited for an explanation from this extraordinary girl.

"Okay. Here's how it works," Katanya said, all trace of her former speech pattern gone. "I'm a *Me*, and almost everybody else—except for my moms and gramma—but most of the kids I know and their folks, people in the 'hood, they're part of *We*. I don't want to be left out of everything, being *Me*. So I talk like the *We*, and I don't get left out."

"I see."

"Yeah?"

"Yes, I do. It's no fun being excluded because you happen to be smart and see things other people don't notice."

"That's *right!*" Katanya said, pleased at being understood. "So okay. My turn to ask you a question?"

"Sure."

"All of this is yours? The house and the barn and the two acres and that big car over there?"

"Yes."

"You have a husband, kids?"

"No."

"You have brothers, sisters?"

"Not that I know of."

"So you might have some?"

"It's possible," Lucinda allowed.

"That's very interesting. Are you rich?"

This time Lucinda laughed. "I guess so." She thought about it, then said, "Yes, actually. I am."

"But you work anyway. Why?"

"I need to."

"Because you live here all by yourself?"

The girl was almost alarmingly perceptive. "Yes," Lucinda answered.

"That makes sense. Have you lived here a long time?"

"It was my mother's house. I inherited it when she died."

"Was she old?"

"She was the same age I am now."

"That's a young age to die. And how old were you?"

"Nineteen."

Her expression serious now, Katanya said, "You've lived here all by yourself for *twenty-seven* years?"

Lucinda nodded.

"You must get lonely. *I'd* be lonely."

Looking away from the girl's eyes, Lucinda nodded again. "Sometimes I do," she said.

"Only people I've seen come here are the UPS and FedEx guys, the mailman. Where are your friends?"

"Around. Here and there. Mostly in California. That's where I grew up. Are you hungry?" she asked, growing uneasy as she looked back at the girl.

"I'm always hungry," Katanya said. "My moms calls me a bottomless pit."

"You're sure no one's going to be looking for you?"

"She might. You could phone her, say I'm with you."

"You know the number?" Lucinda asked, getting to her feet.

"Got it in my pocket."

"Okay. I'll phone her and then we'll have something to eat."

"Can I ask one more question?"

Lucinda smiled. "From what I know of you so far, I think you're going to ask a *lot* more questions."

"Probably." Katanya returned her smile.

"Go ahead," Lucinda said, opening the front door and standing to one side to let the girl enter the house.

"Oh, wow! This is so cool! I *love* it."

"Thank you."

"Some day I want a house *just* like this. Nice and old-fashioned on the outside, all new-fashioned and bright on the inside."

"I'm sure you'll have one."

"I'm going to try very hard."

"I know you will," Lucinda said. "So what was the next question?"

Looking up again at Lucinda, the girl said, "Does it bother you, being the only *sister* in this whole neighborhood?"

Chapter Three

Lucinda felt as if all the air had suddenly been sucked from her body, from the entire house. Shock turned her rigid and she could only stare at the child whose face began to crumple. Upset crept across her features like a shadow and she was, all at once, on the verge of tears, her chin quivering.

"Did I say the wrong thing?" she asked fearfully.

Lucinda was able to shake her head, but not to speak. She had to make a conscious effort to breathe. It hurt.

"Are you mad at me? You want me to go away now?"

Again Lucinda shook her head.

"People around here don't know? Is that it?"

"That's it, but not it," Lucinda managed to get out, sweating in the chilled air. She badly needed something to drink, to clear what felt like an accumulation of dust in her throat.

Taking her by the hand, Lucinda led the girl to the kitchen and indicated she should sit down while Lucinda opened the refrigerator and got two Diet Cokes, popped the tabs, took straws from the cabinet, dropped them into the slots and handed one to the visibly apprehensive child. After a long drink, Lucinda sat down across the table from Katanya, carefully placed her Diet Coke on the table, and said, "What made you ask me that?"

"You're not a sister?" the girl asked, confused and a little frightened.

"What makes you think I am?" Lucinda rephrased the question, ashamed to see that she'd alarmed the child.

"I don't know," Katanya answered. "You kind of remind me of that girl in *Flashdance*. I can't remember her name. You're real pretty, like her. Only her eyes are dark, her hair, too. But one of my mom's friends has green eyes and her hair's for-real straight and almost as light as yours. She's got freckles, though, and you don't. I don't know," she said apologetically, almost helplessly. "You didn't act all white with me. You acted easy, like ... like my mom's and gramma's friends would, not like Mrs. Crane and the people who live around here. We see them in the supermarket or at the CVS and they're all *soooo* polite, *soooo* careful. You know? Trying to show they're not racist. They get all big-eyed and smiley, pretending it doesn't matter to them that I'm a black child. But the way they talk down to me and smile big fake smiles, I know it *does* matter. They say silly-ass things like what nice curly eyelashes I have, and how cute my hair is. And aren't I *lucky* I don't have to sit in the sun to get a tan." She rolled her eyes. "You didn't say stupid stuff. You just talked to me like I was an ordinary girl."

"You're no *ordinary* girl," Lucinda said.

"You know what I mean."

"And *you* know what *I* mean."

"Unh-hunh, I do."

"My father was part black," Lucinda said. "I think a quarter."

"Unh-hunh."

"But I didn't know that until after my mother died."

"How come?"

"It's a long story."

"So, just now, why'd you get so … I don't know, shocked or whatever, like as if nobody ever asked you that before?" Katanya asked, her curiosity outweighing her fear.

"Because nobody ever has."

"*Nobody?*"

"Not one person."

"You don't *want* to be black, have people know?"

"No. I mean, I wouldn't care if it was something I'd always lived with. But that's not … It's very hard to explain." Lucinda drank more of her Diet Coke, then said, "It just never happened before, that's all." She looked down at the table-top then again at the girl. "I'd have liked to know my father."

"How come you didn't?"

"I'll make us some sandwiches and we'll talk about it."

"I can help," Katanya offered.

"No, sit and have your soda. I need to move around a little."

"You're not mad at me for sure?"

Lucinda looked down at the child. "Why would I be?"

"I don't know. Grown-ups get mad at kids all the time for no reason. They just need to be mad and kids can't fight back, so they get mad at us."

"That's true. But if I get mad at somebody, I always have a reason. And I wouldn't be angry with you for speaking the truth."

"Okay. Good. That's fair." Katanya reached for her soft drink as Lucinda opened the refrigerator again and took out cold cuts and lettuce, a jar of mustard. She was running on auto-pilot, placing things on the counter, opening the drawer for a knife, setting out plates, while her thoughts went back to the night her mother died.

She'd been drunkenly dizzy with fatigue from spending days and nights at her mother's bedside, and one of the nurses—the older, gruff-spoken one named Joan, had said, "Go home and rest. The rate you're going, we'll be booking you in here, too, if you don't." So she'd gone home and had fallen asleep, fully dressed, on top of the bedclothes. When the phone rang, it felt as if she were swimming through a sea of glue as she tried to awaken. The phone rang and rang and didn't stop until she broke through the surface and grappled with the receiver.

"Better come on back, hon," the familiar gruff voice said. "And hurry."

Shaky, her coordination shot, she staggered down the stairs and out of the house to the car. Her vision wasn't too good, either, and she couldn't drive as fast as she'd have liked, so it took her twenty minutes to get back to the hospital. Ten minutes too long. Lily was gone, her flesh already cooling. The nurses were busy preparing the body for removal. Respectfully, they'd left the room while Lucinda stared at her mother, trying to make herself accept this. She couldn't. Two hours earlier Lily had smiled at her and murmured, "I'm sleepy." She'd closed her eyes and fallen asleep again, with the remarkable ease she'd displayed for the previous two weeks—just sliding away: awake one moment, asleep the next.

It was the morphine, and the other drugs, on top of the radiation, the nurses had told her. But Lucinda was nonetheless mesmerized by Lily's instant shifts from waking to sleeping. "She's going," Joan had explained in the corridor two nights before. "She'll sleep longer and longer, and then she just won't wake up. It's a blessing, really," she'd said, her good heart on display in the kindness of her gaze. "Poor woman's suffered enough."

That was true: Lily had suffered, just as Beattie had suffered, just as, Lucinda imagined, their mother, her grandmother, had suffered. The women in the family had all died young, their bodies ruined from the inside out by the cancer that started in their breasts and spread to claim every organ. The women died shrunken, their cheeks and limbs hollowed, their breath rancid with the smell of chemicals and inner rot; their hair reduced to a fine stubble of regrowth.

But even knowing it was going to end, having been warned for months that Lily would die, Lucinda still wasn't prepared for it. She sank into the chair beside the bed and studied her mother's lovely, waxen profile. She lifted her mother's hand and was shocked by the cool weight of it. Four months from start to finish. One day Lily said, "I feel lousy, Luce." And, thrown by this atypical admission, Lucinda got on the phone at once to make an emergency appointment with their GP, then drove her mother to his office and waited while Lily was escorted by one of the nurses into an examining room.

"I'm admitting her right away," Dr. Tepperman had said across the desk in his office less than an hour later. "She's got a lump in her breast the size of a golf ball."

Lucinda had felt a chill at the roots of her hair, a sensation as if her scalp was shriveling.

"She knew," he said with some anger, "and she ignored it. Now we have to hope it's not too late."

It is too late, Lucinda thought, knowing well Lily's fear of doctors, of hospitals.

"What'll happen?" Lucinda asked.

"They'll operate, remove the breast, maybe some lymph nodes, then maybe radiation therapy. We'll keep our fingers crossed. I've already got a call in to the best man I know. He's booking an O.R. for tomorrow."

"Tomorrow?"

"Lucinda," he said softly, "this didn't just happen last week or last month. She's had that lump for *months*, maybe a year or more. We've got to move fast."

Twenty-four hours later, Lucinda was sitting beside her mother's bed, listening to Lily moan in her sleep. It was frightful, terrifying. The surgery had been what they called "radical" and the specialist had said sadly, "We couldn't get it all. It's already spread."

"Spread where?"

"Everywhere."

"Everywhere?" Lucinda had repeated, her brows drawing together.

"It's in her lungs, her liver, her bones."

"Then why do the radiation?"

"To buy her some time."

"Time for what?" Lucinda asked.

The specialist had stared at her for several moments before saying gently, "Time to get her affairs in order."

Affairs. The word didn't have the same meaning for Lucinda as it did for the doctor and she had to redefine it so that it became appropriate to the situation. Lily had been famous for her affairs. But this was affairs as in legalities, as in wills, as in getting the paperwork in order. "My mother did all that last year," she said, realizing as she spoke that Lily had known for quite some time that she was going to die. "Maybe she doesn't want radiation," she said.

"She agreed to it."

"She did? When?"

"Before the surgery."

"Oh."

Was Lily hoping for a miracle? Lucinda had wondered. Why had she agreed? It was all too fast, too confusing. Lily always had reasons for the things she did. But maybe this time she was too sick to have a reason.

―

"You'll be okay," Lily told her the day before she died. "You'll never need for anything, Luce. I've made sure of that. Everything's in your name, so you won't get hit with huge estate taxes."

"All I've ever needed was you," Lucinda replied, working to hide her fear.

"Only thing I feel bad about is leaving you all alone. You're just a kid."

"I'm nineteen, not a kid."

"You're a *kid*," Lily argued. "I didn't think *I* was either, at nineteen. I thought I had things all figured out, but I was wrong."

"What things?"

"How I wanted it to be."

"Didn't it turn out the way you wanted?" Lucinda asked.

"Mostly. Some things I'd've changed, if I could've. But I couldn't change the world. Was I a crummy mother, Luce?"

Indignantly, Lucinda had said, "No! You've been great. And look what you did for Gin! You were better to her than her own mother."

"That so-called mother should've been put up against a wall and shot. Gin's a pistol. Hang on to her, Luce. She's for real, an honest-to-God friend. They don't come along too often."

"I know that."

"I mean it," Lily insisted.

"So do I."

"Let Eddie handle the funeral, the press. Don't try to do it yourself. It'll be a zoo, people trying to get next to you. Eddie'll know how to deal with them."

"Okay."

"I'm proud of you, Luce. First one in our family to go to college, and graduating in only three years. Always so damned smart. Whatever you do, be your own person. Don't let anyone tell you how you should live."

"I'll probably keep on with the scripts. I enjoy doing them; they're a breeze."

"Keep your distance, though. The business stinks," Lily said sourly. "It's worse than the cancer. The money was great, but I gave up too much, things I shouldn't have; played by their rules. If I had it to do again, I'd do it differently."

"What did you give up?"

"I'm tired, Luce, need to sleep for a while."

"What did you give up?" Lucinda asked again.

"Too much," Lily repeated. "Thing is, it was the way it had to be. We agreed from the start. I'm gonna sleep now."

"Okay," Lucinda said, wondering what and who "we agreed" meant.

"Love you, Luce," her mother murmured, eyelids fluttering.

"I love you, too, Lily."

After that, she was never fully awake for more than a minute or two. And then, while Lucinda was away for less than an hour, Lily was dead, her hand small and cool, the fingers slightly curled; this surprising weight on Lucinda's hand.

Perhaps twenty minutes later, Joan said, "C'mon, hon. We need to see to your mom and you need to go home." She handed Lucinda Lily's suitcase. "We packed up your mom's stuff." In a confidential tone, she said, "I was a big fan of hers, back when. *Big* fan. Thought she'd be a piece of work when she was admitted, but she wasn't one to put on airs and graces. Your mom was a genuine person, a decent woman. And she adored you, hon. You're all she talked about, to anyone who'd listen. She was so proud of you, telling us how you finished Yale in three years with high honors."

"Really?"

"Really. You were the sun and moon for your mother. And I could tell how close the two of you were. It's going to be rough on you for a time." The nurse put a consoling hand on Lucinda's arm. "You'll keep expecting to see her, to hear her calling to you from another room. You'll be sad and you'll be missing her, but keep reminding yourself she's at peace now. She earned it. So go on home now and try to get some rest. You're going to need it. We've been getting all kinds of calls from the press, the TV people. Hovering like damned vultures. Parking lot's already crowded with them, waiting for the word. Your mom asked me to remind you to get Eddie."

"Right. Okay."

"Now slip on out of here, and take care of yourself, hon."

Lucinda thanked the woman and leadenly moved away. Outside, she put the suitcase in the trunk, then drove home, trying to take in the fact of her mother's death. It didn't seem real, perhaps because she was so very, very tired. Everything felt as if it were happening at a great distance.

Leaving the house dark, she went upstairs to her mother's room and stood in the doorway, studying the shapes of the furniture, breathing in Lily's fragrance. At last, she pushed off her shoes, curled up on the bed—the fragrance strongest here—and went to sleep.

The next morning, ignoring the ringing of the telephone which would stop briefly only to start again, she went out to the car to retrieve the suitcase and brought it to the kitchen where she placed it on the table. While a pot of coffee was brewing, she carefully examined every item in the small bag: three nightgowns, a pair of scuffed slippers, the robe Lucinda had bought for her mother's first hospital stay but which Lily had worn only a few times, several magazines, a stack of telegrams (all of which Lucinda had already seen), a large envelope filled with get well cards and letters (Lucinda had also seen all of these), a toiletries bag that contained a powder compact, two lipsticks, one ancient pot of rouge and another of mascara, soap, a toothbrush, deodorant, a small bottle of her mother's perfume—this she set to one side—and, tucked away in one of the pockets, wrapped in a lace-edged handkerchief, an old deckle-edged black-and-white photograph.

Sinking into a chair, her hands trembling, Lucinda studied the photo, knowing with visceral certainty that she'd found what she'd been looking for. She'd found her father. There were her eyes, her mouth, her cheekbones, the height of her forehead, the slightly squared aspect to her jaw. Her features on a handsome, smiling, light-skinned but undeniably black man.

"I need to know," she told Eddie when she got through to him a few minutes later at his hotel in the city. "I don't want your sympathy right now. Don't patronize me, don't put me off, just *tell* me."

"Sweetheart, there's not a lot I *can* tell you."

"Tell me everything you know right now."

"You sound pretty angry, Lucy."

"I've been fed lies my whole life, Eddie. All those 'affairs,' that was all bunk, wasn't it?"

"She was protecting you ... "

"Are you sure she wasn't protecting herself?"

"Listen to me good, Lucy," he said sternly. "If I know one thing, it's that your mother loved you like a religion. Yeah, maybe she was protecting herself some, but you mattered most of all. You know what would've happened word got out Lily Hunter had a Negro husband?"

"*Husband*? They were married?"

"Yeah. That much I know."

"But how ... ? Why ... ?"

"All I know is they were young, got married when Lily was sixteen, maybe seventeen. Nobody knew, not even your aunt Beattie. Lily had to come clean with me when she got pregnant with you. That's why I worked out the whole French thing."

"Tell me about the 'French thing.'"

"Look, I know you found something and that's why all of a sudden I'm getting the third degree. But I'm not gonna do this over the phone. Okay? I'm gonna go catch the train, you'll pick me up at the station and we'll talk when I get there. Okay?"

"I need to *know*. Can you understand that? I don't know who I *am*, Eddie. Do I have a family somewhere? Aunts, uncles, grandparents?"

"Lucy, I'll be there in a couple of hours. I'll tell you everything I know. But I'm warning you: It's not a heck of a lot. And I don't want you getting a mad-on with me. You think I'm not broken-hearted, sweetheart? You don't think I just lost somebody I loved, too? Almost thirty years, me and your mother were friends. Better than friends. She wasn't just a job for me; it got to be personal. So I'll get there and we'll talk, but I'm not gonna let you beat up on me, Lucy."

Somehow, without being aware of it, Lucinda had made two sandwiches. She stood looking down at them for a moment, then turned to look over at Katanya. "It was the strangest thing," Lucinda said. "I had a father, my mother had a husband, but nobody ever knew."

"How come?"

"My mother was famous. To stay famous she had to keep her husband a secret and tell everyone her daughter was an orphan she'd adopted."

"'Cause your mama was white?"

Lucinda nodded.

"And your daddy was black?"

Lucinda nodded again.

"What was your mama famous for?"

"She was a movie star."

"Yeah? That's cool."

"It wasn't cool," Lucinda said softly, getting two plates and positioning the sandwiches on them. "It was what my mother had always wanted. To get it, she had to pretend for the public to be very different than the way she actually was. And she absolutely could not have had a black husband."

"Did she love him?"

"According to what I was told, she adored him. The thing is, when I found out, all I wanted was to know about him—who he was, what he did, what he was like. I didn't get very far. And then"—Lucinda put the plates on the table and sat down opposite the girl—"then it struck me that I didn't know who, or what *I* was. I wasn't white. I wasn't black. I wasn't anything. I didn't know who to be. Everything about my life was a lie. I know my mother only wanted to protect me and that's why she didn't tell me, but once I found out ... " Lucinda's eyes moved to the doorway. "One day a few months after she died, I just couldn't go out. I was on my way to the post office but I couldn't get past the front door, couldn't even *open* the door. I felt as if everyone who saw me would know I wasn't what I appeared to be. I didn't know how to be a person of color, and I didn't know how to go back to being what I'd been before."

"You got scared?" Katanya asked softly.

"I went far beyond scared. I felt like a complete fake, like an empty closet, like a suitcase somebody left at an airport."

"That's bad. You'd better eat that," the child said. "My gramma says it's a sin to waste food. And you're skinny. I bet you don't eat much."

"Most of the time when I open the refrigerator nothing looks right, so I wind up eating crackers, drinking juice."

"*This* looks right," Katanya said coaxingly, picking up half her sandwich. "Let's eat this." She sat and waited for Lucinda to follow suit. When she did, Katanya took a bite and then, chewing, she signaled for Lucinda to do the same.

Suddenly Lucinda smiled. "I think you could straighten little Jason out in no time flat."

"Sure could," the girl said. "Straighten you out, too, I think."

"Heaven knows, I could use some help."

"Aw, you're okay. You just need to be with people again."

"Maybe I do," Lucinda allowed. "I need to figure out how to do that."

"My moms says it's not like it once was, but it's not where it should be, either. Being Afro-'Merican, I mean."

"For years and years, I'd sit here late at night and wonder about my father's family, wishing I knew how to find them. Then I'd think about how, a few generations back, he'd probably had relatives who'd been slaves."

"Probably. My gramma tells stories her great-gramma told her about bein' a slave. Scary stories about how black people got treated back then, getting hurt 'n' hung. You're not eating."

Lucinda bit into the sandwich, surprised at the richness of the baked ham, the tang of the Swiss cheese, the complementary bite of the hot and sweet mustard. She was suddenly very hungry.

"What I think," the girl said after swallowing another bite. "I think we've got to find you your family."

"I tried for years," Lucinda said. "Even hired detectives. They got nowhere."

"You ever gonna be happy if you don't find them?"

"I doubt it."

"Okay. Then we'll just have to try new ways."

Lucinda smiled again. "*We* will?"

"Sure. I've got all kinds of ideas already. And you said yourself I'm really smart. I could help you. It's not like I'm doing anything but staying outta Miz Crane's way. Uh-oh! We forgot to phone."

"Give me the number and I'll do it right now."

"You eat first," Katanya said. "Five more minutes won't make any difference." She gazed at Lucinda, saying, "Maybe she'll let me come visit with you again."

"Would you like that?"

"I would *love* that. Would *you* like that?"

"Why did you wave to me? What made you think I wouldn't come out and shoo you away?"

Katanya shrugged. "I don't know. Every time I looked, you were at that computer and you didn't look happy. But you didn't look scary or crazy, either. So when you saw me, I just waved to say hi. And when you didn't seem to be mad,

I thought maybe you'd like to have a visit. And you did, didn't you?"

"Yes, I did."

"Your friends ever come to visit you?"

"Not for a long, long time."

"Maybe you should tell them to come. I bet they would."

"Probably," Lucinda said, thinking of Ginny who would, at a moment's notice, catch the next plane. "But ... " she trailed off and looked again at the doorway.

"Well," Katanya said, pulling Lucinda's eyes back to her, "we'll just see how we do today. Okay?"

What a kind and clever child! Lucinda thought, touched by Katanya's extraordinary sensitivity. Most other people—never mind children—would have written her off as nuts and headed for the hills.

"Okay," Lucinda agreed. "We'll see how we do."

Chapter Four

The woman's tone was so obsequious it was patently obvious she knew that Lucinda was Lily Hunter's daughter. In all the years she'd lived here, it had never occurred to Lucinda that she had a certain fame, purely by association. She'd been aware of it when they'd lived in California and had early on learned to take it in stride, to discount the overly friendly people who approached her thinking she'd be a door they could open to get to her mother. But she hadn't given it a thought since her mother's death—as if she, too, had died. Which, in a way, she had. Now that she considered it, she imagined she was spoken of locally as the peculiar woman no one ever saw; the odd, reclusive neighbor who was the daughter of a world-famous movie star. Good grief! Lucinda thought wearily. There were endless ramifications to the facts of her heritage—on every level. Her actions (or lack of them), her very presence in the town, her rare appearances here and there, were noted. And all this time she'd thought she was, in essence, invisible, unknown.

"I was wondering where she was," Mrs. Crane said. "I hope she's not being a nuisance."

Irked by the statement—Mrs. Crane was one of those people who assumed children were bothersome to others because they themselves found children, even their own, a nuisance—Lucinda made a face at Katanya, who laughed, then slapped a hand over her mouth.

"She's an absolute delight," Lucinda said coolly. "Would you mind if she stayed for a while?"

Her voice now positively fulsome, the woman said, "That's awf'ly good of you." She had what Eddie used to refer to as Long Island lockjaw: a manner of speaking that was all clipped consonants and drawn-out vowels. Lily had dubbed it the Katharine Hepburn school of constipated diction.

"I'll have her back in an hour or two."

"Well, thank you so much, Miz, ah Mrs., ah—"

"Lucinda."

"Ah, yes. Lucinda. Thanks *so* much."

The moment she hung up, Katanya laughed merrily. "Ah, yes. Lucinda. Thanks *soooo* much," she mimicked flawlessly as if she'd actually heard the woman's words.

Lucinda laughed with her. "You're wicked."

"That's what my moms and gramma say, too." She brought the plates over and put them in the sink, declaring, "This is *fun!*"

"You're easy to please."

Katanya shrugged. "I like you," she said. "You're pretty *and* you're nice. Most pretty people are mean. Ever notice that?"

"Yes, I have."

"It's like they think cuz they're good-looking they're better than everybody else. And people let them get away with all kindsa rotten stuff cuz of it."

"That is true."

"But you know what I think?" the girl asked, standing next to Lucinda at the counter. "I think the ones who think they're hot aren't even one little tiny bit special. It's the ones who don't know, or don't care what they look like who're the good people. My moms," she said seriously, "is very beautiful."

"I believe that."

"But she's like you. *She* doesn't believe it. And she's nice, too. You'd like my moms."

"I'm sure I would."

"And you know what? My moms'd like you, too."

"You think so?"

"Yup. Know why?"

"Why?"

"Cuz you're nice to me. My gramma says that people who treat kids right are people who remember how it feels to be a kid."

"Maybe that's true. I've never thought of it."

"My gramma's smart, too. Oh! Thank you for the sandwich. It was good."

"You're welcome."

"I wish I was staying with you and not Miz Crane and poor screamin' Jason, and Mr. Crane who can't wait to get away from the two of them every morning. I think he can't even stand comin' home at night. He's always phonin' to say he'll be late, go ahead and eat without him. Anybody tried that with my moms, he'd get away with it once and that'd be the end of him. That's kind of what happened with my dad. He was foolin' around, and one of my mom's friends saw him 'n' told her. Moms packed up all his stuff and left it in the hall, wouldn't let him back in the apartment."

"How old were you when that happened?"

"Little," Katanya said. "Maybe three. I don't remember it, don't remember him, either. After that, my moms dated some but she finally quit. She says men are purely decorative and more trouble than they're worth. That's when we moved in with my gramma so she could look after me mornings while moms worked. When I started school, my gramma went back to her job full-time."

"What does she do?"

"She cooks and keeps house for a family in a great big apartment on Fifth Avenue, been workin' for them my mom's whole life. They're v-e-r-y nice people. But they're old now—*really* old, in their eighties. I worry sometimes what my gramma'll do if they die and there's no more job for her. My moms worries about it, too. Which is why she's been going to college nights for a long time now. See, she does the taxes for everybody we know. March and April she makes enough money to pay for her school and help gramma with the rent. One more year and she'll graduate and be a certified public accountant."

"That's wonderful. Where do you live in the city?"

"A Hundred and Twenty-third Street. You know where that is?"

"I do. How much longer will you be staying with the Cranes?"

"Eight more days. Six days already gone and we haven't done one single thing. Not a thing. Haven't gone anywhere, haven't done anything. She just rents videos, thinks I came to Connecticut to sit inside and watch bad TV shows or dumb kid movies. I'm supposed to be getting *fresh air*."

"Oh, dear. That's hardly a vacation."

"Ex-actly! So, wanna do somethin'?"

"Like what?"

"You're the one who lives here. You must know what-all there is to do."

"I have no idea, I'm afraid. The only places I go are the post office and sometimes to the library to do research."

"We could look on your computer, see what's around. Or," Katanya quickly shifted direction at seeing Lucinda's change of expression, "we could go explorin' in the woods out back, pretend we're on a safari and like that."

"We'd get eaten alive by mosquitoes. There's a stream that goes through there and because of the heat, the bugs are ferocious this year."

"Don't you have anything like Off!?"

Lucinda shook her head. "I'm sorry. I don't."

"How about a drive?" Katanya suggested. "We could just go anywhere, look around."

Dragged past her habitual reservations by the girl's enthusiasm, Lucinda agreed.

———

"You always put on a getup like that when you go out?" Katanya asked as they sat in the front seat of the car.

Lucinda turned the key in the ignition, then got the air-conditioning going full blast. The car's interior was oven-like. "It's just a hat and sunglasses," she said, feeling tremors starting in her spine.

"But you're in a car. You don't need those things. Nobody looks at people in cars."

Her hands damp on the steering wheel, Lucinda said, "It's a habit."

"Why?"

"Another long story."

"Oh. Okay." Katanya sat back and looked out the window, waiting.

A minute went by, then another, and another. Lucinda tried to make herself put the car into Drive, but couldn't. She also couldn't move her hands from the wheel.

"What's the matter?" the girl asked finally, looking over.

"I can't do this," Lucinda whispered, dry-throated again. "I want to, but I just can't."

"That's okay. We don't have to. Maybe we could go for a walk. How would that be?"

"I'm so sorry," Lucinda said, ashamed.

"It's okay." Katanya leaned over and patted Lucinda's arm. "You don't have to be scared. I wouldn't want you to do somethin' scary. That wouldn't be fair."

She was getting lessons in civility from a small child, receiving more sympathy and understanding from this girl than most adults had ever offered. "You have a good heart," Lucinda murmured. "I get this way now and then. Tomorrow I might just climb into the car and go off without a thought. But sometimes it takes me three or four tries to make it to the post office. I really am sorry. You deserve an outing."

"We could try walking up the road," Katanya suggested again.

"Yes. Let's try that." A pause, then, "Do I seem like a crazy lady to you?" Lucinda tried to smile but couldn't quite bring it off.

"Unh-unh." The girl shook her head. "I told you: I think you're nice. I get scared sometimes, too. There's some boys like to hang by our stoop. I see them, I go back to the bodega around the corner and phone Mrs. Garcia. She's big and she can be *mean*. She comes down and chases them away for me, so I can get inside. And sometimes," she went on, warming

59

to the subject, "I can't get to sleep cuz I know there's a monster on the fire 'scape, just waitin' for me to close my eyes. Then he'll come flyin' through the window when I'm sleepin' and eat me up or hurt my moms or gramma. So I stay awake, watchin' the window. Then, in the mornin' when I wake up, I say, 'That was stupid, Kat, you bein' a scaredy-cat.' But in the dark things seem way real sometimes."

"Yes, they do."

There was a silence. They sat in the now-cool air, listening to the plaintive violin music oozing from the speakers.

"Let's walk," Katanya said, opening the door and getting out to stand looking in at Lucinda. "Come on. We'll try. If that doesn't work, we'll think of something else."

By the time Lucinda turned off the car, removed the key from the ignition and got out, Katanya had zipped around the back and was waiting by the driver's side. "You can hold my hand, if you like," she said soberly. "That might make you feel better."

"Thank you."

Lucinda took hold of the child's hand—small and warm and solid—and they started down the driveway.

———

She felt disabled, impaired in some way. Her movements were uncoordinated, her feet responded to every ripple and rut in the road. Any moment now, she'd topple over and be unable to get up.

"Who lives there?" Katanya asked, pointing at the enormous, pastel-painted Victorian Lucinda had always admired. It had a deep wrap-around porch with half a dozen wicker rockers; the front windows had stained-glass panels, and there was just the right amount of gingerbread trim.

"I don't know," Lucinda answered. "I don't know any of the people who live around here."

"It's a pretty house, isn't it?"

"Yes, it is."

"Oh, look! It's got another little house on the side."

"I think that's the garage."

"Yeah? It looks like a little house."

"It does," Lucinda agreed.

"I like your house better," the girl said with newfound loyalty. "How come you don't have any furniture on your porch?"

"We used to, when we first came back from California." Lucinda had to wonder where the porch furniture was. Probably in the barn, she decided. One of these days, she'd have to take inventory of the barn's contents. She hadn't been inside in at least ten years.

"Be nice to sit out on the porch in the evening," Katanya said. "Sometimes, when it's really really hot, me and moms and gramma we sit out on the fire 'scape. Long time ago, we used to sleep out there. But it's too dangerous now. Crackheads and junkies, they'll climb right over you, steal stuff and leave by the front door. It happened to Mrs. Garcia, but she woke up and went after the guys with her baseball bat. Broke one guy's arm and the other guy's knee. Nobody messes with her anymore. But we've got gates on all the windows now. Gramma has to unlock them if we want to go out. An' we got a police lock on the door. You know? The one with the pole that goes one end in the floor and the other end up against the door?"

"I've never actually seen one."

"It's good. Nobody could *ever* get past that."

"That is good," Lucinda said, trying to imagine living with steel gates on the windows and police locks on the doors. It'd be like a prison.

As if reading Lucinda's thoughts, Katanya said, "My moms says we'll move when she graduates and gets work as a certified public accountant. But gramma says that'd be foolish because we'd have to pay lots more rent for a place that wouldn't be any safer or better than the one we've got and it'd probably be half the size. Our place is big," she explained. "We've got three bedrooms. It's rent-controlled, see. Gramma's always lived there. It was her mama and papa's place, and gramma came back to live with them when my grampa went to the war in Vietnam and got killed. They looked after my moms while gramma worked every day for Mrs. and Mrs. Weinburg. Gramma says we're never moving and that if more people were like Mrs. Garcia we wouldn't have any problems at all."

"She's probably right."

"I told you. She's right most of the time. Gramma's *smart*. She was in college when she met grampa. She was studying to be a lawyer. But they made my moms and then he went off to be in the war, so she never got to finish."

"That's too bad."

"Oooooh! *Look* at *that* house! It looks just like a tiny little castle. And there's even a round room. It's so *cute*."

"There are five or six of those houses around town. They were apparently built by this mad architect who'd never sell them, so for years and years they were empty. I suppose he must've died and they were finally sold by the estate. There's nothing else like them anywhere. I've seen three of them. They're all different and not very big, but wonderfully eccentric. I've always loved those houses. I think they looked better empty, though. There was something quite magical about them completely empty."

"Still is, I think," Katanya said. "Wouldn't you love to see what it's like inside?"

"I would, actually. Although when they were empty, you could walk all around and look in the windows. The floors were beautiful white marble and there were rooms with domes, and some that were round, like that one. They all had columns out front, and classical entryways, covered passages that led from one room to another. I always wondered about the man who designed and built them. I thought he must be very wealthy to keep on building these places and leaving them empty, just, perhaps so he could drive by now and then to admire them."

"How old were you when you came here from California?"

"We moved back when I was sixteen and got accepted into Yale."

"Wow! You went to Yale? That is *cool*! I'd like to go to Yale."

"Perhaps you will."

"What'd you study there?" Katanya asked excitedly.

"English."

"And that's how come you do the Internet stuff?"

"Partly. It wasn't what I planned to do; it's just how things turned out."

"What'd you plan?"

"I thought I'd keep on writing scripts. That's what I'd been doing since I was thirteen."

"What? Like movies?"

"That's right."

"You wrote *movies* at thirteen? And they *let* you? Did they get made?"

Lucinda had to smile. "I wrote six of them and they all got made. But they were written under a pseudonym because Lily and I agreed that was the wisest way to go. I wrote most of them for my best friend, Gin Holder."

"*She's* your *best friend*?" Katanya stopped and stared up at her in amazement.

"That's right. You know who she is?"

"Course I do. *Everybody* knows who she is. Wow! *Wow!* Which ones did you write?" she asked excitedly.

"They're old movies. You probably wouldn't know them."

"Bet I would! Which ones?"

Amused, Lucinda named them. "*December Blue, Abby, Rain Days*, and *Power Play*. A couple of others."

"I love *Rain Days*! It's the *best. You* wrote *that*?"

"Yes, I did. You've seen it?"

"Sure. My moms and gramma bought that one. It's their favorite. Wow! Wait'll I tell them! They'll be totally blown away."

"Nobody knows I wrote them, Katanya."

"You mean I shouldn't tell?"

"Only your mother and grandmother. Okay? Do me a favor and please don't talk about me to Mrs. Crane."

"Okay, sure. I don't like her enough to tell her something that important anyway. Are you getting tired? Should we start back now?"

"That might be a good idea. It's awfully hot."

Katanya did an about-face, took hold of Lucinda's other hand and waited for her to turn. "How come you don't write movies anymore?"

"One more long story," Lucinda answered.

"You still best friends with Gin Holder?"

"I think so."

"Don't you know?"

"I'm as bad about the telephone as I am about going places."

Katanya thought about that for a time as they made their way back along the road. "Maybe," she said at last, "next time she phones, you should talk to her."

"Maybe," Lucinda allowed, beginning to feel very tired.

When they arrived at the Cranes' driveway, Lucinda said, "I'm going to leave you now. Okay?"

"Okay. Could I come visit again? I had a *really* good time."

"I think so. Let's see how it goes."

"Thank you very much, Lucinda."

"You're welcome. Go along now." Lucinda released her hand and took a step back. Katanya remained where she was, looking a little sad, a little lost. "Go on," Lucinda said gently.

With reluctance, the girl turned and started up the driveway. Halfway along, she stopped and turned. Lucinda waved. Looking relieved to see that she was still there, Katanya waved back, then skipped off out of sight.

Exhausted suddenly, Lucinda turned and made her way back down the road.

Chapter Five

Once home, Lucinda sat slumped on the living room sofa. She was so tired that it was several minutes before she could reach to remove her hat and sunglasses. Her head felt swollen: a recognizable symptom of sensory overload. She'd said and done more in her few hours with Katanya than she had in years. During her time at university she'd easily spent entire nights sitting in diners, or in off-campus housing, talking with friends; the exchange of ideas had kept her energized. Back then, she'd been alive with ideas, on fire with them; in love with her life and with the process of learning. Now, anything more than a few minutes spent with someone started her brain rocketing, like one of those silver balls inside a pinball machine, bouncing here and there, shooting through gates—bells and totals ringing higher and higher, tension mounting proportionately. Finally, her stomach began to contract and a headache set in—as it did now.

She had to sit for another fifteen minutes before she was able to go reeling to the kitchen for her medication. Leaving the lights off, one hand on the countertop for support, she washed down the pill with half a small bottle of Evian water. Then, back in the living room, trembling, nauseated, her eyes slitted against the glare, she pulled the verticals over the windows and stretched out on the sofa with her eyes closed while fragments of conversation with Katanya repeated again and again. The volume of the words made her head throb. She tried to redirect her thoughts into neutral territory, but random snippets kept returning, playing over and over. Her stomach went up and down like an express elevator. She tried instead to concentrate on her breathing, swallowing every few seconds, hoping she wouldn't be sick. She hated throwing up, hated the feeling she had afterwards of being unable to control her own body, hated the raw throat and the pain in her belly and the vile taste in her mouth.

This was a bad one: the sensation of a red-hot needle piercing her temple, a powerful hand squeezing at the base of her skull, the giddying sensation of the room turning. She shifted onto her side to combat the positional vertigo and, for a minute or two, the spinning stopped. Then it started again. She turned to the other side and gained another few minutes before the world behind her eyelids started to spin once more.

Sliding off the sofa, she lay on her back on the floor, eyes shut, focused entirely on her breathing. Her hair was wet at the back of her neck, her whole body felt simultaneously hot and cold. Her heart beat so hard, so heavily that she knew if she were able to look down at herself she'd see her chest lifting and falling. Breathe out slowly, she told herself; now breathe in. Out slowly, in steadily.

Within half an hour the medication started to kick in and she was able to crawl back onto the sofa. Dragging the mohair throw over herself, she curled up on her right side, cold now to the point of shivering, and pushed her attention back to her breathing. The needle piercing her temple was becoming dulled, the grip on the back of her neck was easing. Her stomach now felt hollow, bruised, but the nausea was passing.

Hands tucked between her thighs, she thought about Katanya waving to her from outside, beckoning her to come out. She thought about her remarkable smile and the startling whiteness of her teeth, about the musical notes of her laughter and the gently caring touch of the girl's small hand on her arm. Tears leaked from Lucinda's closed eyes as she heard again, "You'd better eat that. My gramma says it's a sin to waste food. And you're skinny. I bet you don't eat much."

It was so painful to have someone, anyone, express concern for her well-being. She'd been so successful in closing herself away from people's concern, from their bewilderment and confusion at what seemed to be her rejection of them that now she doubted she had the ability to reconnect. Another lost skill, among so many.

Curled into herself under the throw, gradually thawing, her thoughts slipped back to what she'd long considered to be the beginning of the devolution of her life.

———

"Tell me about him!" Lucinda had demanded, holding up the photograph the instant she and Eddie were inside the car.

"Oy!" Eddie sighed. "Lucy, Lucy. Could we be a little civilized here, sweetheart? I'm sad, I'm tired and I need some coffee. We'll go somewhere, I'll get my coffee, a little to eat, and we'll talk."

Frustrated, she pulled out of the station, heading for the Post Road.

"Slow down, please," Eddie said quietly. "You're making me nervous."

"Sorry," she said automatically, and eased her foot back on the accelerator. "I'm sorry, Eddie. It's just ... I'm so ... "

"I know, Lucy. Me, too. A few more minutes and we'll talk. That's a promise."

She picked the Greek diner because she liked their home fries, because the atmosphere was good-natured, and because the owner's young wife was a very beautiful, soft-spoken woman with masses of dark curly hair and a lovely smile. Often on the weekends during her years at Yale, Lucinda had come in at night to sit at the counter with her textbooks and eat plates of home fries and drink coffee while she studied. The wife (whose name Lucinda had never learned) would keep Lucinda's cup full. She greeted Lucinda or bid her goodbye with a glorious smile. They never once spoke.

"Have breakfast," Lucinda had told Eddie as they slid into a booth with cracked leatherette seats. "It's good here."

"Fine. It's early still. I'll have breakfast."

After they'd ordered and the owner had poured coffee into thick white mugs, Eddie said, "Here's what I know, Lucy. His first name was Franklin, and he and your mother looked at each other like they'd never seen anyone better in their whole lives. I saw him maybe three times. Once was by accident before you were born and we were back east here, doing promotion for one of Lily's early movies. It was in forty-six or -seven. I went up to her room without phoning first from the lobby, got to the door in time to see this fella leaving. I figured he was hotel staff, didn't give it another thought. Next time I saw him was in Paris when we cooked up the fake French film deal." He held up a hand to stop her from interrupting. "Believe me, it took some doing. But Lily had it all figured out. It was the only way she could keep everything secret. You know how she was in public. Nobody ever recognized her. She was counting on that in

France. And it worked, too. There was a rented apartment, a doctor. The whole thing was organized like a military operation. Anyhow, we took a cab to the hotel and he was there, waiting. I remembered him from the hotel in New York and things clicked in my head. A great-looking guy, tall, strong, well-spoken, beautiful manners. Didn't take a genius to see why Lily fell for him. All she said to me was, 'I'm trusting you with this, Eddie. You're the only one who knows.' Then she introduced me to her husband, Franklin. He shook my hand, looked me right in the eye, and thanked me for everything I'd done for your mother. And that was it. I left the two of them there. Five months later I flew back over to bring the two of you home to an arranged press greeting at the airport." He shrugged and drank down the last of his coffee. And as if he'd been waiting, the owner was there, refilling Eddie's cup.

"And the third time?" Lucinda prompted, the moment the man moved away from the table.

"Maybe a year later. You were still a baby. Lily phones me, says she's got to get back east right away. It's urgent. I've got to get her there, get someone to look after you. So I tell her it's no problem, my Estelle would take care of you. She was crazy for you, Estelle. Couldn't get enough of you. So I make a couple of calls to cover what was on my plate, then go pick the two of you up, drop you home with Estelle, then me and Lily head for the airport and catch the red-eye. 'What're we doing?' I ask her finally. And she tells me Franklin's shipping out to Korea. She's got a window of maybe a couple of hours, to see him. I've got to get her to New Jersey." He paused, stirring sugar into his cup. "I always thought she had a whatchamacallit, a premonition."

"Why?"

"I think she knew he wasn't gonna be coming back."

"He *died*?" Lucinda asked softly, stricken.

"Yeah." Eddie's voice thickened. "Just tore her up like nothing I'd ever seen. Couldn't imagine how she felt until Estelle passed. Then I knew. But if it wasn't for her having you, Luce, I think that would've been the end of Lily. She went to pieces for the best part of a year. And she was never the same after. Something just went right out of her. She could pull it together when she had to—for work, you know—but that woman's heart was well and truly broken."

"He died," Lucinda repeated, her grief doubled. She'd lost and found a father in the space of only hours. She had no one now.

They were silent for a time. Lucinda looked at the man across the table, suddenly seeing that somehow, when she wasn't looking, Eddie had grown old. He had to be in his late sixties, although he still looked good. Dapper always, with a full head of dark wavy hair and lively brown eyes, expressive features; an attractive man. He was the only person she'd known all her life, and she loved and trusted and relied on him just as her mother had.

The owner came with their food; they both automatically thanked him and looked down at their plates.

"All that business about Lily and men, it wasn't true, was it?" Lucinda asked.

"Studio dates. A guy so much as laid a finger on her, Lily was on the phone to me to come get her. Outside a sound stage, I never saw her do anything more serious than hold some fella's arm. And that was just for the press. Minute they were gone, she wouldn't even get near a guy, never mind touch one."

"What about Lester? Was any of that true?"

"Some. She did have a girlfriend that worked in the New York office. I forget her name, but they were tight and she knew Lily wanted to act more than anything. So she phoned to let your mother know Foxcroft was in town and on his way to the office, and to get down there right away. Lily laughed when she told me about it. Her and Ann Miller and your pal Gin are three of maybe half a dozen women who made themselves out to be *older* than they actually were to have a crack at the movies. Lily wasn't seventeen yet, but said she was eighteen. Got herself all gussied up, went in there and just *happened* to be at reception when Lester strolled by. He got one look, stopped to talk to her, heard that voice and asked her to audition. Hired her on the spot. He did try to put the moves on her, but Lily kept him at arm's length until she got the contract. Once everybody signed on the dotted line, she told him that she thought he was the dearest man alive but she was underage and she was sweet on a fella in Connecticut.

"To his credit, Lester got a laugh out of it. He could've made things hard for her but he decided to play along. He was crazy about her. That part's the truth. He had a soft spot for Lily 'til the day he died. But Lester was a gent of the old school; he wasn't vindictive and he never played mean. Plus casting her—a complete unknown who walked away with the picture—scored him big points; signing Lily moved Lester way up in the major leagues. So everybody won."

"Your breakfast's getting cold," Lucinda said.

"So're your home fries," Eddie countered. "You eat, I'll eat, too. It's gonna be a rough few days."

Lucinda picked up her fork and speared a potato. "Did she ever say anything about his family?"

"Whose?"

"My father's."

"I'm pretty sure she was in touch with them, but she talked about it just this one time. It was right after she got word that

he died and she said something about how at least his people had a part of him in his grandchild. But you know how
she was, Luce. Lily didn't want to talk, nothing on earth
could make her."

"I know." Lucinda put the piece of potato into her mouth
and chewed. She couldn't taste a thing. Drinking more of her
coffee, she watched Eddie dig into his bacon, scrambled eggs
and paprika-sprinkled home fries.

"This's good," he murmured, eating quickly, pausing intermittently to dab his mouth with a napkin. "Hungry."

"Was he in the army?"

Eddie shook his head. "Navy. Pilot, I think. I seem to recall a remark he made about landing on a ship's deck in bad
weather. Anyhow, the man went to college. That much I
know."

"How do you know that?"

"He was an officer, Lucy, a captain. Not a lot of black cap-
tains in those days. Or now, for that matter. But especially
not then."

"But no last name."

Eddie shook his head again. "She told me one time that
there wasn't so much as a single scrap of paper to connect
her with anyone, not even you. Don't know what she did
with your birth certificate. Some French lawyer probably
made a nice chunk of change getting all the documents together, creating an identity for you so she could 'adopt' you
and bring you stateside. All she ever said was it cost her a
lot of money." He finished a triangle of toast, then washed it
down with coffee. "She went to the embassy in Paris with
those adoption papers and got you added to her passport.
Very smooth. She definitely got her money's worth, 'cause I
know the rag reporters tried every way to Sunday to check
out her story but got nowhere. All the paperwork passed

muster. Nobody believed her, but nobody could prove you weren't adopted. So it got to be old news in a hurry. Just the way Lily wanted it."

"If he was a captain, he had to've been a fair bit older than she was," Lucinda said, thinking aloud.

"Oh, yeah," Eddie agreed. "I figured him to be maybe twenty-eight, thirty when I saw him that last time. Could've been older or younger. Hard to tell, the way some people are. Like you. You look fifteen tops. Here you're nineteen already. And I'm a couple of years younger than Abe Lincoln. Time just gets away on us." He looked out the window at the parking lot, blinking back tears. After a few moments, as if remembering, he put down his knife and fork and pushed the plate away. "I'm gonna miss her. Can't believe she's gone."

"I know." Lucinda had given up on the home fries and sat with both hands wrapped around the coffee mug. "I think that's why she let it go for so long. Because she was lonely; she missed him."

"Let what go?"

"The lump. Dr. Tepperman said she had to have had it for as much as a year. But why did she agree to the radiation? I'm so confused. I have to find his family, Eddie."

"I'll help, but there's not much to go on."

"Maybe they'll come to the funeral."

"Sweetheart, think about it. That's not gonna happen. It'd be nice for you, but I can't see it. It's a long time later. Whatever contact Lily had with those people, there was some kind of agreement in place or you'd have seen them before now."

"But, Eddie! It's not the fifties anymore. It's almost the seventies. That stuff doesn't matter now."

"Let's take it a step at a time here, Lucy. Don't go getting ahead of yourself. First, there's the funeral to get through. Give it a while. Then we'll have a run at it, see what we see."

He was right, of course, and she knew it. Reporters had started phoning at six that morning, without preamble asking imbecilic questions like, "How do you feel about your mother's passing?" or "What's it like being an orphan again?" Insensitive ghouls. She'd slammed down the phone each time and quit answering after the third call, letting the service take messages.

"Let's go to the house and I'll get started on the arrangements."

For a second or two she thought he was talking about starting the search for her family. Then, with a drowning sense of sorrow, she realized he was referring to her mother's funeral. *What's it like being an orphan again?*

When she opened her eyes she couldn't figure out whether it was day or night, or even which day or night. Moving cautiously, she sat up. The headache hovered, perhaps ready to attack again. But it might give up and go away if she took more medication. That sometimes worked. Rising from the sofa, she stood for several seconds, checking her equilibrium. Definitely not a hundred percent. More medication. But first, she needed to clean up. She could smell herself; she hated that.

After she'd showered and washed her hair, she returned downstairs to the kitchen. When she turned on the stove light she saw with a jolt that she'd slept for more than twenty-four hours. She'd returned from her walk with Katanya the previous day at two-twenty. It was now almost three and she'd certainly slept for longer than half an hour. Or had she? Parting the the vertical blinds slightly, she saw it was full daylight outside. After getting a pot of coffee started (always a must with a migraine), she went to the living room to turn on the computer and waited for it to boot up. Knowing the child wouldn't be there, Lucinda nonetheless pushed aside one of the slats to look around. No one.

When she looked back at the computer, the day at the top of the screen read Tuesday. At once she felt guilty, certain Katanya had come to signal to her from the garden only to see the windows covered. She'd probably thought Lucinda hadn't wanted to see her, and she wasn't so bold that she'd come to the door. Katanya was a deeply sensitive child.

Hearing the telltale groans from the coffeemaker signaling that it had finished the brewing cycle, she got up with care and walked slowly back to the kitchen. She'd written that number down somewhere. But where? A visual scan of the kitchen produced no results. She couldn't just go over there, asking could Katanya come out to play. But she couldn't disappoint the child—or herself. She wanted, even needed, to see Katanya again. Something had started that she didn't wish to stop.

Her head starting to ache, she poured a cup of coffee and took her medication with a swallow of the extra-strong brew. Then, annoyed with herself, she said, "The phone book, stupid," and lifted it down from the top of the refrigerator. Trying to focus on the small print hurt her eyes, sending threatening pinpoints of pain into her temples. But she found the listing and with an unsteady hand made a note of the number. Then, not giving herself the time to think it to death, she picked up the handset and tapped out the number.

"This is Lucinda Hunter," she said when the woman answered. "I hope it's not an inconvenient time to be calling, but I'd like to speak to Katanya."

"Oh!" There was an entire spectrum of emotions in that one syllable: surprise, irritation, and the obsequiousness that couldn't be concealed. "Of course. Just a moment, please." Mrs. Crane covered the mouthpiece with her hand and let out a shout that would've done a third-base umpire proud. It was so loud that Lucinda had to hold the phone away, with the feeling that blood might start oozing from her eardrum. At the other end of the line, the receiver was audibly dropped onto a surface—in disgust, disappointment?—and Lucinda risked returning the handset to her ear, hearing the woman say, "Telephone." Then quick squeaky steps as sneakers ran across linoleum.

"Hello?"

"Hi. It's Lucinda."

"Hey, hi. How you be?"

"Oh dear. She's standing there, listening, looking very suspicious."

"That be right."

"The woman needs a hobby."

"Sure do!" Katanya agreed in a gleeful tone.

"I wanted you to know that I wasn't avoiding you today. I get migraine headaches. Do you know about them?"

"Yeah, I do."

"Okay, well I've got one. I just took some more meds, so with luck, I'll be okay by tomorrow. Would you like to come in the morning? I thought we might try for an outing. Something exciting, like the Wendy's drive-thru. I could probably manage that."

"Sure. That be fine."

"Do I need to explain it to her or will she take your word for it?"

"I be takin' cara that. Don'tchu worry none."

"Thank you, Kat. I'll see you tomorrow at, say, ten?"

"Good." Lowering her voice, sounding as if she'd hunched herself over the phone, the girl whispered, "Hope you feel better. I'm sorry you're sick." Then her voice returning to its previous volume, she said, "Yeah, 'kay, 'bye," and disconnected.

Lucinda was smiling as she put down the phone.

Chapter Six

She tried to do some work but knew at once that she couldn't. Merely looking at the blocks of type on the screen hurt her eyes, started her feeling queasy. Pulling up her address book, she sent an e-mail to Craig to let him know she'd be a little later than promised on uploading the edited content to their ftp site.

From habit, she went to her home page to read the latest news and was just scanning the headlines when Craig e-mailed back to say, "You're already way ahead of schedule. Don't sweat it. Everything's fine. We're just doing the html on the copy from last week. So it'll be at least another week before we need that last batch. Take it easy. Great job, as always. Best, Craig."

Relieved, she closed the browser and shut down the computer. The combination of the coffee and the medication had her feeling sleepy but jumpy. She settled again on the sofa and turned on the TV, searching until she found an old black-and-white film. Putting down the remote, she curled up on her side, fascinated, as always, by the sound quality, the edginess of the voices. Modern sound technology tended to dull voices, so the characters' voices were oddly muted, often toneless. She'd always loved the old noir films, with their great cinematography, dark plot lines and interesting actors: *The Maltese Falcon* with prime Bogart and a wonderfully duplicitous Mary Astor; *Sunset Boulevard* which she could watch over and over, marveling each time at the dialogue and the remarkable lighting on Gloria Swanson, the woman's posture and power; Jane Greer's wicked beauty in *Out of the Past*, and a neurasthenic Bergman in *Gaslight*—one of her all-time favorites, which Lucinda considered to be period noir. Moody, dark films with exceptional scripts, outstanding performances.

One of the best films Lily ever made was Lester's only attempt at noir: *Street Crime*. Again having her play against type, he'd used Lily as the cast-aside wife in a dangerous triangle. With a clean-scrubbed, wholesome look, her hair pulled back into a ponytail so that her features, particularly her eyes, had stunning definition, he'd had the costume designer dress her in simple white blouses, baggy slacks and loafers: outfits that played down her by-then famous figure. Lily inhabited the role of an abandoned woman so fully that even though her character was ultimately revealed to be the vengeful villain of the piece and responsible for her husband's death, viewer sympathy was entirely with her. And after an intense courtroom scene, when she was acquitted by the jury, audiences spontaneously erupted into applause. She won the Golden Globe that year for best actress and also got an Academy Award nomination. "I won't win, and I hate those do's, so I'm not going," she'd told Lucinda. A jubilant Lester wound up accepting the award for her while she and six-year-old Lucinda were at a drive-in restaurant, having burgers and fries and chocolate milkshakes—blissfully unaware that she'd won until they arrived back at the rental house to find the street crowded with press and photographers. "Oh, crap!" Lily muttered. "I'm not even wearing lipstick." The shots that appeared in the next day's papers were less than flattering, and Eddie had phoned to say, "*Mazel tov,* Lil. I'm very proud of you. And Estelle is *kvelling.* You'd think she was your mother, she's so excited. But, listen. Do everybody a favor and stay home next time. That way, if you win again, you'll have time to go put on some makeup and comb your hair before the press starts pounding on the door."

At the press conference Eddie organized the next afternoon, Lily was dressed to the nines; her hair and makeup had been done by two women sent over by the studio, and she was sporting her important jewelry—a diamond pendant and rare pink pearl earrings. She was also, Lucinda remembered vividly, genuinely surprised and thrilled at having won. It was one of the rare occasions when she was happy to chat with the press and have flashbulbs going off in her face nonstop. Still, she didn't put the golden statuette on display but kept it in a box on the shelf in her closet. "*They* know I won it and *I* know I won it. What's the point of having it on show? That'd be too much like bragging." She did, though, hang the framed citation in the hallway of each of their several rental homes. But when they moved back to Connecticut, she couldn't decide where to put it, so it sat on her dresser for four years, until she died. Lucinda eventually positioned the heavy award in the living room bookcase and hung the citation on the wall by her desk and every so often she'd look over at it and think about that night at the drive-in. "Wonderful, Wonderful" had been playing on the car radio and Lily had said, "I love this song." When Lucinda asked why, Lily paused before taking another bite of her burger to say, "I just do. Someday you'll know why."

The first picture Lucinda wrote was *December Blue*, an admittedly somewhat derivative noir based on an idea she and Gin cooked up, about a girl who wanders into a Los Angeles police station one December night, wearing a coat over her pajamas. She tells the desk sergeant that she can't remember who she is or where she lives. A detective, played with effective economy by Joseph Cotton, gets his fiancée, Ann Doran, to take the girl in while he tries to uncover her identity. For once playing younger than her age (she was almost eighteen when principal photography started) Gin was thoroughly convincing as sixteen-year-old Arla Blue. In bed in Doran's guest room, the girl wakes up screaming from an horrific nightmare that she insists to Doran, and the next day to Cotton, is not a dream at all but a replay of her mother's murder—shown in fragmented backflashes that are lit as if by lightning, with the assailant only a distorted shadow. Her memory returning in the aftermath of the nightmare, the girl declares that her father has murdered her mother and that she witnessed it.

When confronted, the man disbelievingly laughs it off, telling Cotton that his wife is away, visiting her family in Oregon, and that his daughter has always had an overactive imagination. Since there's no evidence to the contrary and since she's underage, Cotton has no choice but to leave Arla with her father. After Cotton's departure, the father demands to know why she's trying to make trouble for him. Arla just glares at him. And the next day, desperate, she returns to the station and begs Cotton to help her. He tells her that he's been unable to contact her mother in Oregon, but without any proof of Arla's claims, there's little he can do for her. Now frantic, the girl returns home. Her father's away at work, but a cut to the clock shows that it's after four; he'll soon be home.

Agitated, Arla paces back and forth in the kitchen while the camera cuts to the clock, showing the minutes ticking away. She stops and gazes at the cellar door, then suddenly swings into action. She flies down the cellar stairs to her father's workbench. Grabbing a crowbar, she climbs back up and loosens the top board that holds the set of wooden stairs to the floor beam below the door. Satisfied, she returns the crowbar to the workbench and carefully goes back up the now unsteady steps.

That evening during dinner, when her father becomes incensed by her renewed accusations and goes after her, she jumps up from the table and runs down into the dark cellar, slamming the door behind her. Once at the bottom, she pulls the staircase away from its minimal connection with the beam, creating a gap of several feet. When her father comes chasing after her, he throws open the door, steps into space and plunges twelve feet to the concrete floor, breaking his neck.

After nudging him with her foot, then holding her hand over his mouth to make sure he's dead, she pushes the stairs back into place. With a hammer she drives the nails back into the beam. Then she drags the body to the foot of the stairs, grunting with the effort as she shifts the father so that he's sprawled face-down. Satisfied by the scene she's created, she leaves the house by the storm doors, taking care to collect the displaced leaves and twigs and strew them back over the doors. From a pay phone up the road, she calls Cotton to say her father tried to attack her but she ran down to the cellar. When he followed, he tripped and fell down the stairs. Since she is coatless and cold, her shivering creates a believable tremor in her voice.

The police arrive and find not only his body but also (directed by scenes Arla claims she remembers from her nightmare) that of her mother, buried in the back garden. The final shot is of Arla, smiling happily as she sits at the vanity in Doran's guest bedroom, smiling at her reflection in the mirror, while she listens to Cotton and Doran in the living room talking about "that poor kid." As she listens, she opens her shoulder bag and removes several items, one of which is her father's wallet. She counts the money, then puts the wallet back in the bag and pulls out a jewelry box. It is obvious by her expression that this box was her mother's. As she slides a diamond solitaire onto her finger and holds out her hand to admire it, her eyes seem to glow as coldly and brilliantly as the diamond—an effect created by the lighting man who rigged up two tiny spotlights shielded with multipointed cardboard cutouts and shone them directly into Gin's eyes. The effect was creepy and chilling, leaving one to wonder if Cotton and Doran would be her next victims.

The picture got decent reviews (Gin got raves) and did well at the box office, earning a respectable gross. More importantly, it moved producers to take Gin seriously as an actress. It was her breakthrough movie. In hindsight, Lucinda could see holes in the plot but the screenplay certainly was nothing to be ashamed of. And she particularly liked writing about females with a killing bent. It wasn't new; nothing was. But coming up with a different take on old themes was always challenging. What made *December Blue* notable was the combination of a great cast, wonderful cinematography, terrifically creative lighting, and Gin's outstanding performance. "A very decent script, kiddo. You never fail to amaze me," Lily said, giving Lucinda a hug after the sneak preview, when they were well out of sight of the audience. "And you!" she said, turning to put both hands on Ginny's shoulders. "You're going to get one hell of a lot of attention now. You were great, Gin, really great." Turning to include Lucinda, she said, "I am honestly proud of you girls."

Lily was right. Offers began pouring in, and Ginny Holder became Gin forever after, going on to star in more than twenty features and winning some major awards. For the past ten years she'd regularly phoned up, begging Lucinda to get back to work and write a decent movie for her. But Lucinda had—as Gin often said, sounding so like Lily it was a bit unnerving—"Too damned many reasons for saying no and not one of them worth crap."

Now the noir film Lucinda was watching on TV was from the late forties, but she couldn't recall the title. It didn't matter. She liked the look of the era: the lumpy furniture, the pools of light and intriguing dark areas, the men's fedoras and the women's frou-frou dresses. Plenty of snappy back-and-forth dialogue, rich with urgency; faces with mobility and character. The women had thick fake eyelashes, absurdly dark eyebrows and overdrawn mouths, yet were beautiful in spite of the makeup. The good guys had pencil-line mustaches and nip-waisted suits with heavily padded shoulders but carried themselves with dignified authority. The bad guys had visibly cheap suits, bad hats, and they slouched or shambled. Quality physical acting that spoke volumes. She had the sound turned way down and couldn't really follow what was going on, but it didn't matter. It was gratifying to study how the components meshed, creating mood and tension. She loved movies, had once loved being part of the movie-making process. Movies made sense to her in a way nothing in real life did. As well, there was a logic to scriptwriting that had made perfect sense to her and nothing had ever given her quite the degree of pleasure she got from taking an idea and developing it into a screenplay, fleshing out characters and situations, building the momentum. She missed that process almost as much as she missed Lily and her old friends. Sometime soon, she really would have to call Gin. For now, the medication was overcoming the caffeine and her eyelids were getting heavy.

The worst part of a migraine attack was the way time got all chewed up and thrown out of whack. She slept until three a.m. and when she awakened the headache was gone. But her days and nights were going to be skewed until she could reset her internal clock. Wide-awake at three in the morning, she cleaned the coffeemaker and started a fresh pot going before heading upstairs for another shower. Her body was stiff from sleeping on the sofa, so she stayed under a very hot spray until her muscles loosened. Then she dressed and returned to the kitchen to have some toast with her coffee. She heard the morning paper bounce off the front door and went to get it, and read several sections while she had a second cup of coffee.

Then, all at once anxious to be done with the editing so that she'd be free to spend time with Katanya without feeling guilty, she went to the living room and turned on the computer. While she waited for it to boot up, she wondered all at once why this child had become so important to her. Had she finally gone crazy altogether? Placing such significance on a few hours' of interaction with a nine-year-old ... But they were both lonely and felt out of place. What was the harm?

Lucinda was just double-checking the last paragraphs of the edit when she turned to see Katanya skipping up the driveway. Clad in a hot-pink T-shirt and white shorts, wearing her big sneakers, the girl waved and broke into a run.

Smiling, Lucinda got up and went to open the front door as Katanya ran up the front steps, beaming, and ran right to Lucinda to throw her arms around her waist, exclaiming, "I'm so happy to see you!"

Lucinda was so taken aback she didn't know how to respond, couldn't move; she just stood registering the sensation of having this child's arms wound around her waist.

Stepping back, Katanya asked, "The headache better?"

"Gone," Lucinda told her, standing aside so the girl could come in.

"Good. I saw you at the computer, so I figured you must be better. I'm glad."

"So am I. Look, I'm just finishing one last bit of work. If you don't mind waiting for a couple of minutes, I'll get it done and that'll be the end of it."

"C'n I watch?"

"Sure. But there's really nothing to see."

"That's okay. I'll watch anyway."

"Fine."

Lucinda started back into the living room with Katanya beside her. "Know what I really liked yesterday?" the girl asked.

"What?"

"Well, I liked it that you phoned, first of all. That was cool, cuz I was a little worried, thinking maybe you were mad at me or something. So I was glad to know you weren't. But what I *really* liked was you called me Kat. Only my moms and gramma call me that, and a coupla my girlfriends. But it was like ... family, kind of. You know? It made me happy."

For a few seconds Lucinda was so choked up she couldn't speak. Then she cleared her throat and said, "It just came out automatically."

"That's the way it should be," Katanya said, moving to look at the computer screen. "Not like something you planned or like that." Looking back at Lucinda, she said, "What's your nickname?"

"Ah, well." Lucinda slid into her chair and was now at eye level with the girl. "My mother called me Luce. And Eddie— he was my mother's publicist and sort of a father to me—he always called me Lucy. When we were at school together, Gin used to call me Cinders. Fortunately, she stopped by the time I was about twelve. Ever since then she's called me Ella."

"Oh! I *get* it!" Katanya crowed. "Ella Cinders. Cinderella!"

"Right! You're quick."

"Yeah. I am. So what should I call you?"

"I don't know. What would you like to call me?"

"I like Luce."

"Okay, that's it then. I just have to check two more paragraphs and then I'm done."

"Done for today or done for good?"

"Done for good," Lucinda told her.

"Great! Want me to go sit over there or something? Or is it really okay if I watch?"

"You can watch. But nothing's going to happen unless I find a typo."

"What's that?"

"Spelling mistake."

"Okay. I'll look with you."

Lucinda scrolled down to the last page of text and began reading, with Katanya so close that she could feel the girl's breath on her hair. Her senses were so inundated by sensation that it was hard to concentrate, but she forced herself to focus because she wanted, suddenly, to be done with this work forever.

Five or six minutes and it was done. "Spot any typos?" she asked Katanya.

"Nope. But what's that word synergy mean?"

"It's when the combined effects of a number of things are greater than the individual effects. For example, if you had, say, a stomachache and you took two kinds of medication instead of one, the combination would work better than just the one. Or if you wanted to protest something, getting a group of friends to protest with you would be more powerful than just your protesting alone."

"Oh! That's a good word. I'm gonna remember that." Putting a hand on Lucinda's shoulder, she said, "I like bein' with you. I learn things."

"So do I," Lucinda said, made happy by the warmth of that small hand.

Chapter Seven

They were in the kitchen, Lucinda getting juice-boxes from the refrigerator, when Katanya asked, "What's that?"

"What's what?" Lucinda asked, moving over to where Katanya was standing by the window.

"That wood thing."

"The fence?"

"I know it's a fence. But what's it *fencing*?"

"The pool."

Wide-eyed, the girl looked up at her and said, "You have a *swimming pool*?"

"Yes, but—"

"Could we go in it?"

"Come, let me show you."

Lucinda unlocked the back door and led the way to the gate in the stockade fencing. Katanya stepped inside, looked at the neglected pool with its leaf-covered pond of rainwater at the deep end and asked, sadly, "How come it's like this?"

"When we moved back from California my mother had the pool put in for me. If it was warm enough, I used to swim every day, from April until late in October. It was the one thing I looked forward to. Then one year, when the company called to schedule an appointment to get the pool cleaned and filled, I told them not to bother. I didn't even know I was going to do that, but I did. I'm still not sure why."

"How long ago was that?"

"Not too long. Three or four years, maybe five. I've lost track of time the last few years."

Staring down into the brown water, Katanya said, "If you asked them to come back and get it all cleaned up, I'd go swimmin' with you. I *love* swimmin'. When I came on the train, I was all excited because this town is near the water and I thought we'd go to the beach every day. But even though they've got a beach sticker on their car, we haven't gone once. I brought my bathin' suit and everything."

"Well then, I should probably call and ask them to come."

"Yeah! You *should*. Then we wouldn't have to worry about going out in the car or anything. We could *swim*."

"You're right. Let's go back in, and I'll phone them."

"Oh, cool!" Katanya exclaimed. "I'm so *happy*!" Taking Lucinda's hand, she skipped along at her side as they returned to the kitchen, and then Katanya skipped in squeaky-sneaker circles around the room while Lucinda got on the phone and agreed to pay an exorbitant surcharge for immediate service.

"They'll come this afternoon," Lucinda said after hanging up. "By tomorrow morning, it'll be cleaned and filled. So you'll be able to come over and swim. But I'm going to make you wear sunblock," she warned.

"I've got some. My moms made me bring it."

"Good. Because I don't want you getting crisped out there."

"Crisped," Katanya repeated with a smile. "That's funny. You know good words."

"Yes, I do."

"You've got so many neat things. I bet you've got treasures in the attic, too."

Lucinda laughed. "There's tons of stuff up there. But treasures? That would depend on your point of view."

"How come?"

"Mostly, it's my mother's old furniture, this and that. Would you like to go up and see?"

"Definitely for sure. I've never *seen* a real attic. All the old-fashioned kids' books I read always have attics full of treasures—special things, *magical* things."

"Then, maybe, from your point of view, there *are* treasures up there. Let's go see."

"This is gonna be so much fun!" Katanya said, and reached to take Lucinda's hand as they started toward the stairs.

Every time the child made physical contact with her, Lucinda felt as if she was receiving some rare life-giving transfusion that bypassed veins and went directly through her skin into her bloodstream.

On the attic landing, Lucinda opened the door and reached inside to turn on the light. The air was hot and heavy up here. A couple of flies buzzed lethargically, flying lazy, drunken little loops before landing on the ornamental round glass window at the far end and walking, as if in a stupor, over its surface. Thick dust covered everything, except the half dozen cartons or so nearest the door that contained the Lily Hunter memorabilia.

"It's just like the books," Katanya said with awe, "just the way it's *supposed* to be. Betcha anything there's treasures here."

"Like what?" Lucinda asked, amused, leaning against the door frame, arms folded over her chest.

"A chest filled with gold and jewels, stuff like that."

"Ah! That particular treasure chest would be downstairs in my bedroom." Seeing Katanya go wide-eyed again, Lucinda explained. "My mother's good jewelry. But," she said, unfolding her arms and walking into the center of the attic, "there is a box I think you'll like."

Shifting some chairs and pushing aside several large boxes containing she knew not what, Lucinda got to her mother's old dresser which was flush against the far wall. Lifting the flaps to make sure she had the right box, she carried it back to the center aisle and put it down on the floor. "Have a look in there," she said, on her way to the front to turn on the air extractor above the window.

"Wow!" Katanya delved into the heap of costume jewelry, pulling out long strings of glass beads, ropes of pearl, bangles and bracelets, brooches and gaudy paste dress rings. "Treasure," she whispered. "Exactly like in the books."

Lucinda brushed some of the dust off one of the ugly old brocade-covered dining room chairs and sat down, watching Katanya sort through the contents of the box, ooohing and aaahing over items she liked. The extractor drawing off some of the heat and pulling cooler air up the stairs, Lucinda was content to observe the child, remembering how, once upon a time, she, too, had played with these glittery, real-seeming gems. She could, so clearly, see herself sitting on the living room floor of the Brentwood house with this very box, examining the contents while Lily, stretched out on the sofa, studied a script. After half an hour or so, Lily would sit up, holding out the pages, saying, "Okay, help me run my lines, Luce." Dialogue she could remember to this day. Lily putting nothing into her lines in the living room. Then, on the set, there was all kinds of meaning in them.

When she tuned back in, Katanya was looking at her with concern. "You okay?" she asked. "Your headache comin' back?"

"I'm fine. Just hot. I don't handle heat very well."

"We can go back downstairs," Katanya offered, plainly reluctant to be parted from her treasure trove.

"Tell you what. Let's bring that down to the living room where you can take everything out and decide what you'd like to have."

"Have? You mean like for keeps?"

"Absolutely."

"Honest?"

"Honest."

"Wow! Okay!" Katanya quickly began putting everything back.

Lucinda went to turn off the fan, then picked up the box and they left the weighty heat of the attic. Downstairs again, leaving Katanya in the living room with her newfound treasure, Lucinda washed her hands before getting two more juice boxes from the refrigerator.

"The FedEx truck's coming," Katanya said as Lucinda handed her the juice. "Thank you. I'm very thirsty. Whatchu have bein' delivered all the time?"

"Just about everything. Books, groceries, music."

"Groceries? You don't even go to the market?"

"Nope. The post office and the library. That's it. I order most things online."

"I didn't even know you could do that. Wait'll I tell my moms and gramma!"

"Do you have a computer at home?"

Katanya shook her head.

The doorbell rang and Lucinda went to sign for the package—her order from CDnow.com.

"Do you like music?" she asked Katanya, using a single-edged razor blade to open the box.

"Yeah."

"What kind?"

"All kinds. What'd you get?"

"Old music from the fifties."

"You gonna play it?"

"A little later," Lucinda said, setting the opened box on her desk.

"Can I ask you something? I looked in the phone book, but I couldn't find you. So I was wondering would you maybe give me your phone number so I could call you sometime?"

"Of course." Lucinda quickly wrote her name and number on an index card. "We've never had a listed phone number," she explained.

Katanya looked at what was written, then folded the card and slipped it into the pocket of her shorts.

Thinking suddenly that this had to be a boring morning for the girl, Lucinda said, "Maybe I will play the music now," and grabbed one of the CDs, slicing the cellophane wrapper with her thumbnail as she went over to the sound system on the floor-to-ceiling wall unit that housed the TV and VCR, her many dictionaries and reference works, and dozens of books.

"Since I Met You Baby" was the first track. "I love this song," she said, hearing an interior echo of Lily's voice. She had favorite songs and would stop whatever she was doing if one came on the radio, to listen intently as if hearing encoded messages.

"My gramma loves it, too," Katanya said. "She told me Ivory Joe was the first black man to make the white charts. She's got Sam Cooke, Ray Charles, Brook Benton, Ben E. King; all those old guys. It's good music," she said critically. "Okay if I sit on the sofa?"

"Oh, honey, I'm sorry. Of course you can. Good grief! I don't know how to treat people anymore. Please, make yourself comfortable."

"You do so know how to treat people. You just forgot, that's all."

"Would it be okay for me to give you a hug?" Lucinda asked.

"I'd love it!"

Lucinda bent down and lifted the girl. Katanya wound her arms around Lucinda's neck, locked her legs around her hips, and laid her head on Lucinda's shoulder as "My Special Angel" began. Humming low, Lucinda danced slowly in a circle with the child in her arms, just the way Lily used to dance with her when she was little.

—

"What kind of car is this anyway?" Katanya asked.

"It's a Bentley Mulsanne."

"I never heard of a Bentley Mul-whatever. Where'd it come from?"

"It's from England."

"If it's from England, how did it get here?"

"I phoned the nearest dealer, who happened to be in New Jersey. I said I wanted it, they told me how much it cost. I said how much I'd like for the old car, and they said fine. I had my bank wire them the money. Then they drove this one here and went back to New Jersey in the old car."

"What was the old one?"

"A Cadillac. It was my mother's, although she always had me drive her everywhere because she was very nervous behind the wheel. But I never liked the Cadillac. It was too cushy, too much an old poop's kind of car."

Katanya laughed appreciatively.

"Really, it was. You couldn't get any real feeling of the road. I wanted something wonderfully engineered, something special, and this was special."

"Yeah. It's really special, really nice and really big." Katanya turned to look at the rear of the car, then leaned far over toward Lucinda to read the mileage. "It hasn't even gone a thousand miles! Is it new?"

"No, it's nine years old."

"That's the same age as me."

"Yes, it is."

"Well, I like it a whole lot. It's way better than an old poop Cadillac! An' it smells good, too."

"Thank you."

Lucinda got onto the Post Road and stayed in the left-hand lane, signaling for the turn into the plaza where the Wendy's was located.

"What would you like to have?" Lucinda asked as she pulled into the driveway beside the restaurant.

"I'll have the same as what you have."

"You're welcome to have anything you like."

"I want what you're having," Katanya insisted.

There was no one ahead of them at the drive-thru window. Lucinda ordered two bacon cheeseburgers, each with large fries and root beer, then drove around to the pickup window. She handed over a twenty-dollar bill, got her change, then waited for the food. Her heart was racing and perspiration was trickling down her sides, saturating the hair at the back of her neck. Once again her hands were slick on the wheel. She had to keep swallowing, and hoped she wasn't going to get sick. Two minutes and the food was being passed through the window. She placed the bags on the floor of the passenger's side, then headed toward the exit, trying to think of a way to tell the child that she had to go home.

"I think we should go back to your house and eat there where it's nice and cool," Katanya said.

Lucinda glanced over at her, then back at the road. She had to wet her lips before she could say, "Okay."

"Tomorrow, we could make our own lunch and eat at your pool," Katanya went on. "That way, we won't have to go anywhere at all. It'll be great."

Lucinda's chest heaved and she blinked back tears—grateful and ashamed and filled with wonder at how a child so young could be so perceptive, so kind. After a minute or so, when it felt as if the emotional spasm had passed, she said, "You know something? I think you are one of the most wonderful people I've ever met."

"I think you are, too," Katanya said. "You did this for me, even though it scared you a whole lot. I could tell that it did, but you keep your word when you say you'll do somethin'. That's important to children, you know."

Lucinda managed a smile. "Yes, I know."

"Most people *don't* know. Miz Crane sure doesn't. It's mostly the reason why Jason's always pitchin' fits, cuz she says, 'We'll do this or that later or tomorrow, Jason,' and then she never does it. And she thinks cuz he's not even three yet that he doesn't know she just broke a promise. It's not the right way to treat him."

"No, it isn't," Lucinda agreed soberly. "Do you like him?"

"Yeah, I kinda do. He comes to sit with me when she's in the kitchen cooking or downstairs doing the laundry. Snuggles right up, lifts my arm around his shoulder and sucks his thumb. Minute he hears her voice, he jumps up and off he goes. I don't think she's a good mom."

"Maybe she doesn't know how to be."

"Was your mom good?"

"Considering the circumstances, I think she was remarkable. Do you know what a cliché is?"

"I don't think so."

"It means roughly the same as 'been there, done that.' You know? Something that's common; you've heard it or seen it or done it a hundred times before."

"That's another good word. Klee-shay. I'm gonna remember that."

"Well, in Hollywood a lot of the top actresses became clichés. They started getting older and they weren't so much in demand anymore, and that worried them so they'd start drinking. So many of them wound up alcoholics. So many. Sometimes they'd get sober, or they'd find religion. Sometimes they'd get married six or eight times, or they'd get caught shoplifting in some store. Lily was never a cliché. She had a glass of wine maybe once a week. She didn't mess around with men. She walked away while she was still on top because she never wanted to be a has-been. And she treated me, always, as if I was a person and not a nuisance. She was a really good mother."

"'Cept for she didn't tell you about your dad."

"She had valid reasons at the time. She never meant to hurt me. I think she'd be very sad to know I wound up such a mess."

Lucinda pulled into the driveway, put the car into Park and turned to look at Katanya. "I think it would have broken her heart to see how I am now."

"There's not one single thing wrong with how you are now. You are fine 'n' dandy," Katanya asserted. "My gramma says that."

"It's a song title, you know."

"Really?"

"Unh-hunh. I'll play it for you, if I can find the track."

"Okay. Let's go inside and eat now. I'm starvin' hungry. Thank you for the ride in your nice Bentley Muscleman."

Lucinda laughed and pulled the key from the ignition.

Chapter Eight

"I had the best time," Katanya said at the door. "Should I come at ten again tomorrow?"

"That would be fine."

"What about your work? Are you gonna get in trouble?"

"No, no. I'll finish it tonight, then we'll be free to do whatever we like."

"I can't wait. We do neat stuff when I come here." Katanya hugged her around the waist. "Thank you, Luce. 'Bye." She skipped off down the front stairs, carrying her bag of treasures, and went running down the driveway, pausing to wave and blow a kiss before disappearing from view.

Lucinda walked back through the house, paused to take two Cokes from the refrigerator then continued out the kitchen door and into the fenced area to see how the pool men were doing.

The two young men had been working nonstop for more than three hours and had finished removing the rainwater and clearing the dead leaves and twigs from the drains. Now they were scrubbing the tiles with long-handled brushes and were better than two-thirds of the way to the shallow end. She walked over to the first young man and handed him one of the Cokes. His T-shirt was drenched with perspiration and he accepted it with a grateful smile and called over to his partner to come get the other Coke which Lucinda gave to him, saying, "It looks very good."

"Another half an hour or so and we'll be ready to start 'er filling."

"Wonderful. Thank you."

"Thanks for the Cokes. It's hotter 'n hell out here."

She returned inside and was about to take the box of costume jewelry back up to the attic but decided instead to leave it next to her desk. Katanya had had a wonderful time, trying on earrings and necklaces, going back and forth to the downstairs bathroom to admire herself in the mirror. In the end, she'd selected a very pretty rope of bezel-set crystals—"For my moms. She'll like this"—and a coral-colored enamel and gold-toned choker. "My gramma will love this." But she took nothing for herself. "I'll decide tomorrow. I haven't even looked at everything yet."

Lucinda sat down on the sofa, tired but pleased with how well the day had gone and particularly pleased with Katanya urging her to get the pool cleaned. With the pool ready for use, Lucinda would have to dig out her bathing suit. It was probably shot after so many years stuffed away in a drawer. If it was, she'd make do with shorts and a top because now that the pool was going to be usable again, she would definitely use it. The only time she didn't mind being out of doors in the summer was when she was in the water. She kept the temperature in the mid-eighties, having always disliked the initial shock of diving into water so cold her heart threatened to seize up and quit functioning.

Thinking back, she couldn't remember why she'd stopped having the pool serviced—just another example of her ongoing retreat from the world. Not that she'd ever had to interact with the young men; they came and went, skimming leaves and insects from the surface, checking the chemical levels and cleaning the filters. But she had, until just a few days earlier, been sinking deeper and deeper into her recessive trench. Now, so unexpectedly, it had stopped. A little girl had come to admire the garden and, turning, beckoned to her. Her draw was powerful: as if she were true north and Lucinda, like a magnet's needle, had no ability to resist the pull. Nor did she want to, once past the first few minutes in the girl's company.

It was about recognition. She could see herself in Katanya in many ways, could identify with how the child felt and how she viewed the world around her. She truly was a wonderful little being—bright and quick and innately kind. Lucinda had no doubt that she would grow up to be a splendid woman and, for a few moments, Lucinda was filled with envy of the mother and grandmother who would bear witness to Katanya's journey into adulthood.

Once upon a time, Lucinda had thought that she would one day marry and have children. She'd believed she'd found someone to love in Harcourt Lowndes in her senior year at Yale. At a time when most of the students had long hair and were wearing tie-dyed garments, love beads and headbands; when the girls had given up shaving their legs and underarms and abandoned brassieres, when the boys wore bell-bottom jeans and T-shirts bearing anti-war slogans, Cort's only concessions to the era were to abandon his blazers and neckties and to wear his penny loafers without socks. He'd been one of the small group of grad students who were the sons and grandsons and even the great-grandsons of alumnae. They wore the old "uniform"—pastel-colored Brooks Brothers button-down shirts with chinos or cords. Their hair was short and side-parted, they were all clean-shaven and good-looking, giving off a serious air yet smiling benevolently while passing through the chanting, dancing and singing, tambourine-playing crowds on campus. Lucinda had taken the middle ground, wearing short shapeless dresses and her long hair center-parted. She'd chosen comfort over statement but had no problem with any of the factions making themselves seen and heard during her years there. She did hate the idea of young men, still boys really, being sent off to fight a war that made no sense and seemed to be without legitimacy, but she couldn't be angry with the ones who chose to go. They believed they were demonstrating loyalty to their country. She also understood why some of them were heading off to Canada.

Thinking back, she could still see, as if it had happened only hours or days earlier, the hurt and bewilderment creasing Cort's fine features when she'd taken him aside after Lily's service to say, "I can't see you anymore."

"What d'you mean?" he'd asked, not getting it at all. Although why should he have? she'd wondered.

"Things have changed. I mean, I've learned certain facts I didn't know before. They affect everything. It just wouldn't be right for me to keep on seeing you."

"We need to talk about this," he said insistently. "You can't just tell me we're over and expect me to say, 'Oh, okay. 'Bye. See you when I see you.' I need to know about these 'facts' you've learned, and I need a chance to present my case, if I have to. This is hardly the time or place to be having a conversation like this, Lucy. Your mother died. You just got through a memorial service the likes of which I've never seen. Press and TV people all over the place and Eddie stage-managing the event like the ringmaster at a circus. Remarkable fellow, that Eddie." He'd shaken his head, as if in disbelief—and, possibly, displeasure. "Please, give yourself—and me—a couple of days, then let's talk. Today's Thursday. Why don't I drive down Saturday and we'll talk."

"I'll say the same thing Saturday I'm saying now."

"Fine. But at least there won't be crowds of people on all sides; we'll be alone and have a real chance to discuss matters. You're trying to call off our entire future together. Let's at least have the time and privacy we both need. You'll present your case and then we'll go from there. That's only fair."

"You know what I discovered this week, Cort? Nothing is fair, *nothing*. And there is no absolute truth, only degrees of it."

"You're upset, you're sad, you're scared," he said sympathetically. "This is *not* the time or place for talking about breaking up." He stroked her hair and looked deep into her eyes. "I'm not giving you up without a fight. I love you, Lucinda. I'm never going to feel about anyone the way I feel about you."

Oh, you will, she'd thought, studying him intently, storing snapshots she knew would reside in a mental album that she'd be examining intermittently for the rest of her life.

The seriousness of his intent, his determination, were all too clear. He was working on his master's thesis and really had very little free time. But he made the time and drove down from New Haven on the Saturday, as promised. His expression when she opened the door to him stated how certain he was of his ability to change her mind. He embraced her and she accepted his kiss and the welcome of his encircling arms, knowing it would be the last time they'd touch.

There had been a tiny flickering hope inside her that he might dismiss what she was about to tell him and say that it was all completely irrelevant, nothing that would deter him even the slightest bit. But this was Harcourt Lowndes the Fifth, great-great-grandson of the renowned senator from Maine. And while the family was famous for their liberalism and public-spirited generosity and their stands on all matter of civil rights issues, it was a family that placed enormous value on bloodlines. There was no conceivable way—unless he was willing to walk away from generations of history and wealth—Cort would commit to a woman who was one-eighths black. It was one thing to be liberal and to endow colleges and scholarships and to do all sorts of good works. It was another thing altogether to welcome someone of color, regardless of how small a degree, into the bosom of the family. She knew this from the evenings she'd spent with Cort and his parents when they'd driven down from Portland to see their son and his girlfriend and take them out to dinner. To Lucinda's mind, the outcome of the conversation they were going to have was a foregone conclusion. And so her brain recorded one shot after another of this twenty-four-year-old man she'd been in love, and in bed with, for the previous thirteen months.

Find an old photograph and not just one life has ended but many.

He surprised her. At once, he said, "That does *not* matter! I categorically do not care."

"Think about it for a minute, Cort. You may find that you do care."

"I don't *need* to think about it. I love you. I want to marry you. I want to have children with you. We will be happy together and have a good life."

"I'm always, always going to remember this," she said quietly. "And I'll think of you every time with love for saying that it doesn't matter. But there's more."

"More?"

"All the women in my mother's family have died young, of breast cancer."

"That doesn't mean you will—" he began.

"It very definitely means I will. Which is why ... " She faltered and had to take a few seconds to rein in her fear, her sorrow, the sheer horror of what was to come. "Dr. Wilstone, my mother's oncologist, has already booked me for the surgery."

"What surgery? You mean you've already got it?"

She shook her head. "No. It's a very radical step and he's admitted that oncologists are very divided on it, but he believes the only way I won't get the disease is if he removes my breasts. I think he's right, so I'm going ahead with it."

Cort went pale. All at once he looked old, and she knew how he'd look when he was fifty or sixty. He'd be handsome, distinguished; his fine features would acquire authority and he would, in some ways, be even better looking than he was now.

His lips moved as if he was silently repeating the words, but he didn't, or couldn't, speak for quite some time. "Isn't that kind of drastic?" he asked at length in a thready voice.

Feeling a terrible pity for him, and for herself, too, she went on. "I'll be disfigured, but I won't die. I also couldn't breast-feed those children you'd like to have one day." *Now say that wouldn't matter to you, Cort.* Silence. "On top of that, I'd probably pass the genetic predisposition on to any daughters we'd have." *Tell me we could adopt children, Cort.* Continued silence. Eyes distant as the information got processed. "No, it just wouldn't work," she said. "I couldn't do that to either of us. There are too many negatives." *This is how you find out just how true, how encompassing, how deep someone's love is. This is the way you discover that how you look and whose genes you bear have more importance than the person you are—the good and positive qualities you have, your gifts of every sort get discounted by the revelation that secret markers of color and of illness lie embedded within your very cells. It's not possible to separate the subtlest racism from a fear of potentially fatal flaws.* "I know you're trying to get yourself to say again that it doesn't matter to you, but we both know it does."

He got up and walked around the room in a daze, picking things up and putting them down, his tall, broad-shouldered frame diminished, as if the information he'd been given had taken a drastic physical toll, collapsing several disks in his spine. Finally, he stopped a few feet away from her and asked, "When is the surgery?"

"Three weeks from Monday."

"You can't go through something like this alone. Let me at least be with you, see you through it."

"It's kind of you to offer, but no. Eddie's going to come stay with me until I'm better."

"Eddie? The fellow at your mother's service who was directing the media like a well-dressed traffic cop?" His brows drew together. "Why him?" The phrase *of all people* hung silently on the end of his question. It offended her because she did, after all, know about some important things—like loyalty and respect and discounting surfaces because it was the good heart, the solid, steadfast heart that mattered most in the end. And all at once, in a flash of radiant insight, she understood why Lily had loved that song, "Wonderful, Wonderful." Because she and the man who'd been her father had found each other possessed of steadfast hearts; they'd had a love that had never wavered, a love so complete that months of separation were of no consequence. And when he was gone and the separation was permanent, Lily's love life ended forever. If you've known the best, second-best could never be acceptable.

Tamping down her sudden anger, she said, "Eddie's the closest thing to a father I've ever known, Cort. His wife was my second mother. They never had kids of their own, so until I started school at the studio, I spent every day, and sometimes evenings, if there was night shooting, with Estelle. They were my family. When Estelle died, my mother and I were there with him to arrange her funeral and to sit *shiva* every night while the man wept like a lost child. And when my mother was dying, Cort, she told me to let Eddie take care of everything. Because she knew I couldn't handle this alone. And she was right. So Eddie will be with me when I have the surgery. I will not be alone."

As he processed this information, his features slowly cleared, and he regained his height. His bearing was once more patrician, his manner contained yet deferential. Seeing this physical transformation, she knew that it was over, that nothing could be salvaged. What she'd thought for a time was true love had been no more than second-best. So he would make a few more pro forma protestations, but all the while he'd be inching toward the door. And when at last he did go, in his ill-disguised haste neglecting to hug or kiss her or even to touch her hand, she'd watched through the living room curtains as he'd driven off in his red MG without once looking back. She didn't even cry. Her chest hurt, as if she'd taken a blow. But she shed no tears.

He did send an exquisite bouquet of flowers to the hospital with a card that said, "Get well very soon, Love, Cort," and he phoned a few days after she got home to ask how she was doing. But she never saw him again. And a little over two years later, she'd read the announcement of his wedding in the *Times* and thought, with a certain grim satisfaction, I knew you'd find someone else.

Feelings change; facts never do, she thought. And a true heart is for a lifetime—no matter how dated a concept it might seem. She did, in retrospect, think she'd been cruel to the poor young man, hitting him with one harsh fact after another and hoping, impossibly, that he'd have the maturity to deal with the situation. In truth, she'd left him little alternative but to run from her. And considering now how she'd handled matters, she had to admit that she'd been slightly unhinged back then—and likely still was.

Her major regret was that she'd never had an opportunity to tell Lily that she finally understood what her mother had meant that night so long ago at the drive-in, when they'd eaten burgers and fries off trays hooked onto the windows, while Johnny Mathis sang and Lily had said, "I love this song. Someday you'll know why."

Sitting now in the living room of what had been her mother's house, Lucinda whispered, "God, but you were special, Lily. People will never know just how special. And here I am, all these years later, as close as dammit to being an honest-to-god crazy lady, spending my time with a nine-year-old. But you'd love this kid, Lily. She's a pistol."

C h a p t e r   N i n e

The doorbell rang at five past nine the next morning. As-
suming Katanya had come early, Lucinda opened the door
to see a woman who was obviously Mrs. Crane—distraught,
with red-rimmed eyes—with Katanya and little Jason, hand
in hand, on the porch behind her. The woman looked as if
she'd grabbed whatever came to hand and thrown it on: a
short-sleeved white blouse misbuttoned so that it hung
askew, navy track pants, low-heeled black patent dress
shoes, and a heavy-looking black Gucci shoulder bag.

"I'm sorry to just show up this way," Mrs. Crane started
in that tight-jawed fashion Lucinda was coming to recognize,
but with a new element of incipient hysteria, "but there's
a ... a *situation* and I've got an *appointment*. It's an *emergency*
and I need someone to look after Jason until I get back. *Please!*
I can't get a sitter on such short notice. I've tried, phoned
everyone. Nobody's available. I don't know how long I'll be
but ... *Please?"*

Lucinda looked at Katanya who had a long-handled can-
vas carry-all slung over her shoulder, and was wearing an

embarrassed, apologetic expression. The boy looked cross and bewildered, and clung to Katanya's hand with one hand and to her leg with the other as if there existed the possibility that he might, at any moment, be torn away from her.

"Yes, of course," Lucinda said, indicating to the children that they should come inside.

"Oh, *thank* you!" the woman said tearfully as the children slipped past the two women. "She"—referring to Katanya in a manner that made both the girl and Lucinda recoil slightly—"has keys to the house, in case you need anything." Turning, Mrs. Crane ran down the steps and over the path to the Mercedes station wagon that sat in the driveway, the driver's door open and the motor running. Lucinda couldn't help wondering if she'd intended to take the children with her, if Lucinda had refused to have them. Somehow, Lucinda doubted it, but preferred not to think of the alternatives.

Lucinda, Katanya and Jason watched the woman reverse out of the driveway at top speed, spinning the wheel as she sent the car into the road without checking for oncoming traffic, and go roaring off with screeching tires.

At once, Jason's face twisted in a prelude to tears. He was ready to throw himself headlong into a tantrum.

Dropping down to be at eye level with the boy, Lucinda took hold of his chin and turned his face toward her. "Jason, my name is Lucinda. I know you're worried and scared at being left with someone you don't know, but everything's going to be okay."

"And you know what, Jase?" Katanya contributed, squatting next to Lucinda. "Luce has a *swimming pool*! I found your suit and your water wings and I brought them so we can all go *swimming*. Isn't that right, Luce?"

"That's right. Would you like to come inside?"

Sullen, still doubtful, he said, "Okay."

Once inside, Lucinda asked the children, "Have you had breakfast?"

"Nope," Katanya answered. "Something big is definitely up. She was on the phone in her bedroom with the door closed, then she came rushing in to say we had to get dressed right away. Then she drove right over here. I didn't even know she knew where you lived."

"It's all right, Kat. The woman's obviously very upset."

"That's for sure."

"Are you hungry, Jason?" Lucinda asked the boy who was still clutching Katanya's leg.

"Hungwee."

"Let's make breakfast, then."

"We'll help, won't we, Jase?"

"No." He looked around suspiciously yet went gamely with Katanya and Lucinda to the kitchen. "Hungwee," he repeated, letting go of Katanya's hand in order to climb up onto one of the chairs where he knelt with his elbows on the table, chin cupped in his upturned hands, his eyes following Lucinda's every move.

Putting the carry-all down by the back door, Katanya delved inside and came out with a piece of rolled-up paper. "I made you a picture," she said, crossing the room to give it to Lucinda. "You mad at how she dumped us on you?"

"Not really, just confused." She unrolled the paper to study the crayon drawing of a disproportionately tall Lucinda holding a tiny Katanya by the hand in front of a decent rendering of the house. "This is wonderful!" Lucinda told her. "Really wonderful."

"You don't have any pictures on your 'frigerator, so I made you one." Looking over, the girl frowned. "You don't have any magnets."

"Oh, I'm sure I can find some. Let's make breakfast, then we'll search my desk for magnets."

"I brought your book, Jase," Katanya said, going over to get it from the bag.

He shook his head, never taking his eyes from Lucinda.

"Swimmin'?" he asked doubtfully.

"We'll eat, then we'll go out to the pool. Okay, Jase?"

"Swimmin'?" he repeated to Lucinda, as if he doubted Katanya's authority on the matter.

"After we eat," Lucinda said.

"Eat, then swimmin'?" he asked.

"That's what we'll do," Lucinda said.

"*Hungwee!*"

"I'm sure you are." He was a beautiful child, with thick golden hair still damp from being wet-combed, with a side parting so straight and clean it looked as if it had been made with a razor blade; enormous brown eyes, a smudge of a nose, chubby cheeks and a beautiful mouth, the upper lip deeply bowed. In jeans and a blue T-shirt, with sneakers that looked disproportionately large compared to the rest of his small but solid little body, he had an aura of petulance and Lucinda could see that he was still deciding what his attitude in this strange new place was going to be.

Lucinda got eggs and bread, cheese and butter from the refrigerator and set them on the counter, then went back for milk and cream.

"Would you like eggs and toast or cereal?" she asked both children.

"CEWEAL!" Jason shouted.

"Don't *yell*, Jase. It's rude. I *told* you. His mother lets him yell his head off," Katanya said quietly, so he wouldn't hear. "Like I said, the woman has no clue how to raise a child."

Her voice returning to its normal level, she said, "I'll have toast and eggs, please, Luce. What should I do to help?"

"You can get Jason some cereal. It's in the cabinet over there, under the counter."

Down on her knees, Katanya looked over her shoulder, saying, "Guess what, Jase? Cheerios! Your favorite."

For the first time, the toddler smiled. Shifting, he sat on the edge of the table, his plump little hands on his knees. "Jase love Cheewios!"

Delighted by his transformation, Lucinda hoisted him off the table and swung him in a circle that elicited a giddy trill of laughter. Planting a kiss on the top of his head, she sat him back on the table, patted his chubby cheek, then continued organizing the breakfast.

"You get all this food from ordering over the computer?"

"Some comes from the Rowayton Market. They deliver."

"You've got it all worked out," Katanya said, placing the box of cereal on the counter and glancing over at Jason. "When his mom's not around," she whispered, "he's really good, cute as anything."

"He's adorable."

"Wait'll he pitches a fit, you won't think he's one bit adorable." Dropping her voice again, she said, "I think there's *big* trouble. Mr. Crane didn't come home last night. Miz Crane went nutso, phonin' all over the place, gettin' louder and louder. She was on the phone 'til really late, so I went ahead and gave Jase his bath and got him into bed, read him *Goodnight, Moon*. He's crazy for that book. She never even noticed, just kept on phonin'. When I woke up, she was on the phone, as if she never went to bed at all. From what she was shouting this morning, I think she's gone to see somebody at the bank. Some kinda fuss about money. I heard her shrieking, 'What do you *mean*?' Trouble," Katanya said ominously, with a slow shake of her head. "I think the man had himself enough of her and poor Jase and ran off with all the money."

"That would be a cowardly thing to do."

"He's not a nice man," Katanya said soberly. "He comes in, has a big drink, eats what she gives him, doesn't talk to her, even to say thank you, or this is good. And he never plays with Jase. Jase goes running to the door and the man just shakes him off, like he's a bug or somethin'. He's *mean*."

"How did she get my address?" Lucinda asked.

"She took your number off the Caller ID when you called the other day. I saw her writin' it down. I thought it was weird, you know. But then I remembered what you told me about your mom and I figured maybe she wanted to tell her friends she talked to you on the phone or something, to make herself important. Not much she does makes a whole lot of sense. When we got in the car, I couldn't believe it when I saw where she was taking us. I tried to tell her it was a bad idea to just go showing up on people, especially you, cuz you're very shy, but she shouted at me to be quiet. That's when Jase started hangin' on me. She's kinda tightly wound."

"That, honey, is what's known as an understatement. The way she took off out of here without even looking where she was going, it's lucky there were no cars coming by."

"No kidding!" Looping an arm around Lucinda's waist, Katanya pressed herself against Lucinda's side, saying, "I'm so glad we're friends."

"Me, too." Lucinda hugged her back. "Okay, now. Scrambled or fried?"

"Scrambled, please."

"White or wheat toast, or a muffin?"

"TOATS!" Jason shouted. "TOATS!"

"Jase!" Katanya warned. "What did I just tell you about yellin'?"

"Toats," he said more quietly. "Cheewios and toats!"

"Good boy." She gave him a pat on the head and rubbed her nose against his, making him laugh again. "I'll make the toast," she said, and returned to the counter to open the twist tie on the loaf. She pulled open the toaster oven and laid six slices of bread on the rack. "I won't start it until everything else is almost ready. Gramma taught me that. Otherwise the toast is cold when you go to eat it."

"Your gramma knows all kinds of smart things."

"Yeah, she does." All at once, tears welled in her eyes and she said, "I miss her, and my moms."

"Would you like to phone home?"

"They'll be at work."

"Do you think the Weinburgs would mind if you called your gramma there?"

"No, they wouldn't mind."

"There's the phone." Lucinda pointed. "Go ahead and call your grandmother."

"*Really?*" The girl's spirits had picked right up.

"Really. Go ahead. It'll be at least ten minutes before we're ready to eat."

Katanya didn't need further prompting. "Oh, *thank* you, Luce!" She raced across the floor, grabbed the handset from the wall phone, then stood on tiptoe to dial.

Lucinda turned and began breaking eggs into a bowl while Jason, for no apparent reason, began clapping his hands and singing to himself, rocking back and forth—the very picture of a contented child. Lucinda smiled as she poured some light cream into the mixing bowl, then reached for the whisk and began whipping the eggs and cream into a frothy blend.

Behind her, she heard Katanya say, "Hello, Mr. Weinburg. I'm sorry to disturb you, but could I please speak to my gra'mother? ... I'm fine, thank you, Mr. Weinburg. How are you and Mrs. Weinburg? ... Oh, that's good ... Yes, I will. Thank you, sir." There was a short pause, then the girl said excitedly, "Gramma, hi! ... No, I'm at Lucinda's house. She's my new friend .... No, she's a grown-up lady ... Yeah. She's so nice, Gramma. And you know what? She's got a *swimmin'* *pool!* ... Yeah, her very own .... I will ... Yeah, I will ... No, I promise ... I miss you, too, and Moms ... Okay ... Un-hunh ... Okay ... Will you tell Moms I said hey? ... I love you, too, Gramma. 'Bye ... Okay, 'bye."

Replacing the receiver, she came back to stand next to Lucinda. "My Gramma says thank you for lookin' after me."

"Next time you talk to her, tell your grandmother that it's more a case of *you* looking after *me*."

While Katanya was in one of the guest bedrooms putting on her bathing suit and getting Jason into his, Lucinda stood in her room looking with dismay at her old bathing suit. It had lost its elasticity and the foam inserts that had been sewn into the bodice had disintegrated into a pair of lumpy, shapeless pouches. Dropping it into the wastebasket, she looked through the dresser drawers, trying to find something to wear. All she could come up with were an old pair of lined navy blue shorts and an extra-large white T-shirt.

Studying herself in the mirror, she thought she looked like a painted plank. Flat lines from shoulders to ankles. Good grief! What would Katanya make of her? she wondered, and then realized that to a nine-year-old, a flat chest would seem perfectly normal. It wasn't as if she was an entrant in a beauty contest, Lucinda told herself, going barefoot to the linen closet on the landing to get some towels. She could hear Katanya downstairs, talking to Jason, saying, "If you don't wear these, you can't go into the water."

The boy let out a scream of such volume that Lucinda started in shock, her heart sent into overdrive by a sudden flood of adrenaline; her ears aching. The scream ended abruptly, and Lucinda hurried down the stairs to see Katanya on her knees, holding the boy's wrists firmly with both hands. "You don't scream or shout," she was saying, "and you don't hit me, Jase."

He struggled to free his hands, squirming in an effort to escape her grip.

"You don't scream or shout and you don't hit me," the girl repeated. "You understand?"

He kept on struggling, his face twisted and suffused with color. Katanya maintained her grip on his wrists and repeated herself again, more slowly. "You don't scream and you don't hit. D'you understand, Jase? I'm not lettin' go 'til you show me you understand. We can stay here the whole day. Makes no nevermind to me, little boy," she said in tones that Lucinda, watching in admiration from the foot of the stairs, was certain Katanya had heard her mother or grandmother use at some time.

"When you're good, I like you fine. But when you go shoutin' and hittin', I don't like you one l'il bit. You want it so nobody likes you, Jase? Cuz you're not gonna have no friends at all, you don't learn how to behave."

Motionless now, the boy stared at Katanya, as if deciding whether or not to believe her. He tried to shake off her hands, but couldn't.

"I'm not lettin' go 'til I know you understand me, Jase. We'll just stay here all day, no swimmin', no nothin'. It's up to you."

" 'Kay." He finally submitted, defeated.

"Okay what?" Katanya prompted.

"No shoutin', no hittin'." His head now hung in shame.

"Good, Jase." Katanya released his wrists and put her arms around the boy. "You remember what I said and you'll grow up to have lots of friends, cuz I know you want to be a good boy. Isn't that right, Jase?"

His head bobbed up and down.

"Okay. Now we're gonna put on these water wings and then we can go in the pool."

" 'Kay," he agreed, and allowed her to put the inflated wings on his upper arms. Getting to her feet, she put out her hand and at once Jason took hold of it.

"Are we ready?" Lucinda asked, pretending she hadn't witnessed that scene.

"Yes, we are," Katanya said. "Aren't we, Jase?"

"Weddy," Jason agreed.

———

They were sitting on the side of the pool at the shallow end while Jason splashed happily on the three steps descending into the water. Lucinda had put on a broad-brimmed straw hat and her sunglasses when she'd come out of the water. Katanya had come to sit beside her and Lucinda said, "You handled him beautifully a while ago. You're going to make a wonderful mother someday, Kat."

"He just needs to know the rules," the girl said, never taking her eyes off Jason. "His moms and dad make him crazy.

Little kids know it when their parents can't stand each other."

"Yes, they do."

"These people moved into the place upstairs from us about two, three years ago. They had this little girl named Rebecca, same age as me. We played together sometimes. Her mom was always black and blue from gettin' beat on; her nose was all messed up, squashed flat and over to one side; she had this big scar under her nose that went right into her mouth, and she looked *old*. You know?" She turned to Lucinda who nodded. "She was the same age as my moms, but she looked like an ol' lady. We'd hear them fightin' above us at night. He'd be shoutin' 'bout how stupid she was, how useless, and she'd be screamin' and beggin' for him not to hit her. There'd be thuds and bangs and crashes. And I'd wonder where Becca was while all this was goin' on. She was the scaredest girl I ever knew. If you laughed too loud, or touched her arm when she wasn't 'specting it, or somebody shouted on the street, she'd start to shake. It was just pitiful. My gramma told her mom she was gonna get herself killed if she didn't take Becca and get away from that man; Gramma even said she'd help her out with money if it meant takin' some of the fear out of that child. But the woman didn't say one word, wouldn't even look at my gramma or me. She just took Becca home. Coupla weeks later they were gone and we never saw them again.

"I wonder all the time if Becca's okay. I think if you're the moms, even if you're scared, you should look out for your kids. It's like my gramma says. Ain't no man on earth worth more than your children. You don't do right by them, you don't deserve to have them. I don't think Jase's parents deserve him. He'd be a good boy, if they weren't all the time arguin' and hollerin' and slammin' doors and like that. He's smart. He knows what kinda people they are but he's too little to do more than scream when the mood comes on him. And that's pitiful. Don't you think?"

Lucinda took hold of the girl's hand and said, "Yes, I do."

"I'm gonna pray for him, cuz I don't see anybody lookin' out for him, teachin' him how to behave right."

Holding hands, silent now, they watched the boy jumping up and down in the water, laughing and splashing gleefully.

Chapter Ten

When it got to be five-thirty and there'd been no word from Mrs. Crane, Lucinda said, "I might as well do something about dinner."

Getting up from the sofa where she and Jason had been watching TV, Katanya went with Lucinda to the kitchen, saying, "Maybe she crashed her car. Way she was driving, it could've happened."

"Let's hope not. If we haven't heard from her by the time we finish eating, we'll walk over to the house and see if there's an address book or a list of numbers, someone we can call—Jason's grandparents, maybe."

"Yeah. There's a list on the wall phone in the kitchen, with some Cranes on there. That's a good idea."

"What should we eat?" Lucinda said, opening cupboards.

"What've you got?"

Lucinda turned to the girl, saying, "Know what I love best?"

"What?"

"You'll know for sure that I'm crazy when I tell you."

"What?" Katanya was smiling.

"Kraft mac and cheese."

"Me, too! I love it. So does Jase."

"Are you just being polite?" Lucinda asked.

"Honest! I *love* it!"

"I could eat it until I'm sick," Lucinda admitted. She smiled sheepishly. "Isn't that terrible?"

"It is not. I told you: I love it, too. Let's make *lots*."

"Okay, we'll cook two boxes. And a salad."

"Great!"

They heard Jason come running down the hall and turned to see him—flushed from the sun, a big grin on his face. "Whatcha doon?" he asked, flinging himself against Katanya and reaching out to grab a fistful of Lucinda's skirt.

"We're gonna make Kraft mac and cheese, Jase! How great is that?"

"Gwate!" he declared, tugging on Lucinda's skirt. "Tha's gwate! Gimme hug!" he said, extending both arms to Lucinda. "Up, up!"

"And away!" Lucinda laughed and hoisted him into her arms to spin around with him. "It's Superboy!"

"*Soupboy!*" Jason echoed happily, as the doorbell rang.

The three of them instantly falling silent, Lucinda lowered the boy to the floor, and started for the door.

Mrs. Crane had taken the time to change her clothes. The white blouse, properly buttoned now, was tucked into the waistline of white cotton slacks. In one hand, she had a small suitcase. She looked, Lucinda thought, like a bereft missionary on vacation.

Thrusting the suitcase at Lucinda, she said, "I'm leaving the girl with you. Jason's coming with me now."

The two children had followed Lucinda down the hall. Jason was hiding behind Lucinda, again clutching her skirt, this time with both hands. Katanya stood to one side, waiting to see what would happen.

The heat of anger spreading through her like a sudden fever, Lucinda took the suitcase, set it down just inside the door, then straightened and said to Katanya, "Please take Jason to the kitchen while I talk to his mother."

Katanya did as she'd been asked, and once the children were out of earshot, arms crossed tightly across her chest, Lucinda said in a low, cold voice, "You are the most shameful excuse for a person, let alone a parent, it has ever been my misfortune to encounter. You are unforgivably presumptuous, rude and reckless. How *dare* you come to *my* home issuing orders and depositing two children here like so much checked luggage! It's lucky for you that I'm not some sort of depraved predator and that I actually like children. Patently, you do not, or you'd treat both of them with more respect. You go home and pack a bag for Jason, then bring it back here, because he is *not* leaving with you and he'll need pajamas, his toothbrush, and fresh clothes for tomorrow. Don't even *think* of arguing with me! Given the way I saw you drive out of here this morning, I wouldn't allow *anyone*, let alone a small boy, to get into a car with you. One call to Children's Aid and Jason will be in foster care so fast it'll make your head spin. I do that and it could take you *years* to get him back. Furthermore, Katanya is not *her* or *the girl*. She has a name and you will *use* it. She's not some nameless entity you've been burdened with. She's a person and deserves respect.

"Frankly, I don't give a good goddamn what's going on in your life right now. Whatever it is, you probably deserve it, if your appalling behavior today is anything to go by. Now go get Jason's things and bring them here, and I'll expect you to leave a number where you can be reached. Then tomorrow, or the next day, when you're back in what passes for your right mind, Jason will be here, waiting for you, or his father, or his grandparents, or someone with half a brain, decent manners and basic common sense to come get him."

With that, she closed the door in the stunned woman's face, then had to stand for several long moments trying to calm down. Her heart was racing; her neck and ears were on fire. Outside, she heard Mrs. Crane walk across the porch and down the front steps. Seconds later, the car drove off.

"Maybe she'll call the police," Katanya said, running to Lucinda with Jason right behind her.

"She wouldn't dare," Lucinda said.

"You were good, what you said."

"I didn't enjoy it, Kat."

"I know. But you were right."

"Being right doesn't make me feel any better."

"It should."

"Maybe, but it doesn't. I loathe confrontations, scenes, arguments."

"I understand," Katanya said solemnly. "Will it be okay for me to stay with you?"

"Of course. And Jason, too. I will not allow him to be in a car with her."

"I wouldn't, either. You're sure it's okay for me to stay? Because I know it's hard for you, and I could go home on the train. My moms would come get me at a Hundred and Twenty-fifth Street."

"I would be happy to have you stay, Kat. And Jason is not leaving here tonight."

"Thank you, Luce." Turning to the boy, Katanya said, "Hey, Jase. Wanna sleep over here tonight with me and Luce?"

"Yeah!" he said, jumping up and down. "Stay with you 'n' Luce!"

"Okay," Lucinda said, her breathing still ragged and her heart racketing, as if she'd run for miles. "Dinner. Come on, Superboy"—she held out her arms and Jason took a leap into them—"let's get cooking."

Within half an hour, Mrs. Crane returned. She handed Lucinda a small bright red duffel bag and a folded piece of paper. "My parents' number in Greenwich. She ... Ah, Katanya has keys to the house, if there's anything you need. I, ah, I, uhm. Oh my God!" She looked away, chewed on her lower lip for a moment, then looked again at Lucinda. "I apologize for how I've behaved today. I'm, ah ... " She had to stop and cough, struggling to contain herself. "I'm, uh, grateful to you for taking care of the children." Tears suddenly spilling over, she pulled a tissue from her pocket and blotted her face, then blew her nose. "I am truly sorry. I've been a complete bitch. Everything you said was true—except about what's going on right now. Even though I've made a terrible first impression, I honestly don't deserve any of what Todd's done. You'll have to take my word on that because you were right: based on appearances alone, you'd have to think I do deserve it."

Relenting somewhat in the face of this heartfelt apology, Lucinda said, "Drive carefully. You've got a child here, depending on you. Kat and I will look after Jason until you've calmed down and you're ready to come back for him."

Turning to Katanya, Mrs. Crane said, "You're a sweet girl and you've had an awful time with us. This was supposed to be a holiday for you, and it's been anything but. I've treated you badly and I hope you'll accept my apology. There is no excuse for how I've acted."

"It's okay," Katanya said, and then stepped out onto the porch to give the woman a hug. "I know you didn't mean it."

In a croaking whisper, Mrs. Crane said, "You shame me. I was raised to treat people, *all* people, well; to be respectful."

Surprising herself, Lucinda said, "I think that instead of racing off down to Greenwich, you should come in and join us in the Kraft mac and cheese feast we're preparing."

"Me, too!" Katanya agreed, as Jason peered out from behind Lucinda to smile and wave at his mother.

All at once appearing very young and terribly vulnerable, the woman said, "I know it's dumb, but I love Kraft mac and cheese."

"Well then, come in and eat with us." Lucinda stepped aside.

"You're being awfully decent, considering everything."

"Come on, Miz Crane," Katanya urged. "Soupboy's starving."

"*What?*" A half smile began to form.

"Meet the latest hero, Soupboy," Lucinda said.

"Me!" Jason declared, flying away down the hall with his arms outspread like wings. "Soupboy!"

"I want you to know that I'm not usually the way I was today. Or yesterday, or the day before, or the day before that. Todd's been such a complete bastard. He's played so many games, pulled so many stunts, that I haven't known which way was up. I knew something was coming, but when he didn't come home last night … It was as if someone lit the fuse on a stick of dynamite a long time ago and I've been waiting and waiting for the explosion. That was what last night and this morning was like: the big kaboom. He wiped out all the accounts, except for Jason's trust. It's just lucky that I had a feeling he was up to something, so I opened an account in my name and I've been transferring money into it for almost a year now. There wasn't much in the accounts he cleared, but the *idea* that he'd do that ... "

"What's your name?" Lucinda asked.

"God! I haven't even introduced myself. Sorry. I'm Renee."

"If you don't mind my asking, how old are you?"

"Twenty-six."

"I could be your mother," Lucinda said, a little stunned by the realization that she was, indeed, old enough to be this woman's mother. It was perpetually shocking to come up against the reality that while she still thought of herself as young, she was, in fact, well past the halfway point of her life.

"Oh, never!" Renee disagreed.

"Believe me," Lucinda said, all at once weary. "I'm well old enough, and then some." She took a few seconds, marshaling her thoughts, then said, "Renee, if you've been waiting all this time for the other shoe to drop, why are you so outraged and surprised that it's finally happened?"

"I don't know." Renee looked around, as if she might spot the answer printed on one of the living room walls. "I guess because I tried so hard to make it work that everything else went to hell. All I could think about was either getting Todd to stop whatever it was he was doing and put some effort into the marriage, or just admit that we'd made a mistake and sit down to talk to me. We've only been married three and a half years. I thought it was supposed to last forever."

"It's not the end of the world. You'll get the house, if you want to keep it, but best of all, you've got that wonderful little boy. That's a great deal more than some people ever get."

"I know. And I've neglected him so badly this past year."

"You can fix that. He's your son. He loves you. Pay attention to him, give him some guidelines, set some rules, and he'll be fine."

"Have you ever been married?" Renee asked.

Lucinda shook her head. And with the motion came the signs that a fresh migraine (or perhaps the previous one) was about to strike.

"Renee, I'm not accustomed to having people around. I don't socialize—at all. If you'd like to spend the night, you're welcome to pick a bedroom. I have to take some medication now and go to bed." Her hands starting to tremble, Lucinda got unsteadily to her feet. This one was coming on fast. Her skull felt as if it was swelling, while a steel hand steadily closed over the back of her neck; her eyes wanted to slide out of focus from the building pressure against her temples.

"Are you okay? You've gone all white."

"I'm getting a migraine. Stay if you like. Please excuse me now."

Moving as quickly as she dared, Lucinda got upstairs and closed herself into the master suite. In the bathroom she took one of her pills and swallowed it with several handfuls of tap water. Then she sat in the dark on the bathroom floor with her back against the tub, put her head down on her knees and waited for the nausea to pass. Some time later she was able to get to the bedroom where she crawled, fully dressed, under the bedclothes.

There was a light tapping at the door. Lucinda struggled to wake up as she heard the door open and footsteps come padding across the carpet.

"It's Kat," the girl whispered. "I made you coffee." Taking a tissue from the box on the bedside table, she folded it and put the mug down on top of it. "How d'you feel?"

Lucinda managed to sit up and gratefully drank some of the coffee. It was good—strong, with cream. She patted the side of the bed, indicating Katanya should sit.

"Miz Crane went a while ago with Jase. She left you a note downstairs, said to tell you thanks."

Lucinda drank another swallow of the coffee and looked at the time. Ten-fifteen. "This is good, Kat. Thank you."

"I watched how you did it and tried to get it right."

"You got it absolutely right."

"I phoned my moms to let her know I'm here, and I gave her the number. I hope it's okay that I used the phone without asking."

"That's fine."

"My moms says thank you very much for letting me stay with you."

Lucinda nodded her head slowly.

"Still got a headache?"

"Too soon to tell," Lucinda murmured. "I'll know after my shower."

"I'll make some toast, if you want."

"No. Just sit with me, tell me what you've been doing this morning."

"Let's see. Miz Crane left with Jase about eight-thirty. I phoned home, then had some cereal. Then I read your newspaper for a while—I put it back together carefully for you—until I thought it was time to make the coffee. That's all. Oh, I ran the dishwasher and put the dishes away. Took me a while to figure out all the buttons, but I finally did. I know how cuz the Weinburgs have one. One day I'm gonna buy one for my gramma."

After another swallow of coffee, Lucinda put the mug down on the bedside table and said, "I'm sure that would make her very happy."

"Yeah."

"Yesterday was quite a day."

"Sure was," Katanya said, her voice still hushed.

"I feel like yesterday's leftovers. I'm going to take a shower and keep my fingers crossed that the headache's gone. If it is, we'll plan what to do today."

"Okay. You want more coffee? I made a whole pot."

"I'll have another cup when I come down."

"Okay."

Lucinda reached for the girl's hand. "You're a good girl, Kat. A very good girl."

"You're a good girl, too."

Lucinda smiled.

"Well, you are!" Katanya insisted.

"I'll be down in fifteen minutes."

"Okay." Katanya got up and went to the door, then stood with her hand on the knob, looking down at her bare feet. "I love you, Luce," she said, then quickly left, closing the door gently behind her.

———

With the hot water beating down on the lingering knots in her neck and shoulders, she stood with one hand braced against the wall and cried in gulping sobs, overwhelmed by the way the world had begun crowding back into her life, and by a child's unalloyed declaration of love.

It had been years and years since anyone had spoken of loving her; no one, in fact, since Eddie had died eleven years before. The last time they'd talked on the phone—he'd been living alone in the old house, refusing to leave everything that reminded him of Estelle—he'd said, "They wanna put me in the hospital, Lucy. I told 'em to hell with that crap. I'm gonna die, I'm gonna do it here in my own bed. I know you're stuck in that house like a bug on flypaper, so I'm calling to say goodbye."

"Eddie—"

"Let me speak my piece, Lucy. No interruptions, okay?"

"Okay."

"You're the only kid Estelle and I ever had. Lily let us in, let us be family to you. You're probably still pissed off at her about your dad, or maybe not. There's a lot of water gone under that particular bridge. It was a tough break, not finding the man, or his family. But you had us, and we had you. And we couldn't have loved you more if you'd been our own flesh and blood."

"I know that, Eddie. I always loved Estelle and you, too."

"Good. So we're even Steven. It was a silly life we had here, but not terrible. We always said we'd move back to New York, but we never got around to it. Now, I wish we had. At least if I was in the city, there'd have been a chance of seeing you once in a while. But what's not to be is not to be. A beautiful girl, a beautiful person like you shouldn't be spending her life inside, afraid to go out. What does it matter what people think, don't think? Only thing that matters, sweetheart, is what *you* think. One of these days, please God, you'll figure that out. Be good to yourself, Lucy. You deserve it. Get some pleasure while you can, 'cause life is short." He laughed—a sound like dry leaves rustling in a breeze. "Trust me, I know this. So I'm tired and I'm gonna say goodbye now. I love you, sweetheart."

"I love you, Eddie."

"*Geh gesundterheit!*"

"What does that mean?"

"Go with health."

"Thank you. I ... " She'd wanted to say more, but he'd already put the phone down. Lost, she had sat holding the receiver for quite some time before noticing the repeating buzz on the line meant to indicate that the phone was off the hook.

The next evening, Gin had phoned to say, "He's gone, Luce. I wanted you to know he wasn't all by himself here. There was a gang of us who took turns staying with him. Are you okay?"

"No."

"Me, neither," Gin said. "I'm going to hang up and have a big drink. Love you to pieces, Luce. We'll talk soon."

Now that she thought about it, Lucinda realized that every time they spoke—which wasn't often—Gin always made a point of saying how much she loved her.

The spasm ending, she reached for the shampoo, knowing that very soon she was going to have to phone Gin. Perhaps she'd even make the call tonight, after Katanya was in bed. With the three-hour time difference, Gin would probably be sitting out on the terrace, having a liqueur with her coffee while she read the latest batch of what she disparagingly referred to as screamplays.

Chapter Eleven

The note Renee left read:

> *Thank you for looking after Jason and for taking Katanya. I'm still thinking about all you said. And you're right, about everything. Jason and I will be better off without Todd, and I'm going to be a better mother to Jason from now on. I hope you're feeling better. I'll be in touch soon. You've been very kind to all of us. Thank you again.*
>
> *Renee.*

"I'm gonna miss Jase," Katanya said, refilling Lucinda's mug with fresh coffee. "I think he had a lot of fun yesterday."

"I think so, too," Lucinda said.

"D'you think she's coming back?"

"Definitely. It's her home, and Jason's. She wouldn't just leave."

"Good! She shouldn't."

"No," Lucinda agreed. "She shouldn't." She noticed that Katanya was wearing the same shorts and T-shirt she'd had on the day before. Her suitcase was a small one that couldn't possibly hold very much. "I should do the laundry. Do you have things that need to be washed?"

"Unh-hunh."

"Okay, that's the first thing we'll do. Then we'll decide what we want to do today. It looks as if it's going to rain."

"Even if it does, we can still go swimming. We don't have to go out anywhere."

"Have you ever actually *been* swimming in the rain?" Lucinda asked her.

"Yeah, once. It was fun. It was all warm 'n' everything. Nice."

Lucinda had to smile. "Thank you for the coffee, Kat. It's perfect."

"You're welcome. I liked being able to make it for you."

"And thank you for doing the dishes, too."

Somewhat guiltily, Katanya smiled back at her, saying, "I was pretending it was my house and I was tidyin' up."

"For as long as you're here, this *is* your house."

"Really?"

"Really."

"That's four more whole days."

"*This* time," Lucinda said. "Perhaps you'll come to visit me again, and when you do, it will be your house again."

"I'd *love* to come back to visit!"

"Maybe your mother and grandmother would come, too."

"That would be *soooo* cool! I know you all would like each other."

"I'd like very much to meet them. So now, let's gather up the things that need to go into the wash and get that out of the way."

———

"I've been thinking," Katanya announced, sitting on the side of the pool next to Lucinda, their feet dangling in the water.

"Oh?"

"About how to find your daddy." Katanya looked up, reading Lucinda's expression. Satisfied no displeasure was evident, she said, "Did you try all the schools?"

"We tried every single one in the entire state of Connecticut."

"You know for sure he grew up here?"

"Eddie and I believed that he did, based on Lily's age when she got married. We decided she couldn't have been less than sixteen or older than seventeen, which meant that they had to have met while she was still in high school."

"Okay. What about colleges? You try all those, too?"

"We did. We also tried all the branches of the military. It was close to impossible with only a first name to go on."

"Must've been," Katanya sympathized.

"We couldn't do any searches of birth or death records or drivers' licenses. I had a detective agency looking into it for more than two years before I finally gave up. We simply didn't have enough information to work with."

"What about church?" Katanya asked.

"Pardon?"

"Did the detectives check out the churches?"

Lucinda stared at the girl for a long moment, then said, "No, they didn't."

"That'd be the first place I'd go lookin'. Most Afro-'Mericans go to church. Me 'n' moms 'n' gramma go every Sunday. We went to some different ones before we decided on

St. Mark's. Riverside Church has a *black Jesus*. Did you ever hear of such a thing?"

"I think I may have done," Lucinda said interestedly.

"Well, they had one at Riverside. It made me kind of sad and a little mad, too—as if enough bad things didn't already happen to people of color, now Jesus had to be a black man nailed on the cross. I could see how some people might want to think of him like that, but seein' it only made everything too sad. My moms felt the same way, so we didn't go there again. We liked St. Mark's best, and we've been goin' there a long time now, since I was about four. It's got a white Jesus, which is better, because Jesus was a Jewish man who was born in Bethlehem, not in Africa. So I don't think he could've been a black man. Do you?"

"That seems reasonable. And I can understand why you'd find it upsetting. I don't know much about different faiths, Kat. The only religious place I've ever been inside was the synagogue in Los Angeles Estelle took me to when I was little. Lily always said that God was how you treat other people, and if you knew that then you knew everything important so there was no need to go to church."

"That's true," Katanya said thoughtfully. "It's important to treat people right, the way you want them to treat you."

"Yes, it is."

"Do you believe in God?" the girl asked, then without waiting for an answer, said, "I don't think *I* do. Not in an old old man up there somewhere"—she pointed to the sky—"sittin' on a throne and seein' every single person down here. That's not possible. How could one person see everybody? Nobody could do that, and all the churches I've ever been to make God look like somebody's grampa, as if he's just really old and really smart. But even the oldest and smartest grampa still couldn't see *everybody*.

"I pray sometimes, but I decided a while ago that when I do pray, I'm really only wishing very very hard for things to come out right, or for people to be okay, that no bad things happen to my moms and my gramma. But I think the only person hearin' me pray is me, because if the Grampa God could hear me, he'd've answered at least one little prayer by now. And there wouldn't be no drive-bys, wouldn't be crack-heads or plane crashes and wars everywhere."

"I feel that way, too," Lucinda said softly.

"I do like getting all dressed up on Sunday and going with my moms and gramma to St. Mark's. It's a nice place, and everybody's decent when they're inside the church, even if they don't do right every other day of the week. People are p'lite and respectful in church. I just wish they could be the same way outside. You know?"

"Yes, I do."

"And the other part I like about going is that St. Mark's has got really beautiful windows, Luce. My favorite part of the big window is one piece way over on the right-hand side. There's a blond lady at the back, she's maybe a teenager; a red-haired younger girl in front of her is holding some flowers, and next to that girl is a black lady carryin' a little cross. She looks *strong*—as if she's taking care of the other two. I love that window."

"It does sound beautiful."

"Yeah. When we go, I can't stop looking at them, wondering what it means—the three of them together. Anyway, I think if your daddy had a black moms or dad, he'd've gone to church even if he felt the way your moms did."

"That makes sense," Lucinda said, feeling a tiny spark of excitement. "It's something none of us ever considered."

"D'you have pictures of your daddy?"

"I only have one."

"One's all we need. What we do is, we use your computer to get a list of all the churches around here. Then we look at the list and cross off the ones where we know for sure Afro-'Mericans wouldn't go, like here in this town, for example."

Lucinda laughed.

"They wouldn't, would they?" Katanya asked with some uncertainty.

"Oh, I sincerely doubt it."

"So, okay. We make our list, then we get a map and make a circle on it, with where your moms grew up and went to school 'n' everything. And we pick the right churches inside that circle. If that doesn't work, we make the circle bigger and keep on making it bigger until we find what we want."

"I'm not sure I'd know what I was looking for."

"That's okay. *I* would. It's gotta be either United Methodist, or plain Methodist, or Baptist. Could be Catholic, but probably not, cuz mostly it's either Baptist or Methodist where we go."

"What's your idea, Kat?" Lucinda asked, intrigued.

"I'm thinkin' you get a bunch of copies of that picture of your daddy, then you write to the pastor at each church, asking would he show it to the congregation, or put it on the bulletin board, and see if anybody knows the man in the picture. Might be someone who'd recognize your daddy, maybe even knows his people."

The spark was becoming a small flame and for the first time in many years, Lucinda felt the heat of possibility. Extending her arm around Katanya's waist, she drew the girl close and hugged her to her side. "I'd never have thought of that in a million years."

"We're gonna find your family for you, Luce. I just know it."

"You're very clever, and it's a wonderful idea, Kat, but it's never good to hope for too much."

"It's not hoping for too much," Katanya said earnestly. "It's hoping for just enough."

The rain started then, with no warning. Suddenly, the sky was dark and the rain began pelting down. After a minute or two of trying to enjoy it, Katanya jumped to her feet. "It's no fun at all," she cried as she ran with Lucinda to the back door.

"It's going to be a big storm," Lucinda said, as they entered the cold interior of the kitchen. "Straight to the shower," she told the girl. "Make it good and hot and stay in as long as you like. I don't want you catching a chill."

"Me, neither," Katanya said through chattering teeth as Lucinda wrapped a towel around her, and the two of them hurried upstairs.

"I had to wash my hair," Katanya said from the doorway of Lucinda's bedroom.

Lucinda looked over to see that the girl's hair was now a rapidly drying halo of curls. In one hand Katanya held a pick and a brush, in the other a collection of barrettes and bands.

"I can't do it myself, but I can tell you how. It's not hard."

"Okay," Lucinda said. "Let's give it a try."

With Katanya facing the mirror and Lucinda standing behind her, the girl parted her hair into sections with the pick, then said, "Okay. First you braid this part. You know how to make a braid, right?"

"I do."

Katanya's hair was very thick and springy and wanted to resist. "You've gotta pull hard. It doesn't hurt," she said. "Soon's you get the braid done, I'll hand you one-a these"— she held up a stretchy little band with bright red bobbles on either end—"then you twist it 'round 'n' loop one end over the other."

After the first two braids were done, Lucinda had the hang of it. "Do you do this every day?" she asked.

Katanya laughed. "No way! Takes w-a-y too long. Every Saturday my moms or my gramma does it. You're doin' great."

By the time Lucinda finished, the girl's hair looked fairly much as it had before.

"It's good!" Katanya said. "Next time'll be easier. Thank you, Luce."

"You're welcome," Lucinda replied, examining all the sensations that had accompanied this small event. It felt intensely personal and she was reminded of the countless times Lily had handed her a brush, saying, "Do my hair, will you, hon?" and then she'd closed her eyes and sighed contentedly as Lucinda had gently brushed her mother's baby-fine, wheat-colored hair.

Even after they'd whittled down the list, it was still very long.

"You don't have to make the letters personal. Just address them to the pastor at each church," Katanya said.

"If I'm going to be sending out dozens of letters, I'm going to need to rent a post office box for the replies. And I'd better order extra stationery." Lucinda felt both purposeful and somehow overly vulnerable, with the sense that she was setting herself up for a repeat of the disappointment she'd felt every time the agency had reported their complete lack of success for yet another month. It had reached the point, at last, where she couldn't bear any more negative reports; so she'd called it quits, paid the tab, and with overwhelming sorrow gave up the search. Now she was starting again and she wasn't sure she could handle the sick-making swings from optimism to letdown and back, over and over again.

"I'll help. I can put the letters in the envelopes and stick on the stamps," Katanya offered.

"I'll need a box of photographic paper, too," Lucinda thought aloud.

"What for?"

"I'll scan the photo and make copies of it."

"You can *do* that?" the girl was amazed. "I thought you'd take it someplace to have it done."

"I can do it more quickly, for less money. It's easy. I'll show you how. First, I'd better order the supplies."

"Can I watch?"

"Of course. Pull up a chair."

"Okay." For a few seconds Katanya leaned against Lucinda's arm, saying, "I'm so glad we're friends."

"Me, too," Lucinda said, then turned her attention to the screen, thinking how empty the house, and her life, would be in four days' time when Katanya returned to the city. Katanya brought a chair over and sat quietly, taking note of everything Lucinda did.

That night after she'd emptied the dishwasher and readied everything for the morning, Lucinda tiptoed into the guest room to adjust the covers over Katanya, then stood for a time looking down at the soundly sleeping girl in the dim glow of the night-light. It seemed incredible that, after so many years alone, someone else was sharing the house, in her care. She had accepted the responsibility for this child; easily, automatically, she'd set aside decades of habit. As well, her heart—that dusty old machine—had been switched on and was laboring mightily to accommodate emotions it barely remembered.

Back downstairs, she looked at the pages of labels she'd printed out and the sample letter. Once the supplies were delivered, several dozen letters, each with an accompanying photograph, would go out to selected churches within a twenty-five-mile radius—all because a child had thought of something no adult had even considered years before. So simple, so obvious, yet it had never occurred to one of them.

Sitting down at the computer, she got online and went to the Apple site. It took very little time to find what she wanted. From there, over the next couple of hours, she went to several more sites, smiling as she made her selections. By a quarter to one she'd finished and shut down her connection, feeling very pleased.

Outside, the rain continued, causing the trees to thrash about, sending leaves and small broken branches to the ground, bending the flowers low, as if in defeat; rain gushed from the gutters rimming the roof, creating small lakes at the corners of the house. She adjusted the thermostat before heading up to her room, mindful of the child's presence, amazed at how potent one small girl could be.

The deliveries would start in the morning, and she'd have to make a trip to the post office to arrange for a box and to buy stamps. Perhaps, if the rain continued, she'd take Kat to the diner for lunch. She hadn't been there since they'd torn down the old place and constructed a bigger, more modern one. But the owner and his wife were still there; she caught sight of them from time to time as she drove through town on her way to the post office or the library. And she had a sudden craving for those home fries she used to like so much.

Chapter Twelve

For a moment, hearing Gin's voice, she couldn't speak. After Gin's second hello, knowing her inclination to hang up on callers who didn't speak right away, Lucinda said, "Don't die of shock. It's me."

"Oh my God! Ella has actually phoned me." A brief pause, then she said warily, "Did somebody die?"

"No one died. A lot's been going on the past few days, but nobody died. How are you, Gin?"

"Never mind that. I know you, kiddo. What's going on that you're calling me out of the blue?"

"It's a long story, but I've been thinking about you and I needed to hear your voice."

"I thought I'd never hear *your* voice again. I don't care how long the story is, tell me what's going on."

"It has to do with a little girl from the Fresh Air Fund," Lucinda began, then went on to tell her about Katanya, about the day they'd had with Jason, and the confrontation with his mother.

"That sounds like one helluva girl!" Gin said. "One of these days I'll have to meet her and shake her hand. She's a miracle worker."

"She's very special."

"There's an understatement," Gin said. "So, are you going to write me a script, finally, so I can stop reading the pathetic drivel these fools here keep sending me?"

"Gin, I haven't an idea to my name."

"I can give you ideas 'til the cows come home."

Lucinda laughed. "I'm sure you could, but I'm nowhere near ready to write anything."

"What about having a visitor? Are you ready for that?"

"I would give absolutely anything to see you, Gin."

"Okay. I've got a month's work on a decent HBO flick that's shooting all of August. In Toronto. These days everything's shot either in Toronto or Vancouver—Hollywood North, everyone calls it. It's all about the exchange rate on the Canadian dollar. Anyway, when we wrap, I'll fly down from there to see you. It's what? An hour's flight? In the meantime, I've found a book I'm crazy about. Can I send you a copy?"

"You're thinking about an adaptation?"

"Only if you'd do it. I wouldn't trust another living soul with this material. They'd turn it into dog food. If you're as crazy about it as I am, I'll put option money on the table and produce the picture myself."

"I'll read it but I can't promise anything, Gin."

"Oh, now there's a *big* surprise!" Gin snorted. "Read it! Then we'll talk." Her tone softening, she said, "Do you know how happy it makes me to talk to you? I'd almost forgotten how much you sound like Lily. It's as if I've got both of you back for a few minutes. I miss you like crazy, Lucinda Hunter. Nobody else in the world can do what you do; nobody else knows me the way you do. Every day I think about calling you, but I figure you'd play possum with the answering machine and not answer or even return my call. It hurts me. Have I ever told you that? I *know* you're in that goddamned house, listening to me leave my message, and you won't pick up the stinking phone. That *hurts*, kiddo. You mean more to me than anyone else alive and you won't even *talk* to me."

"I'm sorry, Gin. Really. You have to know that. It isn't that I don't *want* to—"

"I know, I know. I just had to get that off my chest. I'll send you the book. And I'll call you in a few days. I love you, you agoraphobic head-case."

"I love you, too, Gin."

"D'you think maybe it's the beginning of the end of it?"

"Maybe," Lucinda said. "I hope so."

"That makes two of us. I've been very lonely for you, kiddo. Nothing would make me happier than to welcome you back to the world, to have us put our heads together the way we used to and come up with earth-shaking ideas."

When she awakened, the aroma of coffee was in the air and Lucinda smiled as she got up and went into the bathroom to shower.

Katanya had set the table: a mug of coffee sat on the place mat, the *Times* beside it on one side, a folded napkin on the other. An apron tied around her waist, a wooden spoon in her hand, the girl said, "Hi," with a big smile. "I'll make you breakfast, if you like."

"Look at you." Lucinda smiled back at her. "A positive *vision* of domesticity. What's on the menu?"

"Anything you want. I can cook. Gramma's been teaching me since I was little."

"You're a lucky girl. Lily never cooked. We always ate out. I learned how to cook by reading cookbooks."

"Gramma says if you can read, you can cook."

"She's right. I'll have whatever you're having."

"Okay! We'll have my special scrambled eggs and toast."

"Sounds wonderful." Lucinda sat down and reached for the coffee, watching as Katanya swung into action. She got a frying pan from the drawer under the stove before opening the refrigerator and starting to place items on the counter. She was lovely, Lucinda thought, holding the mug with both hands, elbows propped on the table. Her features serious, Katanya found a mixing bowl and began breaking eggs into it. Then she located the cheese grater, placed it over another bowl and went to work with a wedge of cheddar.

With a sudden pang, Lucinda simultaneously realized two things: the first was that this had to be how a mother felt, sitting back to witness her child's progress into the adult world; the second was an advance sorrow at knowing that there were only three days left to them. Katanya had managed to take her beyond the habits of her fear and was steadily assisting her in her own voyage back into the adult world. Perhaps, once she left, Lucinda's momentum would go with her.

"I'm going to miss you," she said, her throat thick with emotion.

Katanya paused in her cutting and chopping to look over her shoulder and say, "I'm going to miss you, too. But I'll visit, the way we talked about yesterday."

"I hope so," Lucinda said, then forced her attention to the newspaper, staring down at the headline through a glaze of incipient tears. Another swallow of coffee helped her get past the moment; a few blinks pushed back the tears.

Katanya's special scrambled eggs were a delicious combination of eggs, cream, cheddar, onions and green peppers. Lucinda wasn't in the habit of eating breakfast but under the girl's watchful eyes, she ate everything on her plate.

"That was wonderful," Lucinda told her as Katanya poured more coffee into her cup.

"Yeah. That's my favorite breakfast. I told you my gramma's food is great."

"Thank you, Kat."

"You're welcome, Luce," she said, returning to the table as the doorbell rang.

"That'll be FedEx." Lucinda got up and went to the door.

"Got all kinds of stuff for you today, Miss Hunter," the driver said, holding out his clipboard. "Need you to sign half the page. You've been busy, huh?" Behind him at the foot of the porch stairs was a dolly stacked high with boxes. "Got a couple more in the truck."

"I have been very busy," Lucinda confirmed, signing on the lines he indicated.

"Wow, Luce!" Katanya exclaimed as the man began carrying in the boxes.

"In here okay?" he asked Lucinda from the living room threshold.

"Yes, thank you."

After bringing in the first load, he returned to the back of the truck and was out of sight for a few minutes, reappearing with his dolly stacked high again.

"What's all the stuff?" Katanya asked.

"We'll open them and you'll see."

"This's it," the driver said. "These are light," he said, handing them over to Lucinda. "Have fun!" He smiled and went on his way.

"When did you order all this stuff?" Katanya asked, walking around and looking at the printing on some of the bigger boxes.

"Last night, when you were sleeping."

"You must've been up all night!"

"It didn't take that long. Where should we start?"

Katanya said, "Probably with the boxes that have the paper 'n' stuff, so we can get your letters ready for the post office. We oughta do that first."

"You're absolutely right. I'll start the letters printing while we open everything else." Lucinda found a single-edged razor blade on the desk, sliced the tape on the large box from OfficeToGo.Com and lifted out the package of five-by-seven envelopes, the ream of paper, and the pack of photographic paper. "If you'd like to help, you can start putting the labels on the envelopes while I get the letters going."

"Sure." Katanya accepted the sheets of labels from Lucinda, then sat down on the floor with the envelopes and began applying the peel-and-stick labels. Every few seconds, she looked at the boxes, visibly curious.

As printed pages began whooshing out the top of the LaserWriter, Lucinda organized the boxes into categories, saying, as she did, "When the letter's finished printing, I'll run the photograph. That'll take a little longer because photo files are big and need more memory."

"How do you know so much about computers?" Katanya asked.

"Same way I know about cooking: from reading books. I've always liked the challenge of mechanical things and I bought a Mac the first time I heard about them. I turned it on and opened every folder and every control panel to see what it could do. And of course I read the manual from start to finish. It took me about three weeks to find the software I wanted and get it installed. More manuals to read, of course. But I was enjoying it. And I got online as soon as service was available in this area. There wasn't much to look at then, but it was exciting. Like being an explorer on a new continent. Best of all was e-mail. Right from the start, I loved it, loved the immediacy of it. You'd send something out and instead of having to wait for days, the way you would for a letter, you'd get an answer sometimes in only minutes."

"That must've been really good for you," Katanya said, "You could be in touch with people and not have to go anywhere."

"Exactly! Except for Gin who refuses to have anything to do with computers. She's very non-mechanical."

"Lottsa people like that. My moms had to learn for school and just hates computers, but my gramma loves e-mail. She goes to the library three, four evenings a week to do e-mail with her old friends all over the place. And I have computer classes twice a week at school. So how'd you get to be doing the Web stuff?"

"I kept going to sites that were great but the text was terrible. Techs take material, do the formatting and upload it without ever reading it. That's not their job. They're there to do the html and the programming. Most of them are young guys with attitude. I e-mailed an executive at one of the sites and said that having grammatical errors on a site selling software wasn't going to inspire confidence in consumers. He wrote right back and asked me if I was an editor. I said I wasn't but that I had a degree in English and was fluent in grammar"—she smiled at Katanya, who grinned back at her—"and he offered me a ton of money per hour if I'd fix all the site content. It was something to do and I was bored silly, so I said sure. I got it done so quickly that the company put me on retainer to vet everything that had to be posted on their site. Word got out, and next thing I knew, I was having to refuse jobs because I had everybody and his brother wanting me. In the end, I accepted retainers from five companies and sort of turned into a drone."

"A worker bee!" Katanya offered.

"Right. So I eased out of it after a few years and just took contract work that wasn't quite so boring. And that job"— she nodded at the computer—"is going to be the last one I do."

"Yeah? How come?"

"It's time to stop," Lucinda said simply. "Perhaps I'll do something else."

"Like writing movies again?"

"Possibly. I don't know. I spoke to Gin last night—"

"You *did*? That's great!"

"It was great, actually. Anyway, she's sending me a book she likes. She's hoping I'll do an adaptation for her."

"You mean make it into a movie?"

"That's right."

"Cool, Luce. You should do it."

"We'll see. Let's open some of these," she said. "You choose."

Kat looked at the array of boxes and said, "No. You choose."

"Okay." Reaching for one of the smaller packages, Lucinda used the razor blade to slice the tape, explaining, "This will need to be programmed, which we'll do later this afternoon," as she opened the box and tipped out the contents. "It's for you," she said, passing it over.

"You got me a *cell phone*? Oh, wow, Luce! Wow!"

"That's so you can call me any time you want to, or your mother or grandmother."

"Wow! Thank you!" Katanya studied the Motorola handset, front and back. "It's so little! I love it!"

"As I said, I'll show you how to program it later. Now, let's see." Lucinda reached for a larger package and started slicing the tape. "I had a good time ordering these things, but if there's anything you don't like, don't be afraid to say so, and we'll get something else. Okay?"

"Okay." Wide-eyed, Katanya accepted the box and lifted aside the tissue paper. "Ooooh!" she said in a whisper, then looked over at Lucinda. "It's like Christmas." Removing items one at a time, she held up the shorts and T-shirts and socks, putting them carefully on the floor. Then she clapped a hand over her mouth and gazed again at Lucinda.

"Do you like it? When you talked about getting dressed up on Sundays, I thought you might like something special."

"It's the most beautiful thing I've ever *seen!*" Using just her fingertips, Katanya removed the dress from the box and gazed at the sand-washed, short-sleeved, full-skirted cherry-red silk dress with its white collar and cuffs. "It's so soft." Carefully returning it to the box, she knee-walked over to Lucinda and hugged her, saying over and over, "Thank you, thank you."

Lucinda held her, awed by the compactness of her narrow body and the strength of her embrace. "Thank *you*, Kat," she said. "Meeting you has been one of the best things ever to happen to me." Easing her away, she said, "All of these things are for you."

"All of it? *All* of it?"

"Yup. There's a PowerBook with extra memory and a built-in card modem, a printer, a carrying case for the Power-Book, and I've arranged for you to have Internet service. All you'll have to do when you get home is dial in and log on.

I'll get your browser set up and show you how to navigate before you go home, give you a few lessons."

"My gramma won't have to go to the library anymore. She'll be able to e-mail from home?"

"That's right. And you and I will be able to e-mail each other."

Katanya shook her head slowly. "You are the nicest lady in the whole world, Luce."

"Oh, not at all. And, believe me, I had to exercise a lot of self-control, because I wanted to buy you everything I saw. I'd have got you shoes to go with the dress, if I'd known your size, but I thought maybe we'd see if I can handle taking you to the shoe store in town after lunch today."

"You don't have to give me anything more," the girl protested. "This is *soooo* much."

"I'd really like you to have shoes to go with the dress. If I can't manage the store, we'll try finding some online. Okay?"

"Yeah." Katanya hugged her again. "I think," she pronounced, "you must be an angel."

Lucinda laughed. "Definitely not," she said. "This was incredibly selfish, Kat. I had more fun buying these things for you than I've had in years and years. It was pure pleasure."

"Really?"

"Truly."

"You're a really, really kind person," the girl said seriously. "Most people don't want to give anything to anybody."

"I'm not most people and you're not just anybody," Lucinda said with equal seriousness.

Breaking into a big smile, Katanya said, "That's true! That is true." She looked again at the dress and said, "I've never had a better time in my whole life than I've had with you, Luce. You're like a fairy godmother."

"Oh, no," Lucinda disagreed. "I'm nothing of the sort."

"You are!" Katanya insisted. "From now on, you're my very own fairy godmother!" She paused, looking over at the now silent printer, then said, "We should get the letters ready. Sooner we get them out, the sooner you might get an answer. We can open the rest of the boxes when we get back. Okay?"

"Yes, okay." She liked the notion of being a fairy godmother, but thought that it was just possible that this child was the one with magical powers.

Chapter Thirteen

Lucinda managed to start the car and pull out into the road, deciding as she did to go to the small substation rather than the one in town. She'd already telephoned to arrange a box at the main post office, but she couldn't face the likelihood of the midday crowds there. However, when she pulled up in front of the small branch, her hands seemed to be glued to the wheel and she was suddenly having difficulty catching her breath.

"I could go in and buy the stamps," Katanya offered with what Lucinda was coming to regard as typically heightened sensitivity.

Lucinda swallowed and, with concentrated effort, managed to remove her hands from the wheel and put the car into Park. "I'd appreciate it," she said. "If you take one of the letters in and get it weighed, we'll know how much postage we need for all of them. I'm guessing it'll be around fifty cents." Opening her bag, she got out fifty dollars and gave the money to Katanya. "Thank you, Kat. Once we've got the stamps, we can sit in the car and put them on, then just drop the letters in there." With an unsteady hand, she indicated the box to one side of the door.

"Okay." Pocketing the money, the girl took one of the envelopes from the substantial stack. "Be right back, Luce," she said, and got out of the car.

Through her dark glasses, Lucinda watched Katanya climb the steps and push into the small post office. Her lungs expanding by degrees so that she could breathe more easily, she sat, waiting.

People went in; a few minutes later they came out. But after almost fifteen minutes, Katanya hadn't reappeared. After another five minutes, knowing something was wrong, she was gearing herself up to go in after her when Katanya emerged. Head bowed, she trudged down the steps and slid back inside the car, pulling the door shut. She sat slumped on the edge of the seat, the letter in her hands, her chin trembling, her body curved into itself.

"What's wrong, honey?" Lucinda asked gently.

Chest heaving, tears brimming the rims of her eyes, head still lowered, the girl said, "Everybody kept pushing in front of me, and the lady 'hind the counter just *let* them."

"Was she a fat woman with fuzzy orange hair who talked nonstop and took forever counting out change?" Lucinda asked.

Katanya nodded and whispered, "Yeah."

"That stupid *cow*!" Turning off the engine, Lucinda said, "Come with me, Kat!" and got out of the car, her indignation having pushed ahead of her reticence to dictate her actions. Taking Katanya's hand, she marched up the steps and pushed through the door. Sure enough, the squatty, obese clerk was yattering away to a customer at the counter while seven or eight people stood impatiently tap-tapping their feet or sighing heavily.

"Excuse us!" Lucinda said in a polite but icy tone, going straight to the counter. "Have you finished, sir?" she asked the elderly customer who nodded in surprise. "Then please step aside, if you will."

"Oh, certainly, certainly," the man said, with a guilty glance at Katanya, and moved away quickly, heading straight out the door.

"Perhaps you could explain why you allowed everyone to push past my granddaughter, instead of serving her," Lucinda said imperiously to the open-mouthed woman behind the counter as Katanya's hand gave hers a squeeze.

"I didn't ... n-hum ... I ... yunh ... thought she was just waiting for someone," the woman offered weakly, small eyes darting here and there, looking like an immense, trapped hamster.

Leaning across the counter, Lucinda said, in a low and menacing voice, "You talk too much, you move at a snail's pace, and you are definitely *not* the sharpest knife in the drawer. As if that isn't bad enough, now I discover that you are critically impaired when it comes to children. Obviously"—her quiet tone turned scathing—"my granddaughter was by herself, waiting her turn for service. If you want to *keep* this job, for which you are in no way qualified, you will *never* pull a stunt like this again. One call from me to your supervisor and not even your union will be able to save you. Violating a child's civil rights is a very serious matter, because whether *you* think so or not, she is entitled to the same service as any other customer, regardless of age." Straightening, she turned to take the measure of the people in the line. "How many of you just stood here and watched my girl get pushed aside?" she asked in her previously gelid tone. "At least two of you did, because I saw you come in. But not one of you said a word, did you? You'd probably have shunted her out of the way, too, because nothing a *child* might want in here could possibly be as important as what *you* want. You should be *ashamed*! Your behavior has been unforgivable." Turning forward again, she took a calming breath—feeling the weight of many eyes boring into her spine like ice picks—before saying, in a voice kept steady by sheer force of will, "Kat, go ahead now, honey, and get what you came for."

Letting go of Lucinda's hand, Katanya stood on tiptoe to put the envelope on the scale. "I'd like to know how much postage this needs, please," she said clearly.

The now red-faced, flustered clerk unnecessarily adjusted the letter's position on the scale with stubby fingers whose nails had been chewed to the quick. She glanced nervously at the zip code, then entered the numbers into the computer.

"That'll be fifty cents. Yunh-huh."

"Okay. I'd like one hundred fifty-cent stamps, please," Katanya said, retrieving the envelope.

"Um ... Don't know if I have a hundred ... Yunh ... " She waddled back to her book of stamps and flipped pages until she found the right denomination. Her face still an almost fluorescent red, she fumbled a sheet of stamps out of the book and counted them aloud with maddening slowness, then pulled out another sheet and, incredibly, held it against the first and counted these, too.

Behind them, Lucinda could hear the foot-tapping begin again, and could easily picture the eye-rolling that accompanied the audible sighs of the waiting customers. She wanted to be able, like her favorite childhood comic book character, Plastic Man, to thrust her arms into space and close her hands around this fool woman's throat and twist her head around until it popped right off—like a cork from a wine bottle. Imagining it, she nearly smiled. Thank heavens, she thought, for comic book heroes.

"Yunh, unh-hunh, okay. Unh-hunh. Got a hundred. Okay?" The clerk waddled back to the counter; her eyes flickered to Lucinda, then, not looking at Katanya, she asked, "Um, anything else?"

"No, thank you."

"Yunh, that'll be unh fifty dollars. Okay."

Katanya put the money on the counter. "I'd like a receipt, please."

"Oh! Okay, unh-hunh. Yunh." She made a great show of turning the bills face-side up before putting them into the till.

Lucinda now gave Katanya's hand a squeeze. She'd forgotten to tell her to ask for a receipt.

The clerk then hit a key to complete the transaction—the tapping feet asychronously louder on the wood floor—tore the slip from the printer, laid it on top of the stamps and was about to slide everything across when Katanya said, "Could I please have an envelope for the stamps?"

Someone behind them groaned audibly.

Lucinda whirled around and glared. Instant silence.

"Yunh. Okay, sure. Yunh, unh-humh." She waddled several steps to one side, bent with a grunt, her post office-issue trousers' seams threatening to give way, then after a few seconds of umhing and yunh-huhing, she straightened with an oversized glassine envelope. Her short-sleeved blue standard-issue shirt had spreading damp crescents under each arm. "There ya go. Thanks. Unh-hunh. Yunh. Okay."

"Thank you." Katanya slid the stamps and receipt into the envelope and then, smiling, said to Lucinda, "All done, Gramma," and the two of them, followed by many pairs of eyes, pushed out of the post office, down the steps and back to the car.

In silence, with Lucinda's breathing audibly labored, they divided up the stamps and the envelopes and quickly affixed the postage. Then Katanya took the letters, and went to feed them a few at a time into the mailbox.

They were driving away when Lucinda finally said, "Don't ever, *ever* allow anyone, but especially an adult, to push you aside, Kat. Only stupid or ignorant people do that to a child."

"I won't. Why'd you say that, Luce, about bein' my gramma?"

"Because it was important. It wasn't about me. It was about you."

"But you said I was your gran'child. You were a *sister* in there, in front of everyone."

"Or maybe I was a white woman with a black grandchild. I claimed you, Kat, because what mattered was that you were being ignored, discounted because you're nine years old. We'll never know if skin color had anything to do with it. And that wasn't the issue. I meant what I said. Those people who stood by and watched what happened, those upright citizens who would've done the same thing to you when their turn came, were pitiful examples of the species. No one should treat *anyone* the way you were treated. God, they pissed me off!" Lucinda was on the verge of hyperventilating, aware of her greatly accelerated heart rate.

"No kidding! But you're really good when you get pissed off," Katanya said admiringly. "You say amazin' things. I know you're all shaky and upset now 'n' everything, but, boy oh boy, you sure can give it out, when you want to. I loved it when you said she wasn't the sharpest knife in the drawer. I never heard that one before."

Lucinda's leg was jumping up and down and she was having trouble maintaining the twenty-five mile per hour speed limit.

Kat went on, saying, "If that'd happened at home, I wouldn't've let everybody crash the line. No way. But it's different here. The rules are different."

"The rules are the rules everywhere, Kat," Lucinda said, then paused to catch her breath. "They don't change from one city or town to the next," she went on. "You're a *person*, someone with rights, and people should respect that. I know this seems like another world to you; it seems that way to me sometimes, too. But right and wrong aren't about geography."

"You got so mad, Luce. It was like you were somebody else, the way you jumped out of the car and went stomping in there." Cautiously, she said, "It can be scary sometimes when people get really mad. Cuz if they can get that mad at other people, maybe they'll get that mad at you."

"I scare *myself* when I get that angry. But I can't conceive of your doing anything that would ever make me that angry with you." She glanced over at the girl, then looked ahead again at the road. "Last night I was impatient with Renee, because she was treating you and Jason like groceries; bags she could just park somewhere and come back for later. She was rude, and I cannot *abide* bad manners. But she was terribly upset and her feelings got in the way of everything she'd been taught about how to behave. I told her off because she needed to be made to see that she wasn't acting out in a vacuum, that what she was saying and doing was affecting the people around her.

"What went on at the post office was something very different, something far worse than bad manners." Lucinda took another slow, deep breath. "I don't get angry often, Kat. I don't like how it feels any more than you liked seeing and hearing it. I haven't actually had anything to be angry about for a long time, because I've been safe inside my cocoon."

"So it's because of me?" Katanya asked.

"No, no. *Not* because of you. You haven't done anything wrong. See, when I was little, I went to school on the lot at the studio where Lily was under contract, and I started to notice that bad things seemed to be happening to a lot of the kids. So I told Lily about it. You want to talk about scary! Lily turned to ice. I'd never seen her like that before. She went storming off to do something about it, and I was glad, proud of her, because it made me see that my mother wouldn't put up with anyone hurting a kid. I already knew that, in some ways. I just hadn't known how *much* it mattered to her, until that day." She paused for breath again. "When I saw that she cared and that she meant to do something about it, it taught me a big lesson—one I've never forgotten: that it's the responsibility of adults to hold other adults accountable for their behavior, particularly when it comes to children. That moronic, nail-biting blabbermouth at the post office and those self-important people hurt you, Kat. I could *not* allow that to go unchallenged. I didn't even have to think about it. I had to get in there and let them know, just as I did with Renee, that their behavior was unacceptable. I know they all thought I was crazy. People always think you're crazy if you speak up. But it was the right thing to do. I am sorry, though, that you got scared."

"Secretly, I was glad—like you said you were about your moms—when you said what you did to that fat lady and those people. It made me proud, made me feel like I matter."

"You do matter. But always, always stand up for yourself, Kat. No matter what. If you believe in your heart that you're right, take a stand and don't back down. You know what Abraham Lincoln said?"

"No. What?"

"He said, 'Let no man falter who thinks he is right.' I read that when I was about your age and I've made it my personal credo."

"What's that? Like your rules?"

"In a way. It's one of my personal standards. I've got others, too." She pulled into the driveway and turned off the motor. "Thank you for thinking up the idea of the churches and for helping me get those letters out."

"You're welcome. I like helping you."

"Shall we open the rest of the boxes now?"

"You gettin' another headache, Luce?"

"You know what, Kat? I categorically refuse to have a headache today!"

"Okay! Then I refuse to *allow* you to have a headache today!"

"That might work," Lucinda said.

They smiled at each other, then turned to get out of the car.

"There's so many things," Katanya said. "I can't believe you did all this for me. It's amazin'! But I'm kind of wonderin' how I'm gonna get it all home on the train."

"You won't be going on the train. I plan to arrange transportation for you."

"Oh! Okay. Thank you." The girl looked at the screen of the PowerBook and the Word document Lucinda had been teaching her to create, then back at Lucinda. "Are you hungry, Luce?"

"Good grief! I forgot all about lunch. I'm sorry, Kat. I tend to get so involved when it comes to computers that I forget everything else. Let me show you how to save your document. Then we'll get cleaned up and I'll take you somewhere."

"*Out?*"

"Yes, out."

"Are you sure, Luce? That'll be twice today."

"I'm quite sure," Lucinda said determinedly.

"Well, okay, if you're sure. Where're we gonna go?"

"To the diner, for a late lunch. They have great home fries."

"I *love* home fries."

"Good. Me, too."

Lucinda could feel Katanya's eyes on her, but she conscientiously ignored the rising panic in her chest. Putting the car in Reverse, she looked both ways, then backed out into the road. Her jaws ached from clenching her teeth, and she was damp with perspiration by the time she parked near the diner which, she saw with relief, was practically deserted.

"We don't have to do this," Katanya said. "We could go to the drive-thru back there." She pointed over her shoulder.

"I *do* have to do this," Lucinda said. "You're giving me courage, Kat."

"I am?"

"Yes, you are. I could tell that you were afraid to go into that post office alone, but you did it anyway and went walking up the steps as if it was something you did every day. If you could do something that frightened you, even pretending that it didn't, at the very least, I've got to *try* to do things that frighten me, too."

"Okay. But if you get nervous or headachy or anything, we'll leave. All right?"

"Yes." Drying her hands on the skirt of her dress, Lucinda adjusted her hat and sunglasses. "All right. But I *want* those home fries."

Katanya chuckled. "Loo-cinda, if it's food that'll get you outta that house, I'll get my gramma cookin' right away."

Lucinda leaned across the seat and kissed the girl's cheek, then sat back, smiling.

Lucinda ordered a BLT with home fries and coffee. Katanya ordered a cheeseburger with home fries and a grape soda. The waitress took the menus and went off, and they sat back to wait for their food.

A minute or two later, the owner's wife came to the booth. Offering Lucinda her well-remembered glorious smile, she said, "Is nice see you again."

"It's good to see you, too," Lucinda said, understanding very belatedly that the woman was profoundly shy and that her coming over to say hello had taken monumental effort. "I've never known your name."

"Is Elena. What's you?"

"Lucinda. And this is my friend Katanya."

"Ah." She beamed at Katanya who grinned up at her happily and said hi. "Is ver' nice see you," she then repeated to Lucinda. "Long, long time, uh?"

"Yes, too long. Thank you, Elena."

"Not so long next time see you?"

"No. I'll come back soon."

"Good, good." The woman bobbed her head, smiled again at Katanya, and slipped away.

"I used to come here almost every weekend when I was at Yale," Lucinda explained to Katanya. "I'd sit at the counter and eat home fries and drink gallons of coffee while I studied. They've remodeled the place since then."

"Yeah, it looks pretty new. And no more counter. Did they have those stools you can twirl on?"

"Unh-hunh. They did."

"I like those. How long's it been since you came here?"

"Over twenty-five years."

"And she remembered you. Wow! That's really some-thing."

"Believe it or not, it's the first time we've ever spoken."

"Oh, that's cuz she's shy, like you," Katanya stated know-ingly.

"You don't miss a thing, do you?" Lucinda said, im-pressed.

"Nope. Hardly anything. Gramma says I'm a scary little dudette."

"*Dudette*?" Lucinda laughed.

"Gramma makes up words all the time."

"Such as?"

"Bimbette, dudette, cabette—that's a lady cabdriver—ush-erette."

"Usherette's not something your grandmother made up, honey."

Katanya was surprised. "No?"

"Nope. That was a real term, before the world turned po-litically correct and words stopped being gender specific. We used to have actresses and authoresses, policewomen and usherettes. Lots of other feminine words, too."

"I always thought it was one of gramma's made-up ones, cuz I've never heard anyone else say that."

"I like dudette," Lucinda said. "It's good."

"Yeah." Katanya fiddled with her knife and fork, lining them up on the napkin as she looked around the all but empty place. The only other customer was a middle-aged businessman in a booth at the far end, eating a sandwich while he read a newspaper. "It's nice here. If I was going to Yale, I'd want to come here and study on the weekends, like you did."

"Maybe you will."

"Maybe." The girl looked doubtful about the prospect.

"If it's what you *want*, Kat, it'll happen. Anything's possible. Anything at all."

"I'm not so sure about that—"

The waitress arrived then with their food, putting an end to the conversation.

Chapter Fourteen

That evening, while Katanya sat at the kitchen table examining the contents of the PowerBook's system folder, Lucinda sautéed some diced chicken breasts in garlic-flavored
olive oil with scallions, green peppers, sundried tomatoes,
black olives and capers. She stirred the chicken and veg-
etable mixture into a pot of penne, sprinkled grated Reg-
giano parmesan over the top and said, "Time to put the
PowerBook to sleep, Kat. The food's ready."

" 'Kay, just one sec. I'm customizin' the clock. Made it
green," she said proudly, "with the day of the week
showin'." She finished, then closed the folder of control panels, and clicked the windows closed until she was looking at
the desktop. "Where do I go again to make it sleep?"

"Under the Special menu."

"I like this touch pad; it's cool. Okay," she said as the hard
drive spun down and the screen went dark. "Done." With
great care she lifted the computer to the chair on the far side
of the table as Lucinda brought over the plates.

"This is good, Luce," Katanya said between bites. "Is this from one of your cookbooks?"

"No, it's my own creation."

Katanya chewed and swallowed before asking, "Could you tell me how to make it?"

"I'll put the recipe on a floppy for you."

"Great!"

Later, while Lucinda rinsed the dishes and Katanya loaded them into the dishwasher, the girl said, "Tomorrow's our last whole day together."

Lucinda froze, holding a plate under the hot water, trying to absorb this fact. Somehow, even though she'd been on the phone earlier to arrange for Katanya's ride back to the city, it hadn't been real. Now, suddenly, it was very real, imminent. Lucinda felt a wave of anticipated loneliness that literally shook her so that she had to put a hand on the rim of the sink to keep herself upright. "How," she asked, "would you like to spend your last day?"

"*I* wanna do whatever *you* wanna do," Katanya answered, holding out her hand for the next item to go into the machine.

Surrendering the plate, Lucinda gathered up a handful of cutlery and held it under the faucet. "We really ought to do something special."

"Like what?"

"I'll have to give it some thought." Lucinda passed over the utensils and watched as the girl distributed them among the compartments in the cutlery basket. Everything had to balance for this child, Lucinda noticed, even how knives and forks were positioned in a dishwasher basket. Few adults and fewer children paid attention to details of this sort. But Katanya did instinctively. It showed in how she'd set the table that morning, in how she'd divided the envelopes into equal piles before handing Lucinda one of the sheets of stamps. It was a rare thing, this innate sense of balance, of equality. Also rare was the honesty, curiosity, humor and imagination she'd brought into this house, into Lucinda's life. And suddenly they were on the brink of Katanya's departure. The thought of the child leaving was to Lucinda's mind equivalent to a power outage that would consign her to permanent night-time darkness and unbroken silence. It signified a return to a life unlived for a long, long time; a life on hold. She couldn't stand the thought of it.

"What's the matter, Luce?" Katanya asked, wiping her hands on a dish towel before folding it over the rack beside the stove.

Framing her reply, Lucinda turned off the water, squeezed the sponge and set it on the rim of the sink. "Nothing," she said, drying her hands with a paper towel, then absently wiping the counter with it. "I'm just trying to think of what we could do tomorrow."

"I'd be happy to stay in the pool. And we could have a barbecue for dinner, if that one you got out there works."

"It works. And I have some steaks in the freezer. Do you like steak?"

"Unh-hunh. Love it. See! We're all set."

"That's not very special, Kat."

"It is for me."

I don't want you to go! Lucinda thought, then silently berated herself for being so childish.

"I should probably shut down my computer now and put it away."

"Do you remember how?"

"Think so." Katanya lifted the PowerBook back onto the table, pressed a key at random and grinned as the desktop reappeared. "The monitors at school don't have color. Some company gave us five computers last year, but they're *old.*

This is bee-ew-tee-full." She kissed her fingers and tapped them on the PowerBook's case. "Okay. I go back up to Special again. Right? Pull down the menu and go to Shut Down?"

"Right."

When the screen had gone dark, Katanya gently folded the PowerBook closed, then pulled the power cord from the wall before removing it, as Lucinda had shown her, from the back of the machine. At last, with delicate precision, she placed everything in the purple carrying case and zipped it shut. "I love this case and my computer. I love every single one of the presents you gave me, Luce. I can't wait to show it all to my moms and gramma. Would it be okay for me to phone and tell them?"

"Of course. Go ahead. I'll deal with some of that packaging in the living room."

To give the child some privacy, Lucinda slid a Jacques Loussier CD into the machine and as the first notes of the jazz rendition of "Air on the G String" emerged from the speakers, she began slicing through the packing tape and breaking down the boxes. The new multicolored duffel bag she'd bought would easily hold Katanya's new things. God! she thought. There'd be nothing left to show that the child had ever been in the house. But wait! She'd forgotten Kat's drawing. Going over to her desk, she moved papers aside until she found it. Then, certain she had magnets somewhere, she opened one drawer after another until she found several in an old box that had once held Lily's face powder.

Five minutes later, the girl came skipping down the hall, went straight over to Lucinda and hugged her around the waist. "My moms and gramma say thank you and you've gotta come visit with us. Gramma says she'll cook a feast for you."

"That's very kind of her."

Moving away to look at the stack of flattened boxes, Katanya said, "I told them how you don't go anywhere and my gramma says it's an open invitation. What's that mean?"

"It means that I could come any time at all."

"Oh! Okay, I get it. When I told her about the computer and the Internet, you should've *heard* her! She was *soooo* excited, said I'm a lucky, lucky girl and she hoped I was bein' properly grateful. I *think* I'm bein' properly grateful."

"You are. Very definitely."

"I wouldn't want you think I wasn't, cuz I am, very, *v-e-r-y, very* grateful. You're my angel fairy godmother."

Lucinda couldn't help but smile. "I'm not at all. I just care for you, Kat. I enjoy your company."

"I enjoy yours, too. Wanna watch TV or something?"

"I've got a better idea," Lucinda said. "We could have a swim and then go to bed. I'm pretty tired, and you must be, too."

"But no headache?"

"Nope."

"O-kay! Let's go swimmin'! I'll go put on my bathing suit."

"TV's terrible," Katanya said with disgust, treading water facing Lucinda. "It's the very same here as it is at home. A zillion channels and nothing to watch. Why is that?"

"I don't know. I can hardly ever find anything I want to see. Even on the movie channels, most of the time I've seen the picture so many times I can repeat the dialogue word for word."

Katanya laughed and said, "My moms and gramma watch movies with the sound off and they say all the lines. They do *The Wizard of Oz* and *Raiders of the Lost Ark* and *Forty-sec-*

ond Street, 'n' three or four others. It's *soooo* funny. Gramma always does the wicked witch. 'I'm going to get you, my pretty one,' " she said in a whiny nasal voice, scrunching up her features, " 'an' your little dog, Toto, too.' "

Lucinda laughed so hard that tears came to her eyes. Katanya stopped moving her arms and legs and shrilled, *"I'm melllllltinnnnnng!"* As she began to slip below the surface, in a tiny voice, she repeated, *"I'm melllll-tinnnnnnnnnng,"* and then slid under the water. After a moment, she surfaced, laughing. "They play out all the parts. It's *soooo* funny. What movies do you know by heart?"

"By heart? Most of Lily's films and, of course, the ones I wrote with Gin. I remember lines here and there from famous movies, but not entire scripts."

"Hey! I know. I could sing a song for you, if you want."

"I didn't know you could sing."

"I can, but you have to promise not to laugh."

"Is it a funny song?"

"I don't think so."

"Then I promise not to laugh."

"I think I need to be where I can stand up," Katanya said.

Following the child's lead, they moved to shallower water.

When Katanya's feet touched bottom, she said, "This is good." She cleared her throat, then began.

"Why are there so many songs about rainbows and what's on the other side?"

Looking up at the sky, she sang "The Rainbow Connection" in a voice with such unexpected power and clarity that Lucinda was overwhelmed. She applauded at the end, and begged, "Sing another, please. That was wonderful."

"Okay. Lemme think." Katanya thought for a few seconds, then said. "Okay, I'll do my gramma's favorite." She cleared her throat again, closed her eyes for a moment, opened them to gaze once more at the sky, and sang, "Someone to Watch Over Me." Her voice floated off into the heavy summer night air, and Lucinda came undone. She held a hand over her mouth as tears ran down her cheeks, wanting this bubble of time to remain intact forever.

When Katanya was getting to the end of the last chorus, Lucinda ducked underwater, telling herself to get a grip or the child would think she was deranged. She surfaced again just as the last note was drifting off into the atmosphere, declaring, "You're *such* a good singer, Kat."

"That's my gramma's favorite song."

"It's one of my favorites, too. I think it's time for bed, honey. You must be tired. I definitely am. I was up pretty late last night."

"I bet you were! Orderin' all those things. How'd you get everything to come so fast?"

"Express service," Lucinda told her as she climbed out of the pool, then turned to lift Katanya out over the side. "You go on in now and get ready for bed. I'm just going to make sure everything's put away, turned off and locked up down here, then I'll be in to say good night."

" 'Kay," Katanya said, wrapping herself in a towel as she headed for the gate.

In the kitchen, performing on auto-pilot, Lucinda locked the door, then stood in the darkened kitchen, hearing Katanya's voice inside her head, singing the final poignant lines from Kermit's song. *Maybe someday the lovers and dreamers would find that rainbow connection.* She had to blot her face on the damp dish towel before going to the front of the house.

Up very early the next morning, Lucinda got the crayon drawing from her desk and fastened it to the refrigerator with the magnets. She stood back to admire it for a few seconds before getting a pot of coffee started and removing two steaks from the freezer, setting them out to thaw on a plate. Then she went to the living room. While the computer was booting up, she got the *Times* from the porch, and glanced at the headlines as she carried the paper to the kitchen. Today, if it killed her, she'd take Katanya out to buy new shoes.

After checking for new e-mail and finding only spam, she closed her Internet connection and, inspired, hurried upstairs to her bedroom. It took her a few minutes to find what she wanted and she dropped it into her pocket.

After she had some coffee and read the paper, she went upstairs to wake Katanya only to discover that she was already up and in the shower. She'd made the bed, Lucinda saw, and her clothes for the day were neatly laid out. It gave her a pang, reminding her of how she had, at Kat's age, deliberated over what to wear before laying things out in just the same way. Did all little girls do that? she wondered. She'd probably never know, she thought, going back downstairs.

She was halfway through her second cup of coffee when Katanya came skipping in. "Hi, Luce!" she warbled and skipped right up to Lucinda to kiss the top of her head.

Amused, Lucinda put her hands on the girl's narrow waist and said, "First you'll have breakfast. Then we'll go get your new shoes."

"But, Luce. You've already bought me so many things. I don't need anything more. I've got good Sunday shoes."

"Are they shiny, black patent Mary Janes?"

"What're those?"

"Ah! Childhood isn't *complete* without a pair of Mary Janes. You must have them. It'll be the last thing I buy you."

"I don't want you getting a headache or anythin', Luce."

"I'll try very hard not to get a headache. We will go to the shoe store and come right home again."

"Well, okay, if you're sure."

"I'm sure."

⸺

The elderly man who greeted them at the shoe store couldn't have been more helpful or enthusiastic.

"Before we try on the shoes," he told Katanya, "I would suggest you pick out a nice pair of dress socks. Then we'll be able to get the perfect fit."

"Will that be okay, Luce?"

"Go ahead," she said, and sat down while, with a hand placed lightly on Katanya's shoulder, the old fellow directed the girl over to examine the display of socks. After asking several questions about what she'd be wearing and for what occasion, he lifted several pairs down for her to inspect.

"Personally, I think a very simple sock would be best," he said. "You don't want to take attention away from your new dress."

"No, I don't."

"I would recommend these," he said, draping a pair of silky white ankle socks across his palm. "They'll go well with the dress and the shoes."

Katanya touched them and said, "Okay. These are nice."

"A good choice." He directed her back to the row of chairs, saying, "Now, let's slip on one of these nice socks and measure your foot."

He was courtly and kind, and went off to the stockroom, humming to himself.

"He's nice," Katanya whispered.

"Very nice," Lucinda whispered back, thinking he more than made up for their experience the previous morning at the post office.

After a few minutes, he returned with three boxes. With a wink at Lucinda, he said, "I have several pairs for you to look at." With a ceremonial flourish, he removed the lid from the first box, revealing a pair of black patent tasseled loafers.

"Are those Mary Janes?" Katanya asked, looking from the shoes to Lucinda.

"No, but you might like something else better."

"I'd like to see the Mary Janes, please," Katanya told him.

"Of course." Setting aside the top two boxes, he removed the lid of the last box and lifted out one of the shoes.

"Oh, I *love* those!" Katanya said. "I didn't know that's what they were called."

"Let's see how they fit," he said, and slipped the shoe onto her foot, then fastened the strap. "Have a walk around, see how they feel."

"They feel *wonderful!*" she exclaimed, stopping to admire her foot in the mirror. "Could I try on the other one, too?"

"Certainly."

Kicking off her sneaker, Katanya pulled on the other sock, then allowed her foot to be fitted into the second shoe. She got up and walked around the store, looking down at her feet, unable to stop smiling.

"We'll have them." Lucinda handed the man her credit card.

"Anything for you, madam?" he asked.

"No, thank you."

Returning to the chair beside Lucinda, Katanya held her legs straight out for one last admiring look. "You're right. They're perfect for the dress. I'm *soooo* happy. Thank you, Luce." She leaned over to give Lucinda a kiss on the cheek, then busied herself unstrapping the shoes and putting them back into the box, along with the socks.

"Are you too old for a lollipop?" the man asked Katanya while Lucinda signed the charge slip.

"I don't think so," Katanya said, and selected one from the box he offered. "Thank you."

"Thank *you*, dear."

"Such a pretty girl," he murmured to Lucinda, giving her the receipt as Katanya wandered through the store, looking at the displays.

"She's lovely," Lucinda agreed, thanking him before going over to take Katanya's hand as they left the store.

"Lots of girls at church have them, but I never knew that shoes could have a name. I'll take very good care of them, Luce."

"I know you will."

As they settled into the car, Katanya said, "In some ways, I wish I wasn't going home tomorrow so I could stay with you forever. But I miss my moms and gramma."

"Of course you do. Two weeks is a long time to be away from home."

"I've never been away before."

"It's time for you to go home," Lucinda said softly, feeling just as torn as Katanya did.

The time seemed to go too quickly. Suddenly, it was the next morning and when the knock came at the door, Lucinda went down the hall with an ache in her belly. But instead of the driver she'd been expecting, there was Jason, clutching a bouquet of flowers and shouting, "Wanna see Kat! *Kat!*"

"Soupboy!" Lucinda laughed and scooped him up, smiling past him at Renee at the foot of the porch stairs.

Behind her, Katanya came bounding down the stairs and Jason was fighting to get free of Lucinda's arms, crying, "Kat, Kat!" She set him down, he dropped the flowers, and flew to Katanya, wrapping his arms around her thighs.

"Hey, Jase!" Kat lifted him, and he started kissing her face—forehead, chin, cheeks and chin—so that she laughed merrily.

"The flowers are for you," Renee told Lucinda, coming up the stairs onto the porch to retrieve the bouquet of white freesias and pass it to her. "Hi, Kat! We knew you were leaving today, so we came to say goodbye, and to give you this." She gave Katanya a gift-wrapped package. "I hope you haven't already read it. It was my favorite book when I was your age."

"Thank you, Miz Crane. It's so cool you came."

Just as Lucinda was about to invite them inside, a black Cadillac limousine pulled into the driveway and parked next to Renee's car.

"Who's that?" Katanya asked.

"That's your ride back to the city," Lucinda told her.

"I'm goin' in a *limo*?"

"Traveling in style," Lucinda said. "I almost ordered a stretch but I thought it would be a bit much."

"Wow! Mrs. Garcia's gonna faint when she sees me arrivin' in that!"

"Good morning," said the uniformed driver, arriving at the foot of the steps. "Luggage?"

"Just inside here." Lucinda pointed out Katanya's things: the small suitcase, the duffel bag, the printer in its box, and the computer case.

Slinging the computer case's strap over his shoulder, the man tucked the printer under his arm, picked up both bags with his free hand and carried them to the limo.

Lifting Jason out of the way, Renee moved to one side, while Lucinda bent to talk to Katanya. "When you get there, he'll help you inside with your things. Then you give him this"—she handed Katanya a folded twenty dollar bill—"and say thank you."

"Okay." Katanya tucked the bill into her shorts' pocket, then hugged Lucinda hard, saying, "I love you, Luce. Thank you for everything. It's the best time I've ever had."

"There's one more thing." Lucinda took the necklace from her pocket and fastened it around Katanya's neck.

"What's this?" the girl asked, holding the pendant up to look at it.

"It's my Phi Beta Kappa key, Kat. It's to remind you that you can do anything you set your mind to do. And remember, you can e-mail or phone me any time. I programmed my number into your cell phone. Let me know how you're doing. Okay?"

"I will. Thank you, thank you."

"It's been my pleasure, honey."

Katanya went over to say goodbye to Jason and his mother. Then she came back to take Lucinda's hand and walk with her to the limo. Behind them, on seeing Katanya about to get into the car, Jason let out a scream and struggled so hard that Renee put him down and he came tottering across the grass and down the driveway to fling himself at Katanya. "Kat stay!" he cried. "Kat stay! *Stay!*"

Picking him up, Katanya carried him onto the grass where she whispered to him. Whatever she said made him wind his arms around her neck and sob even harder, shaking his head back and forth, crying, "No, no nonononono! Kat stay wi' Jase."

"I'll come see you, Jase. I promise. But I gotta go home now, see my moms and gramma. I wanna see them same as you wanna see your moms when she's been away for a while. How 'bout I phone you, Jase? Would you like that?"

Nodding broken-heartedly, he said, "Kat phone Jase!"

"I will. I promise. I have to go now, Jase, so I'm gonna put you down. You can't scream. Okay, Jase? I need you to say you won't scream."

He nodded, and she put him down. He looked up at her for a long moment, his mouth falling open in preparation for a scream of protest. She pointed a finger at him and said, "You promised you wouldn't scream, Jase. You gotta keep your promises."

His chest heaving, he wept noisily. Renee picked him up and he laid his head on her shoulder and popped his thumb into his mouth, never taking his eyes from Katanya.

"'Bye everybody," Kat said, blowing kisses as she slipped into the car.

The driver closed the door, slid behind the wheel and the car smoothly backed away.

"Have you come home again?" Lucinda asked finally, looking over at Renee, surprised to see that the young woman had tears in her eyes.

Renee nodded.

"Thank you for the flowers."

"You're welcome." Renee sniffed and reached into her pocket for a tissue.

"Bring Soupboy for a visit sometime," Lucinda said, making her way to the house. She had no idea whether or not Renee said anything; all she cared about was getting into the house and closing the door so that no one would see her go to pieces.

Chapter Fifteen

In the living room, Lucinda sat on the sofa, the freesias forgotten in her lap as she stared at the floor, listening to the silence of the house. There were a few chores needing to be
done: the linens from the guest room had to go into the wash
and the bed remade. But what was the point of rushing to
do that? No one would be coming. She could leave the mattress naked. The trash and recycling bins had to be put out,
but that could wait, too. She didn't feel like moving and
wouldn't have, except that water was leaking through the
wrapping on the flowers and was soaking into her skirt.

With a sigh, she got up and walked slowly to the kitchen,
her eyes going at once to Katanya's drawing on the refrigerator: the oversized Lucinda with a tiny Kat, in front of the
house which had castlelike proportions in this rendering.
Putting the bouquet on the counter, she sat at the table and
studied the drawing from across the room, remembering
how, with astonishment, she'd discovered that Lily had
saved every drawing, every school test, every piece of writing Lucinda had ever done.

It had been a few weeks after they'd moved from California and, aside from their two bedrooms, the house had been filled with unopened boxes and crates. Just getting from one room to another required navigational skills that Lily didn't appear to possess. She kept bumping into things and was acquiring bruises on her arms and legs. Finally, unable to bear it any longer, Lucinda confronted her mother.

"Fly back to the coast for a few days and visit your pals. While you're gone, I'll get this mess organized. Otherwise, you're going to wind up breaking an arm or a leg. Anyway, I can't stand the, the—chaos."

"Luce, you can't tackle all this by yourself." Lily had looked horrified.

"Somebody has to do it. It might as well be me."

"Are you serious?"

"One hundred percent. Go visit Eddie or Jane or somebody; hang out with Gin, but *go*, please!"

"Okay, Luce," Lily gave in. "I wouldn't mind getting away from this unholy mess for a while."

"By the time you get back, it won't be a mess anymore."

So Lily had gone to Los Angeles and Lucinda had systematically opened every box, unpacked its contents, and found places for each item. After four days, there were only half a dozen cartons left and the second to last one that she opened contained stacks of envelopes, large and small, containing everything from Lucinda's earliest efforts at printing, to first drafts of the scripts she'd written. Initially, she wondered why Lily had saved all these things. But very quickly she came to see that if she'd ever needed proof of her mother's love it was there, in the contents of that box. In Lily's eyes, nothing of Lucinda's was too small or insignificant to save; it was an archive, a mother's gallery of her child's accomplishments.

In the end, knowing she had no choice, she'd returned everything to the carton and stored it in the back of Lily's closet. Now and then she'd wondered if Lily didn't sometimes drag out the carton and peruse its contents, in the process being taken back in time to specific moments—depending upon which envelope she chose to open. That carton was now in the attic. Lucinda was as unable to throw it away as her mother had been, and every few years she sat down to go through the items in the box, feeling reconnected to her mother in a singular way—as if looking at her own childhood and adolescent efforts through Lily's eyes.

In time, Lucinda thought now, perhaps she'd feel that way about Katanya's crayon drawing. It was, without question, an encapsulated moment.

As she was about to get a vase, the telephone rang. It took her a moment to recognize the number on the Caller ID, then she grabbed the receiver. "Hi, Kat."

"Hi, Luce. I called because I feel really bad, as if I didn't say goodbye right."

"Honey, you were perfect."

"It doesn't feel as if I was. You gave me this special necklace but I forgot what you told me it was."

"It's my Phi Beta Kappa key."

"But what *is* it?"

"Phi Beta Kappa is a national honor society. The key is given to juniors or seniors who are in the top ten percent of their year."

"You were in the top ten percent?"

"I graduated *summa cum laude*."

"What's that?"

"It means with highest honors."

"Luce, you shouldn't've given me this. It's too important."

"That's exactly *why* I gave it to you, honey: because you're smart enough to get one, too. And when you do, then you can give mine back to me. Okay?"

There was silence for a moment, then Katanya said, "Are you having a headache?"

"No, I'm okay."

"I *miss* you!" Katanya said, sounding choked. "I'm on my way home to see my moms and gramma but I miss *you*. It makes me feel *terrible*, as if I'm cheatin' on them or something."

"You mustn't think that way, Kat. You're not cheating on anyone. Sometimes, our feelings get all mixed up. It's what's meant when people say they're conflicted: it's being torn between your feelings for different people. You'll be fine once you're home and you see your family."

"But I'm still gonna be missin' you!"

"You can phone any time, and send me e-mails. I'll be right here."

"Okay," Katanya said slowly, then: "Luce?"

"What?"

"You're gonna stay in the house again now and not go out anymore, aren't you?"

"I don't know," Lucinda lied.

"You're gonna," Katanya insisted. "And that makes me feel bad, too."

"I'll be fine, Kat. Just think how happy your mother and grandmother are going to be to see you, and how happy you'll be to see them."

"Yeah, I know."

"I'm *so* glad you called, Kat. Really. I was missing you, too."

"Luce, don't stay inside the house all by yourself. You can visit with Soupboy and Miz Crane. And you can always go see that nice lady at the diner and have home fries and coffee."

Lucinda laughed. "I will, Kat."

"You promise?"

"I promise."

"I really love you, Luce. I really, really do."

"I love you, too, Kat."

"Thanks for giving me your Fie Better Cap key. I'll take very good care of it. 'Bye, Luce."

"I know you will. 'Bye, honey."

The headache came that evening. Suddenly it made its presence known as she sat on the sofa, gazing at the TV screen. The familiar vise clamped around the base of her skull, gradually tightening, and the red-hot needle stabbed rhythmically into her temple. Her stomach clenched like a fist and she was sweating and trembling, in the throes of a simultaneous attack of hypoglycemia. Swearing under her breath, she fumbled for the remote and turned off the TV. Knowing the attack would only get worse if she didn't do something about it, she staggered to the kitchen and got a box of crackers from the cupboard. Her hands shaking, she managed to extract several wheat thins from the box and began chewing them, washing down the resulting mouthfuls of paste with intermittent swallows of bottled water.

Dizzy, shivering, deep in the combined grip of the migraine and the hypoglycemia, she took her medication, then gagged down another cracker with more water. Eyes closed, hands clutching the rim of the countertop, she stood, willing the food and the pill to stay down. After three or four minutes, hoping for the best, she made her way back to the living room and lay down on the sofa, reaching for the mohair throw. Curling into herself, involuntary tears trickling itchily down her cheek, she rubbed a fist over her face and focused on her breathing. It was what her Los Angeles neurologist had taught her to do years before, and most of the time it worked. When it didn't, she'd wind up with the heaves, vomiting until her throat was raw and her entire torso ached, as if from a beating. Occasionally she was so weakened in the aftermath that she couldn't leave the bathroom and wound up shrouding herself in towels, falling asleep on the bath mat. Upon awakening—once it was two whole days later—she was fairly crippled from hours on the cold tile floor, and moved like someone in her eighties for a week.

Her Connecticut neurologist had instructed her to make her mind blank—no easy feat—and she tried very hard to do that now, as she tucked her hands between her thighs, trying to get warm even while she continued to sweat. But instead of the imagined blank screen, she found herself thinking about a visit Gin had made some ten or twelve years earlier.

She had been on location in Manhattan and its environs for five weeks, and had come up to Connecticut to spend two days with Lucinda before flying back to L.A. to shoot the interiors. She arrived, typically, driving herself in a rental car, which she planned to return at Kennedy before she flew home. Nothing ostentatious, ever, about Gin. Like Lily, she traveled pretty much unnoticed, never going for glamour in public. "I love my fans; I'm grateful for my fans. But being accosted by the general public while I'm trying to buy tomatoes is more than I can handle. If you don't want to be noticed, most of the time you won't be." Also like Lily, she chose comfort over style, and wore jeans and T-shirts and sneakers in her off-camera time.

Gin had grown up to be a beautiful woman, with the same small body she'd had as a child. Her curves, when required, were still built into her wardrobe. "It's a gift," she'd declared in her twenties. "I'm never going to have to worry about my boobs falling, the way Lily worried." And like Lily, she'd decided by thirty that she'd walk away from the business at the first sign she was reaching the has-been stage. Also like Lily, she had no interest in keeping herself young-looking by means of plastic surgery. "I could give a rat's ass," she'd said on her thirtieth birthday when Lucinda had phoned her. "They don't like my wrinkles, screw 'em."

"You don't *have* any wrinkles," Lucinda had pointed out.

"They're on their way, kiddo. I've got no illusions that old age is some kind of bug I'm not going to catch."

Lily's example was the yardstick against which Gin always measured herself in terms of how she wanted to live. The movies gave her the money; Gin decided how she was going to use it.

On that visit, a dozen years earlier, she and Lucinda had sat outside on deck chairs by the pool late into the night, talking quietly. Thinking back, Lucinda remembered that it had, indeed, been twelve years before because Gin had talked about turning forty.

"It's going to be interesting to see if anything changes, work-wise," she'd said. "Forty's a mystical number to the boys. They expect you to be old overnight or check discreetly into some secret place to get yourself overhauled. Won't they be surprised to see the same old me?" She'd laughed, lighting an after-dinner cigarette.

"You still haven't met anyone?" Lucinda had asked.

"Kiddo, I'm never going to meet anyone. I don't *want* to meet anyone. I would've thought you'd have figured that out by now."

"Figured what out? I'm lost," Lucinda said.

Sheltered by the darkness, by the silence, Gin had said, "Would you like to know what was happening when Lily came charging into old Lloyd's inner sanctum?"

Suddenly, Lucinda had felt fearful, remembering all the zombie children who'd returned from Lloyd's office, and the bloodstain on the seat of Jimmy's overalls. "Only if you want to talk about it," she'd said cautiously, tensed to hear what her closest friend had endured.

"Well, let's see," Gin said, taking a hard drag on her cigarette. "He'd already raped me and wanted to have another go but just couldn't get in. So he had me on my hands and knees, with a pair of socks stuffed into my mouth, and he was—"

"God, *don't!*" Lucinda had cut her off. "I'll have nightmares for months if you tell me any more."

"*You'll* have nightmares," Gin had said mildly, a bitter hint of amusement in her voice. "I spent thousands, *thousands* on shrinks, trying to deal with my *own*. But you're right. You don't need that."

"It's not that I don't care, because I do; you know how much I do. It's just that I couldn't bear to have that picture of you in my head, Gin; to think about you getting hurt that way."

"You have no idea," Gin had said mildly. "He not only put me off men forever, he also destroyed any possibility that I might have kids. Lily had Eddie take me to the hospital. He was such a brick, that man. Carried me out to the car after they'd sewed me up and took me home so Estelle could look after me. Made up some story for my mother. She didn't care. All she cared about was my being able to keep working. The woman really liked the money I brought in." She paused and took another drag on her cigarette. "Next day I was back at school on the lot. Amazing, when I think about it. Kids have such resilience."

"You were remarkable," Lucinda said. "You still are."

"Lloyd was murdered, you know," Gin said without emotion. "They never did find whoever did it. Got his head bashed in with the proverbial blunt object; his fingers were all severed at the first joint. The *coup de grace* was his johnson got cut off and shoved down his throat. I always thought it was the perfect ending for that sick fuck. Probably one of his former victims got tired of *his* nightmares and decided to do kids everywhere a big favor. Whoever you are, wherever you are"—Gin raised her wineglass—"I salute you."

"I knew he'd been murdered. But how do you know all those gory details?"

"Paid good money for them," Gin answered, taking a last drag on her cigarette before crushing it out in the ashtray on the table between them. "A cop I knew sneaked me a copy of the coroner's report."

"Why would you want to *read* something like that, Gin?"

"I *needed* to read it! I needed to know he was well and truly dead and never coming back, never going to hurt any more kids. It was worth every penny of the fifteen hundred it cost me. I read it, then I made a little ceremony of tearing it into small pieces and setting fire to them."

"God, I'm sorry," Lucinda said inadequately. "I'd give anything if that hadn't happened to you."

"That makes two of us." Gin emitted a hoot of laughter that ended abruptly. "So anyway," she'd continued after a moment or two, "that's why I'm happy living by myself with two old dogs and a really good security system. What's your excuse?"

"You know what my excuse is—if anyone could call it that."

"Fear's a bitch, isn't it," Gin observed. "Shapes us in ways we could never imagine. But hell, Luce. It's not as if anyone would ever look at you and say, 'Whoa, that's a black woman, pretending to be white.'"

"It's not about how I look, Gin; it's about not being what I am, or even *knowing* what I am. I don't know how to *be* anymore."

"That is such bullshit, kiddo. It's a mental block, not something real."

"Gin," Lucinda chided softly, "it's as real to me as Lloyd still is to you every time you think back to that day. Something so monumental changes everything, forever. To quote Lily, 'Don't kid a kidder.' If anyone knows how I feel, you do."

"Yeah." Gin sighed. "I know. The sex symbol who has a body double for any skin scene, who can't stand to be touched off camera, and the lovely white woman who isn't actually white but doesn't know how to be black. What a goddamned pair of clowns!"

"It could be worse," Lucinda offered.

"Yeah! We could both be double amputees or paraplegics!"

There was a silence that lasted a beat or two and then they'd both laughed madly, reaching for each other's hands and holding on hard.

Chapter Sixteen

When she came to, she had no idea what day it was. It was definitely day; the light leaking in at the edges of the shutters was definitely bright—too bright to look at for more than a second or two. Her eyes hurt from just a glance at the glaring seepage.

Moving gingerly, she put on her sunglasses before opening the door to get the paper—there were two of them—from the porch. Two days lost; two days gone, thanks to a medicated coma-like state. The sunglasses back on the table by the door, she carried the blue-sheathed copies of the *Times* to the kitchen, performing a mental examination of her working parts as she went. Generalized stiffness from spending a couple of nights unmoving on the sofa, a residual tenderness in the midriff, cramped neck and shoulder muscles, and a taste in her mouth like chemical waste.

She got a pot of coffee started, stood for a few moments to look at Katanya's drawing on the fridge, then went creaking up the stairs to her bathroom.

Leaving the lights off, she gargled mouthwash, then vigorously brushed her teeth. After tossing her clothes through the door into a pile on the bedroom carpet, she ran a hand through her hair, deciding it needed to be trimmed. Any minute now, she'd have completed her evolution into a frowzy-headed skank who'd terrify small people like Soupboy and appall upscale yummy mums like Renee. Cruel, she thought. Renee had redeemed herself quite thoroughly.

She got the good scissors and a comb, leaving them prominently placed on the countertop so that she'd remember to give herself a haircut after her shower.

She was still shaky, but the long, very hot shower helped, as did feeling clean. After a bad session, she invariably felt filthy and wanted to burn her clothes; her nostrils pinching at the reek of her body.

She had to turn on the light in order to see her hair to cut it and tried to avoid actually seeing herself as she dragged the comb through her hair; distorted glimpses of her image caught her eye, but she turned her back, picked up the hand mirror and scissors, and went to work. It always took more time than she expected because she'd inherited (she presumed) her father's thick hair, and had to stop after each cut at the back, to comb it through again, retrieve the mirror and scissors and tidy up the edges. The top and sides took far less time. When she was done, she collected the trimmings to throw into the wastebasket, then blotted up any stray hairs with a handful of dampened tissues. A coating of dusting powder on her neck and shoulders, then she turned on the blow dryer.

Usually, she'd bend over and dry her hair from underneath but she was afraid to risk it. There was a good possibility that if she did bend, the headache would come roaring back. But the heat of the dryer was making her feel sick, so she gave up, got dressed and went downstairs to have several cups of coffee while she read the papers. Every couple of minutes, she went still, listening. But there was nothing to hear; the house was as empty as a tomb and the only sounds were those of the refrigerator and the gentle rumble of the air-conditioning unit outside. Deathly quiet. She looked over at the crayon drawing. Like any mother or grandmother, she was now the possessor of refrigerator art. It made her smile, then she wanted to weep. She'd forgotten how excruciating the pain of loss could be, and she missed Katanya terribly; missed the squeak of her sneakers, her sweet features and uncommon sense. In only a matter of days the child had so successfully penetrated Lucinda's defenses that she was now in a state that too closely approximated grief.

With nothing else to do, she went online. There was e-mail. Three messages. The first, from Kat, read:

> Dear Luce,
> You were right and I do feel better now that I'm home. My moms and gramma couldn't believe all the stuff you got me, and they loved the jewlry you let me take for them. I hope you're OK and don't have a headache. You promised you'd go see the lady at the diner, so you have to.
> Love, Kat. xoxo

The second, from Kat's grandmother read:

> Dear Lucinda,
> This is Jeneva, Katanya's gran. I wanted to thank you for being so good to our girl and for all the wonderful presents you got her. She

hasn't stopped talking about you since she got home. I hope you will come to visit us sometime. Loranne and I would truly love to meet you.
Sincerely, Jeneva Washington.

The third, with the subject PS, was from Kat and said:

Dear Luce:
I forgot to tell you that I wear your fi better cap key all the time. My gramma knew what it was right away when she saw it and she said she couldn't believe you'd give it to me. But she said it seems tipical of you. I'm not sure what she means by that but I don't think it's anything bad because my gramma thinks you're great. My moms does too.
Love, Kat. xoxo

Lucinda at once replied and then, feeling better, she shut down her Internet connection and went back to the kitchen to have a piece of toast with her last, now-cold cup of coffee.

It occurred to her several hours later, with the laundry done, the blue box and string-bound bundle of flattened cartons ready to go out later; with no work to do and none forthcoming, that she felt positively desperate. Katanya had, for a brief time, given her days dimension and purpose. With the child gone, Lucinda couldn't think of what to do with herself. She tried to read but gave up when she found herself rereading the same page over and over, with no sense of the book's content. She thought about going out to the pool but her eyes still hurt when she encountered random bands of light slicing the cool darkness of the house, so she knew she'd have to wait until after sundown to have a swim.

She paced through the downstairs rooms, stopping repeatedly to look at Katanya's drawing, and each time she did, she felt diminished somehow, shrunken. At this rate, she'd disappear and go floating off into the dust motes that hovered in those blinding slashes of light that found their way into the rooms through the slightest openings—in the verticals, or the mini-blinds, or the curtains. The only safe room in the house was her en suite bathroom, where she could, if she closed the door, find perfect darkness. The downside was that she became immediately claustrophobic and couldn't breathe with the bathroom door closed. So back downstairs she went, to continue prowling through the rooms, searching for something that wasn't there, and returning again, again, again, to the crayon drawing.

By the time evening came, she couldn't be bothered putting on shorts and a T-shirt; it was too much trouble to go out to the pool. She had no appetite but, fearing another hypoglycemic attack, she ate a piece of cheddar and several crackers, then flopped onto the sofa to watch the NBC news. Once the news ended, there wasn't a thing, on any channel, that captured her interest. She powered off the set, and sat looking around the living room, feeling trapped and bored and anxious. She considered e-mailing Kat but upon seeing that she hadn't received any response to her e-mails of that morning, she abandoned the idea. She didn't want to drown the child with her attention.

When she finally remembered her promise to go to the diner, it was too late. Only bars stayed open late; the restaurants closed early, especially on weeknights. And with its transformation from diner to restaurant, her diner closed early, like all the other restaurants. She certainly wasn't going to try any of the other diners on the Post Road, all of which remained open until midnight or later. Just the thought of going into one of those places gave her the shakes. But maybe tomorrow, she told herself, returning to the sofa to run through the channels again.

She was in time to catch an episode of *Law & Order* that she hadn't seen in a while, one of the early shows with Chris Noth. Something about him was so compelling; she'd never been able to assess the particulars. He had humor that, within the context of the character, flirted close to being sardonic without ever actually becoming bitter. He didn't seem to be the sort of man who took himself too seriously. But perhaps he was sufficiently talented to conceal his true self completely beneath the role. What did it matter? All it really meant was that the old episodes had an edge to them that captured her attention.

By 2:00 a.m. she was still watching—an old black-and-white on AMC—and fighting to keep her eyes open. Why? What did it matter if she fell asleep on the sofa, with the TV set on? It mattered, she thought, forcing herself to sit up, because she didn't want to wind up one of those old people whose only companion was a goddamned television set. With due deliberation, she shut everything off and went upstairs to bed.

The next afternoon, when she was positive she was about to lose her marbles, Gin's package arrived. The enclosed note read:

> "If you don't like this, I will eat my entire wardrobe, never mind my hat.
> Love you, Gin."

The cover was atrocious, a hodge-podge of embossing and foil and bad art. But trusting Gin's judgment, Lucinda sat down to read. When at last, reluctantly, she stopped to take a break, six hours had gone by and she was better than halfway through the book. Going to the kitchen in search of something to eat, she gazed at the drawing on the refrigerator, while the book's characters moved about in her head; people so fully realized that she knew them intimately. Distracted, she made a sandwich and sat at the table to eat it with a Diet Coke as she read on, hoping things wouldn't fall apart—as so often happened—in the second half of the book.

Five hours later, at one-thirty in the morning, she picked up the telephone.

"Why have I never heard of this woman before?" Lucinda asked.

"Beats hell out of me! Good, huh?"

"It's wonderful. The cover's an abomination but the book ... It's perfect for you, Gin. I think you're the only actress alive who could play this."

"Me, too. So will you do it?"

"Ah, God!" Lucinda was already starting to plummet from the high she'd attained, reading the book.

"Don't you dare wimp out on me now! It's not as if you have to leave the house to do it."

"No, I know. But it's been so long ... Gin, I don't know if I *could* do it."

"Oh, please. We both know you could do it with one arm tied behind your back. I need to know, kiddo. Because if you won't do it, I'll keep my money in the bank."

"Let me think about it."

"I let you think about it, you won't do it. You'll get so tangled up in your many, many reasons for being scared that you'll probably lock yourself in the basement and stay there 'til kingdom come. If I'm not scared to *play* it, why should you be scared to *write* it?"

She had a point, a big one. If Gin was willing to play someone horribly disfigured and take the biggest risk of her career—given she could even get the financing—didn't Lucinda owe it to her to bolster the effort with the best possible script? It didn't require leaving the house, as Gin pointed out, but it did require a commitment. And she'd forgotten how to make them.

"I can hear the little wheels turning. Don't think yourself out of this, Ella, please. I love this book; I love this character. I want you to take this incredibly *interior* book and turn it into an accessible script. There's not another living soul I'd trust to do this justice. Nobody could. You're the only writer I know who could crawl around inside this woman's head and capture the dark humor and the spirit of this. She's a goddamned heroine, who's off on a road trip, trying to find the courage to kill herself and instead finds a reason to live. You have *got* to do this for me. I want to go out with a big bang."

"What d'you mean 'go out'?"

"I'm sick of the biz, kiddo; sick of the bullshit, the ludicrous demands and expectations. Yeah, I'm still getting the offers, but I'm going to be fifty in a couple of months. I want out of here."

"Literally?"

"I don't know. Maybe. I like it back east; it's different. I'll freeze to death but that's why they sell coats and heating oil."

"You'd move here?" Lucinda was so shocked she could scarcely absorb what she was hearing.

"Sure. I've got this mental image of the two of us living close enough to see each other more than once every few years. You're the only person I really give a shit about. I'm sick and tired of going out for lunch, looking around, and everybody's auditioning. Not just the waiters. You expect that. But the goddamned customers. They're all busy looking past each other to see if there's somebody more important at the next table or coming through the door. Nobody *listens*. The only good stuff coming out of this city is either made for the cable networks or from the edgy, new independent guys who sell out the minute they come up with a winner. And everything they make after that is crap, remakes of classics that aren't broken and don't need fixing, salads made with head lettuce and plastic tomatoes."

Lucinda laughed. "You should write this adaptation yourself. You're getting very eloquent in your advancing years."

"Do it! I want to hear you say you will."

"You're giving me heart failure, Gin. What if I screw up and turn this divine book into yet another salad?"

"In your whole life, you've never said or done one thing that's been ordinary. Even becoming a goddamned shut-in, you had to turn yourself into a Web editor, whatever the hell that is. And don't explain it again! It gives me a headache. Say you will do it!" she commanded.

"God! Okay! I'll do it."

"I knew you would." Gin laughed happily. "I'll throw money at it right away, call her agent in the morning. As soon as we've got the go-ahead, I'll let you know. But don't let that hold you back from getting a jump-start on this."

"I want to read it again, at least once more, maybe twice. What kind of budget are you thinking of?"

"Small. Three or four million tops. I'll do it for scale with a cut of the gross, see if I can round up some of my pals to do the same. We're talking two leads, four or five supporting. What I love is how *contained* it is. You know?"

"Unh-hunh."

"Now you're turtling on me," Gin accused.

"No. I'm missing Kat. I love that girl. I can't stand the house now, without her here."

"So drive into the city and see her."

"Was that a joke?"

"No, it was not. Get into your fancy-ass vee-hick-ule and go see her. It's not as if you're an actual honest-to-god ago-raphobe. You got scared a long time ago and it's taken over your life. This kid sounds like a champ. You miss her, so go see her. It's that simple."

"This is too much for me to take in in one night, Gin. I'm going to go to bed now. It's late."

"Please don't tell me you're getting a migraine. The guilt'll kill me."

"No, I've just gone into sensory overload. I need to get some sleep."

"Kiddo, this is going to be great! You make your comeback and I make my swan song, all in one fell swoop."

"I'm not 'coming back,' Gin. It's just this one last time, and only because it's you."

"Love you to pieces. Go sleep. I'll call as soon as I know anything. And do yourself a favor: go see the kid. You're not going to be happy until you do."

She actually slept hard and awakened feeling purposeful. But by midday, the silence of the house was getting on her nerves, and she was beginning to feel shaky. She sat down and tried to reread the book but couldn't get past the first page, convinced she'd made the mistake of a lifetime in agreeing to take on this job. She hadn't written anything in over twenty years. What if her former ability was gone? Gin would lose her money. She hovered over the telephone, wanting to phone and tell Gin she wasn't up to the task. But she knew how much this meant to her friend, how badly Gin wanted to make a final statement before leaving a career that had, after more than thirty-five years, gone from being her greatest joy to a burden.

Lucinda couldn't do it. She couldn't, with a single phone call, deprive Gin of that dream. She was going to have to pull herself together and write the screenplay. But pulling herself together meant much more than merely directing her focus to the book; it meant doing the one thing that frightened her the most: leaving the illusory safety of the house and driving into Manhattan to see Katanya again. If she couldn't do that, her life, to all intents and purposes, was meaningless. She needed to borrow courage again from the child, and that had to be done in person.

Chapter Seventeen

It was stupid, completely stupid. But the car was dusty, with leaves caught in the trim, and bird droppings on the trunk and she just couldn't make such a momentous trip in a dirty car. So she got the hose and the brush attachment from the barn, donned her hat and sunglasses, and began to wash the car. It was something she usually did every two weeks in the summer, but hadn't done for nearly a month. Annoyed with herself for setting up unnecessary chores that would delay the inevitable, but unable to stop herself, she squirted detergent into the bucket of warm water, then started lathering the car as if it were an immense, improbable baby.

She was just hosing off the coating of soapy grime when, seemingly out of nowhere, Soupboy came chugging across the lawn. Arms spread as airplane wings, making loud *vrrrmm-vrrrmm* noises, he homed in on her like an unsteady little missile. She turned off the hose, then ducked down to catch him. Hot and solid and smelling of grass and milk, he let himself fall happily backward in her arms and laughed at the sky, saying, "Swin' me, Luce. Swin' me wound 'n' wound."

So she swung him around and his giddy laughter poured onto the slight breeze and went drifting off. Peripherally, she saw Renee coming toward them, smiling. And suddenly Lucinda realized that Katanya had brought more than just herself into Lucinda's life; she'd also brought this child and his mother. Lucinda's isolation had effectively been ended without her knowledge or consent, but most certainly with her relief. What she'd been powerless to change for so long had been changed for her because lifelong curiosity had prompted her to respond to a child's beckoning signal to come outside.

"Hi! Jason wanted to see you," Renee said, her smile holding as Lucinda came to the end of a final swing around. One more spin and she'd have been sick.

"Soupboy!" Lucinda said, unreasonably pleased. "You wanted to come visit me?"

"Ya!" he declared. "Soupboy see Luce." He grabbed a handful of her hair and held it like the strap on a subway train as he again let himself hang backward over her supporting arms.

"You got your hair cut," Renee said. "It looks good. I wish I had nice thick hair like yours."

Lucinda took a long look at the younger woman. She had even features and a good complexion, shoulder-length, side-parted glossy brown hair; a plain-faced woman who became pretty when she smiled to reveal her flawless teeth. She appeared to have abandoned her Long Island lockjaw for a relaxed manner of speaking that was considerably more agreeable to Lucinda's ears.

"You have good hair," Lucinda said. "I have more than I need."

Renee laughed and Soupboy lifted himself upright, bringing his face so close to hers that Lucinda's eyes went out of focus.

"Wanna go swimmin', Luce! Le's go swimmin'!"

"Jason, you can't go inviting yourself. You have to wait to be asked," his mother told him.

"Have you got your water wings?" Lucinda asked the husky little boy.

He shook his head.

"Tell you what," she said. "If you and your mother come tomorrow with your water wings, you can go swimming then. Okay?"

At impossibly close range, she could see his eyes shifting as he processed the information, gazing at her sunglasses as if he was, in fact, a superboy and could see through the mirrored lenses. At last, he said, " 'Kay. Kat come too?"

"Kat had to go home to the city, Jason," Renee said. "I told you that."

He shook his head, dismissing her, and repeated the question to Lucinda. "Kat come too?"

"Your mother is telling the truth, honey. Kat had to go home."

At this, his lower lip began to quiver and he dropped his head onto Lucinda's shoulder, murmuring, "Want Kat."

"Me, too," she whispered, knowing in that moment that she was going to make the drive into the city, even if she had to stop at a drugstore first, to buy a box of Depends in case her fear really did get the better of her. She kissed the top of his head, then smiled—amused at the idea of donning adult diapers—at Renee.

"We'll come and swim with Lucinda tomorrow," Renee said, reaching to lift Jason from Lucinda's arms. "Thank you. He's mad about you, but he loves the pool even more."

"The story of my life," Lucinda said wryly, stooping to retrieve the hose. "Always a pool maid, never a guard."

With a burst of surprised laughter, Renee said appreciatively, "That's *funny!*" and started back toward the house, with Jason waving vigorously over her shoulder.

It was after four by the time she'd showered and was ready to set off, but she got stuck at the door. Her hat and sunglasses sat at the ready beside her keys on the hall table, but she stood, rooted in place, unable to move. Behind her, she could hear the *tick-tick* of the wall clock in the living room—an audible reminder that she was losing precious time. It would take an hour, give or take, to drive into the city. She had the address written down on a piece of paper that was growing damp in her hand; she also had the phone number, having done an online search for Jeneva Washington. In the unlikely event she got lost, she could call for directions from the phone in the car. Of course, that would ruin the surprise, which was the last thing she wanted. There was something almost pathetic about the notion of having to phone someone she didn't know, who wasn't expecting her, for directions to her home. No, she knew Manhattan well enough to find her way. While all kinds of things might have changed, the layout of the streets would have remained the same.

Looking down at the floor, she wondered abstractedly if Jeneva was a combination of Jennifer and Eva. And what about Loranne? Could that be Lorraine and Anne combined? Katanya, for that matter, might have been a blending of Katharine and Tanya. People did strange things, when it came to naming their children.

"Oh, for heaven's sake!" she said angrily. "What on earth does it matter? When you get there, you can ask them. Quit stalling and just go!"

With that, she jammed on her hat, pushed her sunglasses into place, looped her bag over her shoulder and snatched up the keys. But now, in self-imposed darkness, she got stuck again, caught up in mental scenarios of how her arrival on One Hundred and Twenty-third Street might go. What if they weren't even home? She'd have made the trip for nothing. But no, she reasoned. Even if no one was home, she'd have gone farther afield than she had in twenty-seven years. That, in itself, was a major accomplishment. And she was going; she was. She just had to make another trip to the bathroom.

She removed her hat and sunglasses, put the keys and piece of paper down on the table and went to the downstairs bathroom. She actually did need to go. Nerves always sent her on multiple trips to the bathroom, as if her bladder was directly connected to the fear center in her brain.

Back in the hall, her hands already growing wet again, despite her having just washed them, she put on her hat and sunglasses, picked up the keys, pocketed the piece of paper. A deep breath and, not allowing herself further time to find reasons not to go, she opened the door, pulled it shut, made sure it was locked, then went across the porch, down the steps and over to the car—clean and gleaming in the late afternoon sunlight.

She was panting like a long-distance runner by the time she'd fastened her seat belt and was reversing out of the driveway. Her leg was jittering, making her foot unsteady on the accelerator, but she kept her speed steady, aiming for the Post Road and the entrance ramp to I-95.

As she waited at the stoplight opposite the on-ramp, she saw that the traffic was bumper to bumper on the northbound side. Rush hour. But on the New York-bound side cars and trucks were moving steadily, if not at great speed. The light changed and she inhaled deeply, then accelerated through the intersection and put on her turn indicator as she looked for a gap in the oncoming traffic.

Mercifully, she loved driving; always had. And joining the flow of cars actually had a calming effect as she navigated the Bentley into the middle lane and stayed there, reaching to adjust the volume on the radio which was tuned to an all-jazz station on Long Island.

The traffic was heavier than she remembered, but what hadn't changed was the way cars with New York state plates, driven by very young men, shot across lanes, from the outside to the inside, passed slower cars in the center lane with mere inches to spare, then, at speeds twenty to thirty miles above the limit, shot back into the passing lane only to slam on their brakes to avoid rear-ending yet another vehicle that was going too slow to suit them. She wondered what it was about young men that led them to behave with such arrogant stupidity. One more thing that hadn't changed was the fact of I-95's being one of the most dangerous highways in the country. It was ill-designed for the volume of traffic it carried from Maine to Florida and she was forever hearing on the local radio stations about multi-car collisions and fatalities near this or that exit. No doubt the majority of those crashes were caused by young men who believed they were immortal and could therefore drive as if they were taking part in the Indianapolis 500, recklessly charging from one lane to another—never signaling—to get ahead of the pack.

From long-standing habit, Lucinda checked the rearview mirror every few minutes, and as she headed toward the Hutchinson Parkway exit, she had to ease back on her speed several times in order not to get hit by yet another small car cutting in front of her. Lily had refused to drive on this highway—and that had been long before it had become so harrowing an experience as it was now. Not that Lucinda was especially bothered. She was a good driver, confident and aware, with strong defensive skills. Gin, too, drove well. But poor Lily could hardly stand even to be a passenger back when Lucinda had had to take her anywhere that involved getting on the highway.

She was aware of glances from other drivers, their puzzled expressions as they wondered who she might be. Was she somebody famous, this woman in sunglasses at the wheel of one of the few (if not the only) Bentleys they'd ever seen— this stately mobile black dowager of the roadways, owned by the peerage, wealthy sheiks, and those few dot-com overnight millionaires who didn't think a Lamborghini was the ultimate driving machine. She faced straight ahead, concentrating on the traffic, on the eighteen-wheelers that pulled up and stayed on her bumper until there was an opening in the inside lane that would allow them to pass her. What had happened to the truck drivers who used to be called The Knights of the Highway, those mannerly men who were always quick to help a driver in trouble and who obeyed the rules of the road? Gone like the dodo, she thought. Replaced by young men dry-swallowing uppers to keep them awake for their cross-country hauls, in such a hurry that they often ventured into the passing lane, risking massive fines. All the men on the road, it seemed, were in a mad rush to get somewhere, and all the women were holding their own, refusing to be intimidated.

She had a fifty-dollar bill at the ready but, to her surprise, there was no longer a toll and the traffic eased somewhat once she crossed the New York state line. It was, though, heavy on the Hutchinson. She was making good time, she saw, with a glance at the clock. Then, taking the exit for the Bruckner, her nervousness returned. Her hands grew moist on the wheel, and she had to keep swallowing. Still, it was too late now. She was more than halfway there. And her reward, if she was lucky in her timing, would be the sight of Katanya, once she got to One Hundred and Twenty-third Street. She hoped she wouldn't have to drive up and down, street after street, looking for somewhere to park. Why was she anticipating problems before they arose? When had she developed this particular bad habit? she wondered. Good grief! You've got to stop this nonsense! she told herself. If worse came to worst, there were bound to be parking lots or garages somewhere in the area.

Recalling her conversation with Gin a few nights earlier, she couldn't help wondering if Gin had really meant it when she said she was considering moving east. It would be such a joy to have her nearby, to be able to see her regularly. Of all the friends Lucinda had once had, only Gin had hung in, refusing to give up on her. It was, Lucinda believed, due to their shared history—those ten years in L.A. before Lily had declared, "That's it! We're getting out of here!"—and a three-man team from the moving company had come to pack up their possessions. For almost seven of those years, Gin had, when not away on a location shoot, lived with them. And during that period, she and Lucinda had been prodigiously creative, and probably happier than either of them had been since—with the brief exception of Lucinda's three years at Yale and her short-lived romance with Cort.

In 1967, when Gin turned twenty-one, having just signed to play the lead in a new film for a staggering (to her) three quarters of a million dollars, she had taken the two most important steps of her life. The first was a lump-sum payment of one hundred thousand dollars made to her mother via her lawyer with the proviso that her mother sign off on any future claims against Gin's income; the second was her purchase of the Spanish Colonial house in Whitley Heights.

Lucinda smiled, recalling Gin's excitement when she'd arrived in the red Mustang she'd bought the previous year to drive Lucinda to see the new house. (She still owned that Mustang, and she'd said more than once that every time she stopped to buy gas someone offered to buy it on the spot for exorbitant sums of money. "And I'd *walk* home. Sure. I don't think so. I plan to be buried in that car.")

"It's so great, Ella," she'd told Lucinda as they flew along the Hollywood Freeway that day years before. "It's got that classic look: white stucco, with red clay roof tiles. There's two big palm trees out front, and great gardens, front and back; it even has a pool. It's kind of on the empty side right now and it needs some work, but it's *mine*. And I'm getting a puppy, too. I always wanted a dog but *she*'d never let me have one. I've got my eye on a cocker spaniel who's going to give birth any minute. Hell, I might even buy two!"

It was, indeed, a lovely house, with a massive, arched, multipaned window at one end of the fifteen-by-twenty-foot cathedral-ceilinged living room that was a separate wing forming the bottom of an el. The rest of the two-story house ran along the upright of the el. The only furniture back then had consisted of two folding chairs and a bridge table in the kitchen, and a mattress centered on the floor of the master bedroom. Over the next few years, Gin slowly acquired random pieces of furniture: a bed frame, a dresser and a night table; a pair of armchairs and a side table; a madly ornate fifties' screaming red Formica and chrome kitchen set she found at the Goodwill, the best security system available, and a second cocker spaniel puppy.

Now, seeing the sign up ahead for the One Hundred and Twenty-fifth Street exit, Lucinda got into the right-hand lane.

She couldn't imagine Gin giving up that house, even though she, too, had been getting calls from Realtors for years. The Whitley Heights house was worth at least a million and a half dollars, perhaps more. Half that amount would buy something very nice in Connecticut—if she was serious about leaving the city of her birth, the only place she'd ever lived.

As if her visit had been destined, there was a parking spot directly in front of the building. Lucinda pulled in, then sat with the motor running, looking at the six-floor walk-up tenement. A middle-aged woman was positioned at the first-floor window to the right of the stoop, arms resting on a pillow as she studied the Bentley with interest, and Lucinda wondered if this was the fierce Mrs. Garcia of whom Katanya had spoken.

Facing ahead again, Lucinda realized she hadn't brought a gift—not so much as a bunch of flowers. She hadn't even thought of it—something that had once been automatic. Following Lily's lifetime example of never arriving at anyone's house empty-handed, Lucinda had always stopped to buy flowers, or a bottle of wine, or a scented candle: something to present to the host or hostess at the door. Yet here she sat with not a thing in hand to ease her entry. It felt like a terrible oversight and there wasn't a corner store nearby where she might go to purchase something.

This was starting to feel wrong. Bad enough to show up uninvited, but to show up with no offering of any sort ... She could feel the woman in the window watching her intently. This was awful! For a few seconds she was tempted to pull out and head back to the highway. But she couldn't. She'd made the trip; she was outside the building where Katanya lived. She couldn't just give up and drive away now, when she was so close.

Her shakes returning, she turned off the motor and pulled the key from the ignition. Getting out of the car, she looked again at the building. The woman was gone from the window. Lucinda locked the car and walked around it to the sidewalk. Throbbing, bass-heavy music poured from one of the nearby open windows, loud even at a distance. A variety of cooking smells hung in the hot, heavy air: something garlicky battled the stinky-sweatsock reek of overcooked broccoli. On the opposite side of the street, several boys loitering on the stoop were watching her. They'd probably vandalize or steal the car the moment she was out of sight. She didn't care. Cars were replaceable.

"You're Lucinda, right?" The woman from the window was standing on the sidewalk not two feet away.

"Yes. Are you Mrs. Garcia?"

Breaking into a wide smile, the woman said, "Yeah, I'm Gloria. Katty told you 'bout me?"

"She certainly did." Lucinda offered her hand. "It's good to meet you."

Somewhat bemused by the gesture, Mrs. Garcia hesitated for a moment before taking hold of Lucinda's hand in both of hers and beaming up at her. "Don' worry 'bout your car," she said, releasing Lucinda's hand to shout something in Spanish to the boys across the street. Two of them came at a run, their feet seeming huge in unlaced top-of-the-line Nike sneakers.

"This my son Geraldo, nephew Hernan," she introduced the teenage boys. "Is *Lucinda*!" she announced momentously.

"Yo!" exclaimed Geraldo with a grin that produced dimples in his cheeks and instantly shifted him from potential thug to neighborhood romeo. "You famous in the 'hood, mama." He threw out a large hand and pumped hers enthusiastically. He emitted a low whistle as he looked at the car. "Man, that be some *beast*," he said admiringly. "What it is?"

"It's a Bentley."

"Never hearda that. 'S *coooool*. Me 'n' Hernan, we look after her. Don' worry 'bout it. Man"—he bumped his cousin's shoulder—"say hey!"

Smaller, shyer, Hernan soberly gave Lucinda's hand a quick, solid shake. " 'S a Mulsanne," he said softly. "Eighty-seven?"

"That's right," Lucinda said. "You know your cars."

"Yeah. 'S a beauty. Never actually seen one up close."

"You go on up 'n' see Katty," Mrs. Garcia said. "Nothing gone happen to your car. My boys look out for it."

Hoping she wasn't about to commit a faux pas, Lucinda pulled out the fifty dollar bill she'd had at the ready to pay for tolls and offered it to the boys, saying, "It would make me happy to buy you and Mrs. Garcia dinner"—she looked at the woman to see that she approved—"if you don't feel like cooking in this heat."

"*Muchos gracias*," she said, indicating to Geraldo that he should accept the money. "Katty said you was kind."

"Yeah, thanks," said Geraldo bashfully, taking the bill.

"I could maybe see under the hood later?" Hernan asked.

"Absolutely," Lucinda said.

"He's studyin' to be a mechanic," Geraldo said. "He be fixin' all the cars 'n' bikes 'round here. Nothin' Hernan don't be knowin' 'bout cars."

"That's wonderful. If you like, next time I come to visit, I'll take you for a ride."

"No kiddin'?" said Geraldo.

"No kidding," she confirmed.

Geraldo high-fived his cousin who regarded her with an expression of grateful amazement that she found touching.

"That's a promise," she said, and patted him on the arm before starting up the stairs.

She'd driven into the city; her car was safe and so was she; and up four flights was Katanya. Everything was going to be just fine.

Chapter Eighteen

The building was clean and well lit, with four apartments per floor. The stairwell grew hotter as Lucinda climbed higher and here, too, cooking smells were caught in the air so that she passed through a layer of air laden with the potent aroma of curry on the second floor. On the next landing the smell was of something badly burnt and she covered her nose as she went quickly up the next flight of stairs where, surprisingly, someone had recently sprayed air freshener. It helped tamp down a smell that belonged to no food category she could recognize.

After giving herself a few moments to catch her breath, she knocked at the door, then quickly dried her hands on a tissue.

The woman who came to the door was about five foot five, slender and stunningly beautiful, with the same heart-shaped face, long neck and huge, thickly lashed eyes as Katanya. She wore a sleeveless, scoop-necked short yellow dress that emphasized her rich cocoa skin; she had clear red lipstick on the most perfectly formed mouth Lucinda had ever seen, and a hint of color on her slanting cheekbones. Her hair was done in dozens of small braids gathered together at the back of her neck with a bright yellow ribbon. She looked at Lucinda blankly for a moment, then clapped a hand to her mouth, staring, before exclaiming, "Oh my God! You're Lucinda!"

"Yes."

"Oh my God!" she repeated. With a hand on Lucinda's wrist she pulled her inside, saying, "I'm Loranne, Kat's mama. Come in, come *in*. This is wonderful! Kat's going to be so happy. *I'm* so happy. I've been wanting to meet you so I could thank you for everything you've done for my baby. But you're so pretty and much younger than I thought you'd be ... I'm babbling. Sorry. It's just that I'm just so excited. Please, come meet my mother, Lucinda, then I'll go get Kat."

Smiling away, her expression one that was close to wonderment, she led Lucinda by the hand through the living room to the kitchen doorway where she stopped to announce, "Mama, it's *Lucinda*!" and the woman at the stove looked over as if thunderstruck.

An older, somewhat shorter and more rounded version of her daughter, Jeneva's straightened hair was pulled back into an old-fashioned bun that suited her well, allowing a full view of her handsome face: a high, rounded forehead with the large eyes she'd passed on to her daughter and granddaughter, a generous mouth and strong jaw. She was wearing a dress identical to her daughter's, but in a burnt orange color.

"Oh my!" she said softly, drying her hands on a tea towel. She approached and reached for Lucinda's hand as Loranne hurried off, saying, "Be right back."

"Lucinda, what a joy to meet you. And you're just as lovely as Kat said you were."

Never knowing how to respond to compliments, Lucinda could do no more than smile. These were warm, friendly people and yet she felt completely out of her depth. Those social skills she'd once possessed had apparently atrophied to such an extent that they were all but useless. She wished she could just sit in a corner and watch them go about their lives, getting to know them through their actions, their daily habits. Her jaw actually felt rusty, as if it needed to be oiled. She thought of the Tin Man and had to smile again, thinking it might be a good idea if she started carrying a small oil can around with her.

"Come sit down," Jeneva said, removing her apron and directing Lucinda into the living room where, thanks to a good-sized unit in the window, the air was comfortably cool.

Lucinda stood near the sofa as Jeneva asked, "Could I get you something to drink, Lucinda? Some iced tea, or a soda?"

"No, no. I'm fine, thank you very much."

"I'll just turn the heat down under those pots and be right back. Please, sit down."

Just then, Katanya came racing in and leaped at Lucinda, so that she had to brace herself to catch the girl who wound her arms and legs around her tightly, crying, "*Luce! You came!*"

Eyes closed, Lucinda held her, breathing in her scent and relishing the feel of her. "I missed you so much, honey," she whispered. "I just had to come see you."

"I missed you, too," Katanya whispered back. "I'm *soooo* happy to see you, Luce."

"Me, too," Lucinda said, opening her eyes finally to see the girl's mother and grandmother, standing side by side in their matching colorful dresses, gazing on with patent approval.

"She's talked about you nonstop since the minute she got home," Loranne said.

"Kat, let the woman sit down now," Jeneva told the child. "I'll get us all some lemonade. I just made it fresh."

"I don't *want* to let go," Kat said, leaning away to gaze at Lucinda. "You *did* it, Luce!" she said, sounding like a proud parent. "You came to see me. I kept my fingers crossed that you would. And here you are!"

"Here I am, indeed."

"Did you drive by yourself, or did you have that nice man bring you in the limo?"

"I drove. Mrs. Garcia's son and nephew are looking after the car," Lucinda explained as she lowered the girl to the floor.

"Hernan's learnin' how to be a mechanic. He's probably gone spaz over the Muscleman," Katanya said, flopping onto the sofa and patting the seat beside her. "Sit with me, Luce."

Lucinda put her bag on the floor and sat down next to the girl who at once scooted closer and looped her arm through Lucinda's, saying, "You got your hair cut."

"I trimmed a couple of inches," Lucinda said. "I was starting to look like someone who'd frighten small children."

"Get outta here!" Katanya scoffed. "You'd never frighten anybody! Even old Jase liked you."

"Okay, then. I was starting to frighten myself."

"That's so silly, Luce. I keep *tellin'* you: You're really, really pretty."

"Thank you, Kat. But it's different from the inside, looking out."

"That's what my gramma always says!"

"Well, she's right."

Loranne perched on the edge of one of the two armchairs, saying, "You're going to suffocate the woman, you keep holding on to her that way, baby."

"No, I won't. Will I, Luce?"

"It's okay," Lucinda told both mother and child. "You don't look old enough to be Kat's mother," she said truthfully. Loranne looked no more than eighteen.

"I'm plenty old enough," she said, with a smile that showed her very white teeth. "And I'm satisfied with my girl. I figured I might not get it right the next time, so I quit while I was ahead."

"Kat says you're close to getting your degree."

"Is there anything you *didn't* tell her?" Loranne asked her daughter. To Lucinda she said, "Yeah, I'm just about there. Four more credits for this last course and I'm done. It's taken forever, but I'm hoping it'll be worth it. I can't wait to have some evenings to myself again, instead of having ten minutes to eat when I get home, before heading off to school."

"It's a great accomplishment," Lucinda said. "You should feel very good about it."

"I'll feel good about it once I've got that paper in my hand and the decent job that degree's supposed to get me."

"I think there's always a need for CPAs," Lucinda said encouragingly.

"I sure hope so," Loranne said. "Eventually, I wouldn't mind having my own office. But I need something to put on a résumé first. You know?"

"Of course," Lucinda said, knowing that no matter what you did or where you tried to do it, you had to have something down on paper that said what you'd done before. All the L.A. waiters who wanted to be actors called it the Big Catch: Until someone gave you work, you couldn't *get* any work. Which was why the majority of résumés in circulation were complete fabrications. The part you played in the Thanksgiving production in fourth grade got translated into the lead role in *The New Pilgrims*, or some other bogus show.

Jeneva returned carrying a tray with four glasses and a clear glass jug of lemonade that had slices of lemon and sprigs of fresh mint floating in it. "You'll stay for dinner," she told Lucinda—a statement rather than an invitation—as she poured the lemonade. "C'mon, Kat, fetch a glass for Lucinda."

Katanya jumped up at once to do as she'd been told.

Lucinda took advantage of the brief lull to absorb the details of the good-sized room. Glass sparkled, freshly polished wood gleamed; the air was faintly redolent of cinnamon and lemon oil. Teak furniture from the fifties, similar to the pieces her aunt Beattie had once given to Lily; a bright Rya rug in brilliant primary colors, family photographs grouped on the wall over an upright piano, off-white sheer curtains on the windows, the old hardwood floors shiny from regular buffing. Against the wall between the windows was a sturdy, wide shelf unit, packed full of books, and a stereo system positioned at chest height with racks of CDs and cassettes surrounding it. In the kitchen straight ahead and to the left was a yellow Formica and chrome kitchen set that Gin would have loved, being the same vintage as her set but minus the excess ornamentation. To the right, four doors opened off the hallway. Three had to be the bedrooms Kat had spoken of, the fourth was the bathroom. There wasn't a speck of dust anywhere. Even the screen of the TV set angled into the corner formed by the kitchen wall was immaculate. It was one of the cleanest, tidiest homes Lucinda had ever seen.

"I like your apartment," she told Jeneva. "It's very nice."

"Thank you." Jeneva settled in the armchair next to the one where her daughter still perched. "My mama and daddy moved in here when they came up from South Carolina in 1922. After my Jimmy died in Vietnam, I came home with Loranne, and I've been here ever since. Now, they'd have to pry me out with a crowbar." She laughed softly, and Lucinda smiled. "And you're Lily Hunter's daughter. She was a wonderful actress."

"Wonderful," Lucinda echoed, apprehensive about where this might go.

"We watched *Street Crime* two nights ago. And last night we watched *December Blue*," Katanya said. "Your moms was gorgeous, Luce. And your friend Gin's gorgeous *and* cool."

"I'll tell her you said so," Lucinda said.

"Kat was telling us you wrote that movie when you were just a child," Jeneva said.

"I was thirteen. Gin and I worked on it together, actually. By the time it went into production I was fourteen and Gin was almost eighteen. When I think about it now, I realize we were just babies." She felt awkward, as she always did, talking about another life in another era; fearful, too, of having people she initially liked turn rabidly curious and reveal that their interest had never been in her but in her relationship to famous people.

"*Talented* babies," Jeneva said thoughtfully. "I remember seeing that movie when it first came out. I was shocked and fascinated by Arla. I'd never seen anything like it. Oh, I saw *The Bad Seed*, and that child was quite something. But it's very dated now. I saw it again not so very long ago on AMC and thought the actors were very good, but the movie is very fifties. You know?"

"I do," Lucinda agreed, able to relax a little at learning that Jeneva liked movies. "I so admired Eileen Heckart's performance as the drunken mother of the boy Patty McCormack killed. She was touching and completely believable. She should've had an Academy Award for that performance. Dorothy Malone wasn't even playing in the same ball-park."

"No, I agree. I didn't care that much for *Written on the Wind*."

"You're a film buff!" Lucinda said, delighted.

"Yes, ma'am. Always have been."

"Me, too," Lucinda confessed in a rush, knowing now that she was safe, that these women had no hidden agenda. "You'd think that growing up on the inside of the business I'd have been immune to the magic—having seen all the wheels turning, all the tricks of the trade—but that made it even more intriguing. It was like a gigantic puzzle that started with a script and ended up involving dozens of people, each with a specific task. For six or eight weeks or a couple of months, they worked—sometimes together, sometimes completely apart—doing their different jobs, and then, when the editor was done, the answer print was okayed, and the soundtrack was finished, you had a ninety- or hundred-minute story—from beginning to end, everything integrated. *If* you were either lucky, *or* good, *or* both. The main thing was that every single component had to mesh. If just one thing was even a little out of whack, you had a bomb."

"I *lived* at the movies as a child," Jeneva confided. "I'd go see *anything*; it didn't matter if it was a western, or a musical, or a horror story. I'd sit through a triple-feature, happy as can be. When it was over and I was outside in the street, on my way home, I'd still be back there, playing out the parts in my head; living in whatever I'd just seen. It'd be hours before I came back to myself. And I was always disappointed that it was over."

"Because," Lucinda rushed to say, "it was so much nicer and better in the movie!"

"*Yes!*" Jeneva was exultant. "You are the *only* person I have ever met who understands that."

"Outside of some of the people I grew up with, so are you," Lucinda told her.

"You and I are going to have to go see some movies, Lucy!"

"I would love that," Lucinda said, "just love it."

"We're going to be great friends," Jeneva declared. "I had a feeling in my bones, when Kat started telling me about you. I just knew you were special."

"Oh, no," Lucinda said softly. "*Kat* is special. That's why I had to come to see her, to see all of you. She's my courage."

"She's our courage, too," Loranne said quietly.

Katanya squirmed, saying, "I hate it when you start talkin' about me that way."

"Then we'll stop," Lucinda said. "We won't say another word about you."

"Matter of fact," Jeneva joined in, "we might just pretend you're not here at all."

"You don't have to do that," Katanya said. "Cuz I *am* here. Just don't talk about me as if I'm not."

"You're quite right," Lucinda said. "It drove me nuts when I was a kid and people did that. Sorry, Kat."

"It's okay," the girl said, threading her fingers through Lucinda's. "Did you get any answers yet?"

"Answers?"

"To the letters."

Lucinda had completely forgotten them. "No," she said. "I think it's too soon to expect any replies."

"Did you go check your box at the post office?"

"No, I didn't."

"You should," Katanya said seriously.

"I will. To be honest, I'd forgotten all about it."

"Well, you can't *do* that. From now on, you'll have to check every day."

"I don't know about that—"

Kat cut her off, asking, "D'you want something important about your family just sitting there for days and days? You *have* to *check*, Luce."

"Okay, I will."

"You promise?"

"Kat, stop badgering Lucy!" her grandmother said.

"No, she's right," Lucinda said. "I promise," she told Katanya, thinking she could go very early in the morning when no one was around, before the service window opened. Not that she expected to find anything. But it might be a good exercise, something to help her get used to leaving the house regularly. "Starting tomorrow," she said, "I will go to the post office every day."

"Good!" Katanya said, satisfied. "I'll betcha anything you're gonna get answers, and find your people."

"I might not, Kat. It's been a very long time. It's possible there's no one left."

"Oh!" Katanya was deflated. "I hadn't thought of that."

"What's really important," Lucinda said, "is that you had the idea, and we tried. It was very clever of you to think of it, when none of the professionals I hired ever did."

"You're just trying to make me feel better."

"No, it's the truth. And guess who came to see me today."

"Soupboy!"

"That's right. He and his mother are coming over to swim."

"He liked you," Katanya said soberly.

"He loved *you*," Lucinda said. "He was heartbroken that you weren't there."

"Yeah?"

"I think you should all come for a weekend very soon," Lucinda said, looking from Katanya, to her mother, to her grandmother. "We could even," she offered Jeneva, "take in a movie or two."

As she extended the invitation, she was already thinking about getting the rooms ready, picturing the house alive in a way it had never been.

Chapter Nineteen

Katanya hadn't misrepresented. Her grandmother's cooking was exceptional. There was fried chicken with a crisp peppery batter, creamy potatoes mashed with shredded onions and cheddar, green beans sprinkled with parmesan and olive oil, and thinly sliced carrots with ginger and dill: combinations of flavors Lucinda had never imagined might go together. But they blended perfectly.

"No wonder you missed your grandmother's cooking!" Lucinda said to Katanya, then, turning: "This is the best meal I've ever had, Jeneva."

"Have more," the woman urged. "There's plenty."

"I don't think I could manage one more bite."

"That's the most I've ever seen Luce eat, Gramma," Katanya said supportively.

"You're too thin," Jeneva said. "It's not healthy."

"No," Lucinda agreed. "It probably isn't. When we lived in L.A. starvation was a way of life for most of the women we knew, and some of the men, too. It always fascinated me. Lily never had a problem with her weight. Neither did Gin.

But almost everyone there was—is—obsessed with camera weight. To look good onscreen, you've got to look under-nourished in real life. My mother was tiny. Gin is, too. But she's been working out like mad for the past eight or ten years. She turned one of the bedrooms of her house into a little gym. She lifts weights, runs on a treadmill, rows on a machine. She hates it, but she's very disciplined. I've always admired that about her. I hate exercise, aside from swim-ming. But I take after Lily and don't gain weight, even when I eat properly—which, I admit, hasn't been for a very long time. It's too much trouble, cooking for one."

"Have to say I'm not fond of exercise, either. But I walk a good deal," Jeneva said. "And this girl"—she indicated Lo-ranne—"never walks when she can run. She won't wait for an elevator. She'll run up ten flights of stairs without a sec-ond thought."

"I've always got to *be* somewhere," Loranne explained. "I don't have *time* to stand around, waiting for elevators. Any-way, I hate being crowded in with a bunch of strangers, everybody avoiding everybody else's eyes. I'd rather take the stairs. I can make good time and I'm not shoved up against ten other people, all of us breathing in the same air. *That's* not healthy."

"I've never liked elevators, either." Lucinda smiled over at Katanya's mother, perpetually awed by the young woman's unselfconscious beauty. "But I tend to be claustro-phobic. I don't like crowds in general."

"Me, neither," Loranne said. "Church is about the most I can handle. And even then, when we're all leaving at the same time, and there's a crowd going out the doors, I start feeling kind of panicky. All those bodies and the smell of dozens of different perfumes and aftershaves has me feeling sick until I can get outside into the air where I can breathe again."

"I never knew that," Katanya said to her mother. "Why do we go, if you feel that way?"

"We go because we're showing our faith, Kat. Some things are bigger than we are."

"Our faith in what?"

"Oh boy!" Loranne rolled her eyes. "In a power greater than ourselves, Katanya. Whatever you believe in. I refuse to have another discussion with you about who or what God is. This girl," she told Lucinda, "could worry the wings off a gnat."

Lucinda laughed.

"Don't go making faces at me," Loranne told her daughter. "You know it's the truth."

"I can't help it if I need to know what things mean," Katanya defended herself.

"I think we've got a future lawyer on our hands," Jeneva said with amusement.

"You *always* say that, Gramma. I don't know that I want to be a lawyer. Maybe I'll be a teacher or a doctor or a CPA like moms. Or maybe I'll become a singer and star in a Broadway show. I haven't *decided* what I'm going to be."

"Whatever you decide to do," Lucinda said, "you'll be very good at it."

"Yes, I will," Katanya said. "I will be very *very* good."

"Will you have some coffee with dessert, Lucinda?" Jeneva asked.

"Yes, please. I don't know that I could manage dessert, though."

"It's just fruit. You'll manage."

Loranne got up to help clear the table. Lucinda moved to help, too, but Jeneva said, "There's not enough room in this kitchen for three grown women moving around. You just sit, Lucy."

Every time the woman called her that, Lucinda felt a little sizzle of warmth. There was something of inestimable value in meeting a person who felt sufficiently secure about herself to use a diminutive of a person's name as a sign of automatic acceptance. It had happened only a few times in Lucinda's life and she'd had a powerfully positive reaction each time, because it indicated an immediately established level of trust—which was certainly the case here.

"May I ask you something?" Lucinda said.

"Of course," Jeneva answered over her shoulder, stacking the dishes next to the sink.

"It's about your names. They're so unusual."

"We've each been named for folks who've gone before," Loranne said. "Mama was named for her two grans, Jessamine and Neva. I was named for *my* two grans, Love and Angeline—"

"And *I* was named for my great aunt Kara and mama's great aunt Tamar," Katanya interrupted. "But moms and gramma couldn't make them fit, so they went with Katanya."

"We couldn't see calling the child Katamar or Karata," Jeneva said with a laugh. "No matter which way we turned it, it came out sounding terrible."

"Katamar." Katanya made a face. "I'd've died of embarrassment."

"Oh, no doubt," Loranne said coolly. "You'd never have been able to live it down."

"No, I *wouldn't've*. I'd've had to change it to something *good*. Katanya's a good name. *Karata*. Yuck. Have you got a middle name, Luce?"

"As a matter of fact, I do. Lily named me after herself. She said it was so the two of us would always know that I really was her child, even though the world was told I was an orphan she'd adopted. So I am Lucinda Lily Hunter. But I've never used my middle name."

"Why not?" Katanya promptly asked.

"Because Lily was my mother. It didn't feel right."

"Oh! Yeah, I guess I'd feel funny if I was Loranne." The girl mugged at her mother.

"What brought your parents to New York?" Lucinda asked Jeneva who turned on the coffee maker and returned to the table.

"My daddy was a musician, played cornet, trumpet, trombone—any brass instrument he laid his hands on. He could make the sweetest sounds you ever heard. My mama sang and played piano. They were part of a big migration of black musicians to the north in the twenties. They worked in the clubs around here, and there were a *lot* of them back then. Daddy played with Fletcher Henderson for a time, and he was in Ellington's jazz orchestra at the Cotton Club. My mama was a fine blues singer and she played the smaller clubs. But after I was born—she was getting on in years by then, forty-four when she had me—she stayed home and gave piano lessons. Which is, of course, how I learned.

"They were doing very well, but Daddy got caught up in the stock market fever in 'twenty-seven and 'twenty-eight and lost all their savings in The Crash. He went to pieces after, just couldn't pull himself together for the longest time. It was mama's piano lessons that kept them going until one day in 'forty-eight, I think it was, Daddy got a call from an old musician buddy to fill in on a recording gig for a trumpet player who was sick. He polished up his instruments— all of them—and went off that afternoon to do the session.

A few days later, he got a call to fill in on a club date, and from then on he never stopped working for more than a week or two—playing clubs and recording sessions—until he died in 'seventy-four of a heart attack. Overnight Mama lost all her energy and took to sitting in a chair by the window, as if she was waiting to see him come walking up the street with his horn case tucked under his arm. She lasted seven months without him. I got up one morning in April to get ready for work and she'd just gone to sleep forever in that chair. She looked very peaceful when I found her. I think she didn't know how to live without my daddy. She'd been with him since she was fifteen years old. Once he was gone, I think she felt that her life was over, too. She was only marking time, waiting to be with him again."

"So Kat inherited her talent from you and her grandparents," Lucinda said quietly, well able to see the vivid panorama Jeneva had painted of her parents' life.

"She surely did. My mama was a little thing, but she had a great big voice—just like *this* little thing."

"I sang for Luce," Katanya told her mother and grandmother. "She liked me."

"I more than liked you," Lucinda said.

"Well, we'll have to have a little concert before you go," Jeneva said. "Loranne sings like an angel. You have to hear these two sing harmony, Lucy. It'll give you chills."

"I don't doubt it," Lucinda said. "I just have to keep an eye on the time. I don't like driving on highways after dark," she explained. "Too many drunk drivers. I either have to stay well behind them or speed up fast and get as far ahead of them as I can. Connecticut is terrible for that. Or perhaps it's changed. It's been so long since I've driven any distance that I may be completely wrong. It certainly *used* to be that way."

"People drinking put me on edge period. You just can't ever *know* what a drunk's going to do," Loranne said. "I see anyone take more than two drinks, I start to get nervous. I don't want to be near somebody who's about to go out of control. I don't want to *see* it or *hear* it. They either turn nasty, or they start tellin' you how much they love you. I can't stand it, either way. I just want out."

"Drunks scare the hell out of me," Lucinda said. A montage of party scenes flashed across the screen of her memory and she saw a beautiful woman, makeup smeared, eyes bleary and mouth loose, one hand flat on a wall, bracing herself as, standing spraddle-legged, she urinated in the corner of an elegant living room while a dismayed crowd looked on aghast; she saw handsome men whose faces had become rubbery masks, staggering through rooms, bumping into chairs, tripping over low tables or one, in particular, falling backward through a glass patio door. "People literally become ugly when they drink too much," she said with a slight shudder, remembering Lily whisking her away from those scenes, hustling her up flights of stairs, or outside into cars, her features tight as she tucked Lucinda into bed, or drove them away. Lily hadn't liked drunks, either. "They give me the heebie-jeebies," she used to say. "They either behave like animals or they're all over you, telling you how wonderful you are. It's sickening."

"I guess we all agree on that matter," Jeneva said, going to the refrigerator to get a large bowl of diced fruit. "Now don't tell me, Lucy, that you don't have room for a little watermelon and cantaloupe."

"I honestly don't," Lucinda said apologetically.

"Okay, but if you change your mind, just go ahead and help yourself."

Loranne and Katanya were doing the dishes. Jeneva and Lucinda were back in the living room with cups of coffee—Lucinda on the sofa, Jeneva in the armchair next to her—when Jeneva said, "Kat was telling me about how you're looking for your daddy's people."

Lucinda nodded. "I'm not very optimistic. It's a long time later and I have very little to go on."

"Kat's idea was a good one," the woman said. "The church is the heart of any black community. And people have long memories. Something, or someone, may turn up."

"I'm not expecting anything."

"No," Jeneva said. "That's probably wise. I hope you don't think my granddaughter's indiscreet for telling us, but she's a deep-thinking child, as you've noticed, and she's been very worried about you, afraid you'd go back inside and stay in your house for another twenty-seven years."

"I don't think I'll be able to do that now," Lucinda said truthfully. "I seem to have lost my flair for concealment."

Jeneva smiled. "You do have a fine way with words."

"I have my moments." Lucinda returned the smile.

"I hope you won't think I'm presuming, but there's something I'd like to say to you."

"Go ahead, please. It couldn't be more presumptuous than my showing up on your doorstep uninvited."

"You *were* invited," Jeneva corrected her. "But never mind. I understand. What I want to say is this. According to what Kat tells me, you found out about your father and you got scared, not knowing who, or what, you were anymore. It's understandable. But here's the thing. I've met a lot of people in my life and just a few of them have been what I call color-blind. They see the outside, all right, but it's not as important to them as what's inside a person. You're color-blind,

Lucy. And that's what'll carry you through. It truly doesn't matter to you what someone looks like. I was at the window and saw you pull up; I saw you talk to Gloria and to those hulking boys who would scare the devil out of most people, male or female; I saw you smile and shake all their hands and give the boys money. It doesn't matter what it was for. You treated Gloria and the boys with courtesy and respect; you made them smile and feel good about themselves. Maybe you were scared, maybe you were feeling shy. That doesn't matter either. You took the time to allow introductions, to offer your hand; you talked, you listened, you showed interest in what those three people had to say. You weren't all full of yourself, even though you arrived in a car that's going to be talked about for *days*, maybe even weeks around here. The point is, that in this part of town, it's a rare person who behaves the way you did.

"I knew I'd like you when Katanya phoned and didn't sound miserable for the first time in six days, because she'd met a nice lady who gave her lunch and talked to her. I'm color-blind, too, and it wouldn't have mattered to me if your skin was pure, one hundred percent white, or some shade of yellow or brown or red. I'm not naive. I've encountered my fair share of racists—of all colors. Some of the people at our church embarrass me with their biases. But you were kind to a child who'd never been away from home before—never mind out of the city—who was having a bad time in a house where the marriage was falling apart. Kat, as you've seen, doesn't miss a trick. She had that household figured out in no time flat. So she took herself off and she found you. You found each other. You'll never know how happy and grateful we all are that you did.

"So what I'm saying is, it's not about who your daddy might have been, Lucy. To all intents and purposes, you are what you've probably always been: a generous, gracious soul. Having some black blood in you doesn't change that. Your mama raised you well. Maybe she made a mistake, trying to cover up the past, but you and I both know it would've been scandalous if she hadn't. We're the same age, you and me. We both grew up in the fifties and we both know that she'd have lost everything, just the way my daddy did, buying on margin in the stock market. She did what she had to do to protect you. And she wasn't wrong."

"No," Lucinda said. "She wasn't."

"You're not angry with her?"

"I've never been angry with her. I adored Lily. She was magical, in her own right, the way Kat is in hers. It's an incandescence. Lily glowed because she was entirely real, flaws and all. She never pretended to be anything but what she was. She hid things from me, quite a lot of things actually. In the end, none of it mattered. I got tangled up inside myself. I got scared. Kat got me to step outside—of the house, of myself. It feels odd to be out, to be here with you and your family, to be having this conversation and to hear the street noises, the traffic going past. But as odd as it is, it's exhilarating, too. I'm not going to be able to stay inside now because I'll need to see all of you again."

"Good!" Jeneva leaned forward to place her hand on Lucinda's knee. "Because we'll need to see *you* again, too. I have a list of movies I'm dying to see."

Lucinda placed her hand over Jeneva's and confessed, "So do I. I've been making my list for years."

Jeneva asked, "When's your birthday?"

"May eighteenth. When's yours?"

"May twenty-second."

"I guess I'm the older twin." Lucinda said. "It's a pity they separated us."

Jeneva looked at her for a long moment, then they both sat back, laughing.

All the way home, Lucinda felt giddy, glutted with good food and good sensations. Like a child again, having made a new friend, she was euphoric. And like a soundtrack, atop her review of that day's extraordinary events, Katanya and her mother sang while Jeneva played a flowing, effortless accompaniment. It seemed for that half hour as if the entire block was listening, so quiet had the street below been. The bass-heavy rumble of someone's boombox had suddenly been stilled; no shouts or laughter had emanated from the stoops nearby.

Nothing she'd ever experienced in the early L.A. days of fabulous, catered and fully staffed house parties, attended by the jewel-bedecked celebrities of the day could compare to the sudden thrill of hearing those two sweetly blended, potent voices lending themselves to old songs that were made completely new again by this mother and daughter's renditions.

By the time she left I-95, she knew it would be hours before she'd be able to sleep. But that didn't matter. Her senses were fairly overwhelmed, even overloaded, but she was calm. There was no hint whatever of a looming headache. She just had a great number of things to think about.

Chapter Twenty

When the telephone rang the next morning just after nine, she'd only been asleep for three hours. Glancing at the Caller ID, she picked up the receiver and said, "Renee, I got to bed very late last night so I can't talk right now. But I haven't forgotten. Would you like to bring Jason over at around two?"

"That'll be fine. Go back to sleep and we'll see you later. 'Bye."

Lucinda fumbled the receiver back into the cradle, hovered on the edge for a minute or two, then plunged back into sleep.

When she awakened it was almost eleven and she discovered at once that the euphoria of the previous night had fled, leaving in its wake a darkness bordering on depression. As she showered, as she pulled on shorts and a T-shirt, as she got the newspaper from the porch, and as she mechanically went about making a pot of coffee, she probed this darkness, examining its depths, its origin. She felt fearful again, and foolish. Yes, she had broken past self-imposed barriers and taken to the highway to see Kat and meet her family. But she'd read far too much into the hours she'd spent in that tidy apartment in Harlem.

Jeneva had spoken wisely, kindly; they'd enjoyed each other's company. But Kat and her family were *there*, and she was *here*, and little, really, had changed. Last night, performing her mental post mortem, she'd endowed the event with far too much significance. She had met two fine women and seen darling Kat again; she'd made the acquaintance of Mrs. Garcia, the guardian of the entry to the tenement, and her son and nephew. But it was all no more than a bubble in time, a ripple on the otherwise motionless surface of the shallow pond her life had remained for more than a quarter of a century.

Yet there she'd been, wandering through the house in the small hours of the morning, a Gershwin compilation CD playing, as she imagined Kat and her mother and grandmother in this house—seeing them in the living room or the kitchen or outside by the pool. She'd even—madly, she now believed—thought about the barn and how, if redesigned and outfitted, it would make a decent-sized guest house where the three of them could come to stay in complete privacy. She'd considered the tremendous desirability of barns in this part of the world, and how New Yorkers, with dreams of owning one, searched endlessly for something to convert to fit their idealized rustic images. They even placed ads in the *Times*. **Wanted. Barn suitable for conversion to residence.** And here she was, with a barn that had been used for decades solely as a repository for gardening tools and items for which she had no immediate use. A large, genuine barn with massive, heavy beams, where hay had once been stored in the loft, when the house had stood as the centerpiece of a working farm. Cattle had grazed in the now overgrown wooded field behind the house and by the pond which was now, year round, overrun by Canada geese whose migratory patterns had been forever altered by well-meaning dolts who, despite posted warnings, had insisted on feeding the birds. The entire eastern seaboard was suffering from the massive presence of non-migratory geese who'd taken up refuge on golf courses and condo complexes—anywhere with available water. And since it was illegal to kill the birds, the local papers regularly ran articles about the problems caused by the geese (they destroyed lawns and left copious quantities of green droppings everywhere) and possible ways in which to get them to go away or to resume their previous migrations south. Let the pests go bother the people in Florida!

Good grief! She'd spent half a dozen hours in the city, and as a result she'd been brimming over with plans for a future that included three people whose lives were well-established and unlikely to be relocated as a result of the wishful thinking of an aging, slightly desperate, recluse.

As she drank her coffee and paged her way through the *Times*, the heat of shame had her sweating. She was retroactively mortified by her naiveté and by the transparency of her newly revealed neediness. She was beyond distressed at her sophomoric castle-building fantasies of the previous night. Yes, undoubtedly, she would see these people again. But their lives and hers had not suddenly, miraculously, become intertwined. And how *could* she have made that idiotic remark about their being twins, separated at birth? God! No doubt about it: she had lost a large measure of her rationality. Sane people said, "Thank you. I had a lovely time," went on their way, and that was that. They didn't arrive home and start spinning dreams like some chronically flawed spider creating asymmetrical, off-kilter webs.

Getting to the end of the paper with no awareness of what, if anything, she'd read, she poured herself more coffee and stood drinking it by the counter, staring blankly into space. Somehow, she was going to have to reintegrate the now-scattered bits of herself and find again the calm focus that had allowed her to go about living her so-called life before she'd allowed it to get upended by her attachment to a lovably imaginative child.

She had work to do, if she could manage to get herself back on track. She needed to reread that book at least once— probably twice—more in order to distill it down to a series of key scenes that would form the skeleton of the screenplay. Then, she'd go back and forth from the book to the script, lifting dialogue and action sequences to wrap around the skeleton—gradually building an entity that would be faithful to the author's narrative, but in an entirely different medium. That, however, wasn't going to happen today, what with Renee bringing Soupboy to swim, and Lucinda's being as tired as she was, having had several hours less sleep than usual.

Why the hell had she been such a goof the night before? Mercifully, only she knew about her dream-weaving and imagined reconstruction plans. She hadn't, as she'd been tempted to do, phoned Gin to tell her about her trip into the city. God! It was unnerving to think she'd almost done it. At the last minute, she'd decided it was too late, even with the three-hour time difference. Gin tended to be in bed by midnight. And when she was on a shoot, she went to bed by nine so that she'd be sufficiently rested to put in a full day's work—even if that work consisted of three or four hours of waiting between set-ups and perhaps two or three hours of actual takes. Sitting on the sidelines, costumed and in full makeup was as enervating as the repeated takes.

Moving on auto-pilot, Lucinda finished her coffee and went to boot up the computer to check her e-mail. She was surprised to see half a dozen items in her inbox. One piece of spam invited her to click on the link to see Tiny Teens Naked; another was an invitation to view naked celebrities. One e-mail promised her a huge income if she wanted to work at home. She shook her head as she deleted it, saying to herself, "Right! Just what I need." The next was yet another in the seemingly endless entreaties from the wife (it was always some family member—a son, a brother, a cousin) of a former Nigerian diplomat who needed some kind person to help them get fourteen, or twenty, or forty million dollars out of that country. As she hit the delete button, she wondered how many people got sucked into that scam. Something that seemed totally transparent to her might seem genuine to some poor soul in the Midwest who'd fork over thousands of dollars to assist in this bogus claim.

The remaining two items were e-mails, from Kat and Jeneva.

Kat's e-mail read:

> Dear Luce:
> I'm so happy you came to see us. My moms and gramma think you're great and were talking after you went home about how nice you are and discusing when we could maybe come on the train to see you. Mrs. Garcia came up this morning to say Hernan is in love with your car and how he and Geraldo couldn't believe you said you'd take them for a ride when you come see us again. She told us how you bought them dinner and she called you something in Spanish that sounded like linda. She was all happy too that you came. I wish you could

come again soon but my moms says I'm too
pushy. Lots of love, xoxo, Kat
PS: don't forget you promised to check the
box at the post office.

Jeneva's e-mail said:

Dear Lucy:
What a joy to meet you! It's the first time in
years when someone new felt like someone I'd
known forever. All of us are anxious to see
you again very soon. I hope your drive home
went smoothly, with no drunken drivers to be
seen anywhere. Kat is itching to phone you but
I've asked her to be conservative about using
the cell phone you so kindly gave her. Please
know that you have an open invitation to come
any time. You will always be welcome in our
home. I mean that truly.
With love, your twin Jeneva

Smiling, Lucinda reread both e-mails before sending
replies—assuring both Kat and Jeneva that any or all of them
could use the cell phone as much as they liked, asking them
please to come visit, and thanking them for a wonderful
evening. As she shut down the Internet connection, she was
wondering why she'd been so full of doubt and self-recrim-
ination. "You're such an idiot," she said aloud. Faithless. In
truth, she hadn't lost her marbles. She really had made a new
friend; she hadn't said or done anything stupid. And she
would see Kat, Loranne and Jeneva again. Either she'd drive
into the city, or they'd come to the house for a weekend. She
could send the limo for them, or they could take the train.

And just like that, as easily as it had descended upon her,
the darkness lifted; she was no longer depressed. She was

also no longer euphoric but had slipped into a mood of gratified acceptance. Things *had* changed. *Your twin Jeneva.* And tomorrow, to keep her promise to Kat, she would drive over to the post office to check the box she'd rented—even though she was certain that it was not only too soon to expect any replies but that it was also unwise even to hope for them.

Soupboy sat on the middle step at the shallow end of the pool, joyfully splashing his water-winged arms up and down, sending showers of water everywhere. When he tired of that, he'd stand on the second step and "dive" into the water, each time, crying out, "Watch me! Watch me!"

Dutifully, Lucinda and Renee looked over each time to watch, congratulating him when he climbed back up the steps.

"He's a complete water baby," Renee said. "If we let him, he'd stay here until he was blue from head to toe and shivering, and he'd scream his heart out when I said it was time to go. He'll do that anyway." She shrugged. "His screaming drives me crazy. I don't know how she did it, but I noticed that Katanya could get him to stop. The minute she was gone, and we were home he started up again."

Deciding it was safe to discuss it, Lucinda said, "She gave him a little talking-to, and laid down the rules about screaming. It was quite impressive, really."

"I'll bet it was. She obviously knows something I don't."

"It's not that complicated. Children need rules, Renee. We all do. Logic is a learned skill. I don't think you can reason with a boy who's not yet three. But you can set down some rules and make sure he understands them."

Her brow furrowed, Renee asked, "How do I do that?"

Borrowing a page from Kat's book, Lucinda said, "Perhaps you could take hold of him and not let go until he promises not to scream. It might take a few minutes but he'll get the message."

"Take hold of him how?"

"Hold his wrists, not too hard. Just enough so that he can't break free."

"That's all?"

"Unh-hunh. Just hold on firmly until he agrees. Then, when he does, give him a hug and tell him what a good boy he is."

"That's amazing," Renee said, looking over at her son. "I'll have to give it a try."

"I think you'll find it's very effective."

"Gosh! Thank you. I will definitely try it next time he starts that terrible screaming." Turning back, Renee said, "You seem—different today, very cheerful."

"I feel quite happy," Lucinda admitted. "I drove into the city yesterday to see Katanya and her family. We had a lovely visit."

"You're keeping in touch with her. That's great."

Lucinda studied the younger woman's expression. She seemed sincere, meeting Lucinda's eyes straight on. "I've developed quite a fondness for Kat," Lucinda said with studied offhandedness.

"From what I saw, it looked very mutual," Renee said. "She's a very bright girl. *Very* bright. A sweet child altogether. I just wish her visit could have been ... better. The timing was unfortunate, to say the least."

"These things happen. I'm curious. What book did you give her?"

"Don't laugh," Renee said. "It was a Nancy Drew."

"That's perfect. I'm sure she'll love it."

"I read them all when I was a kid," Renee said, as if confessing to something illicit. "I still have my Nancy Drew moments now and then."

"I think we all do," Lucinda said, feeling her energy starting to flag.

Renee was smart enough to notice and not overstay her welcome. She got up and went to the shallow end of the pool to tell Jason that it was time to go. At once, he began to emit eardrum-shattering screams. It was all Lucinda could do not to hold her hands over her ears, feeling the rending noise like a hacksaw slicing into her brain. Then, to her surprise, following Lucinda's advice, (*A quick learner*, Lucinda thought with approval.), Renee sat on the top step of the pool and took hold of Jason's wrists. Talking very quietly, she held on while the boy screamed intermittently, struggling mightily to break free. This went on for a minute or two, then Jason went silent, listening at last before he relented and his sturdy little body went pliant. Renee released his wrists and gave him a hug, smiling over at Lucinda as she did. She looked surprised and proud.

"Come say goodbye to Lucinda now," Renee said, bringing him by the hand to where Lucinda was sitting.

" 'Bye, Luce," he said. "Fank you fo' wettin' me swim."

" 'Bye-bye, Soupboy." Lucinda clasped his cool wet body to her and then, surrendering to impulse, planted kisses on his edibly chubby cheeks. He laughed happily, put his hands on her face and kissed her nose.

"Jase come back amorrow?" he asked.

"Let's wait and see what kind of weather we have. Okay?"

" 'Kay."

Wrapping him in a towel, Renee said, "Thank you, Lucinda. For everything."

"My pleasure."

After they'd gone, Lucinda slid into the pool and floated on her back, looking up at the sky, trying, and failing, to do a recollected inventory of the contents of the barn. She couldn't come close to remembering everything in there, but she did know that the old wicker porch furniture was inside and she thought it was high time to get it out. When Kat and her mother and grandmother came, they'd be able to sit out on the porch in the evening.

A cursory examination of the furniture a short time later convinced her that long disuse had rendered it worthy only of the trash. The paint had long-since peeled off and the wicker had split and broken after so many years in the cobwebby barn. The place seemed to be chock-full of items fit only for the trash. The smart thing to do would be to hire someone with a truck to come and haul it all off to the dump. In the meantime, returning to the house, she got online and ordered new wicker pieces for the porch—a settee, four armchairs and two side tables.

Satisfied, she went to the kitchen and studied the contents of the refrigerator. Seeing nothing that appealed to her, she got a small can of Heinz baked beans in tomato sauce from the cupboard, removed the top and sat down with a spoon to eat the cold beans directly from the can. It was one of her favorite snacks. Gin used to tease her about it relentlessly when they were young.

"Jeez! You'd think you were one of the extras in *The Grapes of Wrath* or something, eating cold beans. It's just sad, kiddo. Next thing anybody knows," she'd said countless times, "you'll be panhandling with a tin cup of pencils on Wilshire. Couldn't you at least put the damned beans in a bowl?"

"I like them this way. And you should talk! Aren't you the girl who eats raw hot dogs cold?"

"At least I put bread around them! I don't eat them out of the package!"

"Aren't you," Lucinda would go on, "the girl who has Miracle Whip and white bread sandwiches with lettuce?"

"What's wrong with that?"

"It's just as sad as my eating baked beans from the can."

"I've got an excuse. I grew up with the greedy seamstress from Anaheim whose idea of a classy spread is Miracle Whip. What's *your* excuse?"

By now laughing, Lucinda had always surrendered at that point, saying, "I give up. You win. You are a genuine waif and I am merely a pretender."

The beans consumed and the can rinsed and ready for the blue box, Lucinda picked up the phone.

"I may just have a heart attack," Gin said in feigned shock. "Two calls from you in one week. This is right up there with the miracle at Lourdes, or one of those zany women seeing religious visions in oil slicks on the road."

Laughing, Lucinda said, "I hope you're sitting down because I have to tell you that I actually drove into the city last night."

"Oh my *God*! I think I've got a pain in my left arm. Yes, I definitely do. A shooting pain. This is it! It's the big one. No, wait! It's not the big one after all. Okay, Ella. Hold on and let me grab a cigarette." There was a pause of a minute or so before Gin returned. "Okay," she said. "I'm all set. Tell me everything."

Chapter Twenty-One

Early the next morning, Lucinda donned her hat and sunglasses and drove to the post office. As expected, the rental box was empty. What was unexpected was the stab of disappointment she felt at seeing its emptiness. Returning to the car, she was forced to acknowledge that she'd allowed Katanya's enthusiasm to infect her, and that she must fight it off. Even to hope for an answer was unrealistic. After all these years, Franklin's family was probably long gone, or scattered to distant states, possibly to different countries. Still, she'd promised Katanya that she would check the box and she had done that. Expect nothing, she told herself, and you cannot be disappointed. *Expect nothing*, she kept repeating silently, trying to battle off the depression that, in spite of all her gains, was creeping back to cast a shadow over her good mood.

Home again, she made a fresh pot of coffee and carried a steaming mug to the living room where she tried to go back to the book and her note-taking. But she couldn't. She'd slipped into a holding pattern because of sending out all those letters, and she had no idea how to break it. Her fondness for Kat and her family, and her long-term love for and obligation to Gin seemed to have been partitioned off in an area she couldn't access. She lacked the energy to boot up the computer or to put on a CD. All she could do was sit and drink the coffee while she stared at the TV screen—looking but not really seeing—setting down the terms of an emotional contract she was making with herself. She would, the contract stipulated, give herself one more week's worth of visits to the post office. When that week was ended and she'd received no response, she would with all due care pick up the dropped stitches of her life. She would make a firm invitation, by telephone, to Jeneva to invite her and Loranne and Katanya to come for a weekend visit; and she would make good on her promise to Gin to write the screenplay. She could not and would not attempt to think beyond that. Those were her immediate goals.

The next morning she again checked the post office box, struggling against feeling progressively more foolish. Dialing the combination and opening the little door to gaze at the interior of the empty box was becoming an utterly demoralizing exercise.

She returned home and sat in front of the television set, a bit surprised—when she thought of it—at not having heard from Renee. Soupboy had to be nagging his mother from morning to night, wanting to come play in the pool. But perhaps Renee was fearful of wearing out their welcome and so was giving the boy some variant on the perennial parental theme of, "We'll see." Too bad, Lucinda thought. She'd have enjoyed the distraction of a visit from Soupboy and his mother.

The following morning just before eight, she spun the numbers on the box's small combination lock, got the door open and went rigid, gazing in disbelief into the interior. A single letter leaned against the wall of the box, but she was afraid to touch it. As the seconds ticked by, she continued to look at the letter, aware of someone entering and walking purposefully past her; she heard that someone open a box, remove its contents, then walk smartly away. Silence. Locked in place, her mouth dry, she imagined what message might be contained within the off-white, expensive-looking stationery. There was an embossed return address on the flap. She couldn't read it from where she stood, but she studied the raised lettering—Was it blue or black?—for quite some time. All but paralyzed, she listened to the sound of her open-mouthed breathing, aware that her senses seemed simultaneously both heightened and dulled—a state of being she'd never before experienced.

Again, footsteps clicked across the floor behind her. She heard the door of a box open, peripherally saw hands lifting out a stack of mail, then the box door clicked shut and—feeling eyes touch on her briefly—the person left. The silence again closed around her, and she had, as if viewing the scene from above, a clear picture of how she must appear: a thin woman of above average height whose features were concealed by a curtain of shoulder-length, dark blond hair beneath a broad-brimmed straw hat; with sunglasses riding low on her nose so she could see over top of the rims; bare-legged in a knee-length, shapeless blue sundress; her long narrow feet in what her classmates at Yale had called "Jesus Sandals." Unpretty footwear, nondescript clothing on an unspecial, slightly peculiar-looking woman. She presented the near-perfect picture of a classic oddball, somebody people avoided for fear she might at any moment start an incomprehensible, impassioned rant. She thought she had to seem to an observer like someone who might, without warning, go out of control, waving her scrawny arms about and shouting imprecations, while clots of spit collected in the corners of her mouth. It was such a viable picture that she could almost see herself behaving that way. Except, irony of ironies, she was far too shy and too proud to allow anyone, ever, to see her out of control. The only time she'd come close to losing control was with Eddie, the morning after her mother died. And even then she'd managed to keep from going completely to pieces. With tremendous force of will, she'd contained herself. Only later, safely locked into the bathroom, huddled on the cold tile floor with her back against the tub, did she relinquish control. It was, she had always thought, an ugly display of raw injury. She had never, before or since, undergone such racking pain, such burning anguish.

Good grief! she thought now, deeply bothered by the possibility that she might strike strangers as one of those lost souls who were a few cards shy of a full deck. Completely unacceptable! She reached into the box, withdrew the envelope, closed the door to the box and hurried out to the car. The envelope in her lap, she drove home, parked, and flew up the walk and into the house.

In the kitchen, she emptied the now-cold coffee from her mug, refilled it, then leaned against the counter, staring at the envelope which lay on the table next to the as yet unread *Times*. Completely ridiculous, but she was afraid. And so she dawdled, sipping the hot coffee, studying the envelope from a distance until, suddenly, terribly annoyed by her behavior, she put down the mug, grabbed a bread knife, snatched up the thing and sliced it open.

Inside was a note, written on heavy, expensive stock that matched the envelope. And a photograph.

The note, written in the beautiful old-fashioned script of someone elderly who'd learned handwriting at a time when it was considered to be an important skill, read:

> *Yes, I know the man in the photograph. He was Adam Bentley Franklin. Do you know the young woman in this photograph?*
> *Sincerely, Elise Franklin.*

It was a color shot of Lucinda in her cap and gown, taken prior to her graduation from Yale. She remembered how the photographer had processed kids against a blue drop sheet, one after another, for several days. Lucinda had planned to skip the sessions, but Lily had insisted.

"This is something that's going to happen once. Just once. I want a picture, Luce. Humor me. Someday you'll be glad I asked you to do this."

And so on an unusually hot late April afternoon, Lucinda had joined the line of graduates waiting to be photographed by the quick and efficient middle-aged man with the rolled-up shirtsleeves and the polka-dot bow-tie who'd had, surprisingly, a good eye for lighting. Almost everyone (except a pair of notoriously vain girls who made a great show of tossing their sets of proofs in the trash) was pleased with the resulting shots.

Now, all these years later, one of the prints had found its way back to her. She sat holding the photo in her hand while she admired the fountain-penned handwriting, thinking that Eddie had got it wrong. He'd forgotten Lily's habit of using the last names of people she especially liked. Undoubtedly, Eddie had been rattled by the circumstances on that trip to France, because Lily had always called him Rifkin and had only used his first name when referring to him in conversation with others. Gin was always Holder, Lester was always Foxcroft. And her father had been Franklin. Adam Bentley Franklin.

———

At ten-thirty, thinking it was a reasonable time of day to call, she picked up the telephone and dialed the Westport telephone number printed discreetly below the address on the stationery. Perspiring, she waited while the phone rang once, twice. Then it was picked up and a crisp, English-accented voice said, "Franklin residence. This is Gwyn. How may I help you?"

Thrown, Lucinda said, "Ahm, good morning. This is Lucinda Hunter. Could I speak to Elise Franklin?"

"Ah, Ms. Hunter, yes. Please hold the line for a moment."

Whoever Gwyn was, she'd been expecting Lucinda to call. This was all very strange. She waited quite some time, starting to feel chilled. Then, just when she thought she might have been disconnected, Gwyn came back on the line, saying, "I do apologize for keeping you waiting so long. Would it be possible for you to come to the house?"

Lucinda hesitated, trying to process this. "I could do that," she said at last. "When?"

"Four would be ideal, if you could manage it," the woman said pleasantly. "In time for afternoon tea."

"Tea," Lucinda repeated. Afternoon tea? "Today?"

"That's right. If it suits."

"I think so," Lucinda said.

"Oh, good. Do you need directions?"

"No. I'll find it."

"Just ring at the gate when you get here."

"All right."

"Splendid! We'll look forward to seeing you at four."

Lucinda hung up, bewildered. Some Englishwoman named Gwyn had invited her to *afternoon tea* at the *gated* Franklin residence at four. Her imagination running riot, she tried to make sense of the information she had. She couldn't. Instead, she went to the living room to look for the Fairfield County Directory. Bringing it back to the kitchen, she sat down to look up the Westport address and find the best route to it.

Having jotted down the directions, she returned the directory to the bookcase in the living room, then sat down on the sofa, trying to put her thoughts in order. There were things to do. She had to find something to wear—a decent outfit and proper shoes. She couldn't possibly arrive at an estate in her faded dress and Jesus sandals. Should she bring a gift? How could she, when she didn't know who she was going to see? Flowers! They were always safe. She could go into town and get long-stemmed roses. Yellow ones; they were neutral, always a good choice. Everyone loved yellow roses.

If her handwriting was anything to go by, Elise Franklin was elderly. Was Gwyn her secretary or her nurse? Or was she, perhaps, a daughter or sister? This was a genuine mystery. And somehow Lucinda had to get through the next five hours before she'd get any answers. She wanted to phone someone, to talk to somebody. But there was no one to call. It wasn't even 8:00 a.m. in Los Angeles. Jeneva and Loranne would be at work, and she didn't want to call Kat until she actually had something to tell her. She'd been out of touch for so long with everyone else she'd ever known that it would take hours just to bring them up to date. Hopeless. But she could kill some time by going out to buy the flowers. She'd do that. Getting through the day until the afternoon was more important than her fear. Collecting her bag and her keys, she left the house.

———

She was pulling out onto the Post Road—the beribboned white box of yellow roses and baby's breath on the passenger seat—when all at once she knew exactly where to go.

Parking in the shade, she locked the car and walked toward the diner. It was too early for the lunch crowd so only a few of the booths were occupied. A young waitress showed her to a booth, left a menu on the table and went off to get the coffee Lucinda had ordered.

Two or three minutes passed, then Elena came with the coffee. Setting it down on the table, she offered Lucinda one of her beautiful smiles.

"Will you sit with me for a minute?" Lucinda asked.

Pleased, the woman said, "Sure. I sit," and slid into the booth opposite her. "Where the little girl?" she asked. "You friend?"

"Katanya had to go home, to the city."

"Is good girl," Elena said. "Smart, huh?"

"Yes, very smart."

"Is nice you come again. How you are?"

"I'm not sure. I think I'm going to meet one of my relatives today."

"How is this?" Elena looked very interested. It was precisely what Lucinda had hoped for.

"I never knew my father. I've been looking for his family for a very long time. I'm going to see someone this afternoon. I think she may be my grandmother."

"Yes?" The woman read Lucinda's eyes. "So you be happy then, huh?"

"I think I will be."

"And you friend, the little girl, she come again?"

"Oh, yes," Lucinda said. "With her mother and grand-mother."

"So you have lottsa people then," Elena said. "It's good."

"Do you have children?" Lucinda asked.

"Two. Boy and girl, big now. Boy married. Girl at school, finish soon to be a dentist." Her pride glowed in another radiant smile.

Lucinda smiled back at her. "A dentist. That's very impressive. What does your son do?"

"He makes another rest'rant, in Fairfield."

"That's wonderful."

"His wife have baby soon. Three months."

"You'll be a grandmother!"

Elena pretended to frown. "Yeah. Gra'ma. I think I too young, huh?"

"You are definitely too young," Lucinda agreed, and the two of them laughed softly.

"I get you home fries?"

"I'd love some."

Elena slid out of the booth and paused a moment with her hand on Lucinda's shoulder. "You come back, tell about family?"

"Yes. I'll come back and tell you all about it."

"Good. Good."

———

By the time she'd managed to put together an acceptable outfit, Lucinda had worked herself into such a sweat that she had to take a second shower. While she was in there, she decided she might as well give her hair another washing, too.

She was using up minutes in chunks, trying to get through the hours until it was time to leave the house and make the drive to an area of Westport just past the Merritt Parkway. It was tough getting through the time. Her trip into town had only lasted just over an hour, including a stop to fuel the car. Organizing what she'd wear had taken the better part of another hour, with her trying on the few decent items of clothing she had left. One of these days, she told herself angrily, she was going to have to buy some decent new clothes. Most of her good dresses were horribly out of date or a bit ratty and fusty smelling from having spent too long in the closet.

She had to settle finally on a dress she'd bought the previous summer from the J. Crew catalog: a simple, ankle-length, pale blue linen garment with short sleeves and many small buttons down the front. On the top shelf of her closet she'd found a pair of flat white sandals she'd ordered from a Sak's catalog a couple of years earlier but had never worn. For luck, she would wear Lily's diamond stud earrings and the gold watch she'd bought on a rare impulse at Tiffany's one afternoon when she and Lucinda had gone into the city to meet some of the old L.A. crowd for lunch. With a round face, Roman numerals on the dial and a black suede strap, it was slim and good-looking without being ostentatious. Lily had taken off her old watch, dropped it into her purse and had worn the new one out of the store.

"This is me, don't you think?" Lily had asked.

"It is completely, absolutely you," Lucinda had said teasingly. "It's the most you thing you've ever owned."

Swatting Lucinda's hand, Lily had grinned, saying, "You're awfully cocky now that you've got that diploma."

"That's me, all right. Cocky as all get-out."

Six months later Lily was dead. She'd worn the watch perhaps a dozen times. Lucinda had been faithfully winding it, making sure it was in good working order for twenty-seven years. Today, for the first time, she was going to wear it—taking a small part of her mother with her when she went to meet Elise Franklin.

Chapter Twenty-Two

She had the air-conditioning going full blast in an effort to keep from soaking her dress with nervous perspiration as she drove along the route she'd mapped out. She'd allowed forty minutes for the trip but arrived at the gates in under half an hour. Would it matter that she was fifteen minutes early? Did she care at this point? If she parked somewhere to wait, she'd lose her nerve, turn around and go home. She couldn't risk it, and pulled up in front of the impressively high wrought-iron gates. The window open, she pressed the button on the speaker box. At once the English-accented voice asked, "May I help you?"

"This is Lucinda. I'm—"

"Do please come in, Lucinda," the voice cut her off and the gates began to swing inward.

Closing the window, Lucinda whispered, "Good grief! This is right out of a Daphne du Maurier novel," as she put the Bentley in gear and started forward.

The driveway was a long, curving one—lawns sweeping away on either side to heavily tree-lined perimeters—that brought her to a circular driveway at the front of a white-painted Victorian mansion with three stories of sparkling windows framed by black shutters. A deep porch with several groupings of furniture ran the width of the near side of the house; baskets of bright flowers hung every few feet from the porch roof. Massive terra cotta urns filled with more flowers flanked the steps to the porticoed front door. Several cars were parked in front of the three-car garage that looked to have living quarters above it (no doubt for the staff). One of the cars was a beautifully maintained vintage Rolls-Royce, possibly from the thirties or forties, that was parked in the shade of a massive copper beach tree. There was a late-model Mercedes sedan and next to it a Ford station wagon that looked like a poor relative. Lucinda parked beside the Ford and sat for a few seconds, taking deep breaths. Then, carrying the box of flowers, she made her way to the front door which, she now saw, stood open.

Her lungs were constricted as she climbed the steps, trying to see into the darkness immediately beyond the open door. As she arrived at the threshold a slight figure separated from the shadows and moved forward.

"I have waited such a very long time for this moment," a low, richly accented voice said. "You are just as I knew you would be."

Taking another step forward into the light, Lucinda saw a petite, impossibly erect, exquisitely dressed white-haired woman. She was elderly, but just how elderly was difficult to determine. She was very fair-skinned with delicate features beneath a subtly light application of makeup—a touch of color at her cheeks, mascara on her eyelashes and warm pink lipstick. She was lovely.

"I am Elise," she said, extending a cool, manicured hand, "The mother of Adam, your grandmother."

Speechless, Lucinda took hold of the hand that closed with surprising strength around hers.

"I wished to have today alone with you," Elise said, "before introducing you to the others."

"Others?" Lucinda repeated, trying to make herself believe this was real and not some overwrought dream brought about by one of her severe headaches. It had the feeling of an out-of-body experience—something more appropriate to a dream than to reality. Was this actually happening?

"Your aunts and uncle, the cousins. All will come to meet you when next you visit."

"All?" Lucinda was certain she sounded mentally impaired, suffering, perhaps, from some arcane malady like echolalia—in the grip of which one meaninglessly, mindlessly repeated over and over the words of another.

The old woman smiled, her hand still closed firmly around Lucinda's, her deep-set hazel eyes (*Like mine*, Lucinda thought) very clear, lively with intelligence and humor. "You have two aunts, one uncle who is the husband of my daughter Adele, five cousins—my *other* grandchildren. Also eight great-grandchildren, two great-great-grandchildren. When I received the telephone call from my grandson who saw your letter on the board at his church, *many* calls were made. Very many," she added with what appeared to be amusement.

"I'm not sure I understand."

"But no, of course not," Elise said with a sympathetic tilt of her head.

Lucinda found her accent intriguing. At moments it had French inflections, then British.

"I see Lily in you," the elderly woman said. "And your father, too. You are so like him. I had feared I might never know you. It has been so long a time. You are now, what? Forty-five?"

Lucinda shook her head. "Forty-six. You knew about me?"

"Oh, yes, always. We knew of your cleverness; we knew of the films you wrote, of your academic achievements. Lily wrote and telephoned always; she sent photographs, even magazines with foolish stories and pictures of the two of you at birthday parties and so forth. But we were obliged to honor Lily's wishes to remain separate, apart from your life. And then, when she died—too young, so very sad; we all loved her very much—we had to wait for you. We could not come to you. It was uncertain, you see."

"You mean whether or not I knew about my father?"

"Precisely. It was Lily's great secret and we could not know just how great a secret it might be."

"It was very great." Lucinda used the woman's own words, finding them appropriate in their idiomatic formality. "I didn't know of him—about Adam—until after she died. I found a photograph and I knew at once that he had to be my father. I could see myself so clearly in his features. But I had the name wrong," Lucinda tried to explain, her thoughts jumbled, her senses fairly overwhelmed. "I hired detectives. They searched for years. Finally, I had to give up because we got nowhere at all."

"The wrong name?"

"Eddie, the only one of my mother's friends who met him, thought Franklin was his *first* name. So we were looking for someone with no surname."

"Ah, no! This explains so much. A pity, indeed. But you are here at last, and that is all that matters. I am so happy." She paused a moment, then gave Lucinda's hand a squeeze, asking, "The flowers, they are for me?"

"Oh, God! Yes." Released, yet still feeling the impression of that small hand around hers, she presented the box to Elise Franklin.

"You are too gracious, my dear. Thank you." Rising on tiptoe, she kissed Lucinda on one cheek, then the other. It was the sensation of a hummingbird flirting close to her, then away, leaving behind the faint fragrance of lilac. "Come inside, please." Turning, Elise led Lucinda through the cool, marble-floored foyer with its broad, curving staircase climbing off to the right, and into a vast living room on the left.

"Let us sit," Elise said, and rang a small silver bell that sat on a side table. "We will have tea and become acquainted. Gwyn will come now."

As if she'd been waiting nearby, a good-looking brunette in her late thirties or early forties came smiling into the room with her hand extended. Her clothes were understated but expensive, and her shoes, Lucinda saw, were classic cream-and-black Chanel pumps. "Hello!" she said cheerfully, giving Lucinda's hand a brisk shake before deftly taking the box of flowers from Elise. "How lovely to meet you! I'm Gwyn, Elise's assistant. I'll take care of the flowers. And I'll have cook bring the tea now, shall I, Mrs. Franklin?" she asked the old woman.

"Please," Elise said, easing herself into one of the pair of wing chairs positioned at an angle to the left of the wide fireplace whose deep mantelpiece held many ornately framed family photographs that Lucinda longed to examine. "Sit, please," she told Lucinda with a graceful flutter of her hand as Gwyn went off with the roses. "I'm sure you are very curious about us," she said. "So I have put out the family albums for you to see." Another graceful gesture indicated a table laden with eight or ten large old-fashioned leather-bound volumes positioned before the row of front windows where sheer curtains lifted in the breeze, allowing light to enter but keeping the heat at bay. The room was filled with beautiful things—an art deco bronze statuette of a nude woman, arms uplifted, atop a pedestal, spotlit from above; an exquisite painting that looked to be a genuine Rouault, also spotlit, on the wall to the right of the fireplace; a pair of down-filled sofas and a wide, glass-topped mahogany table positioned on a fine old Aubusson carpet. Deep inside the room, far to the right and positioned at an angle was a grand piano, its top holding more photographs as well as stacks of sheet music. Atop the built-in bookcases flanking the fireplace were collections of small items: a cluster of paperweights on one side, an assortment of cobalt glass pieces on the other. *Treasures*, Lucinda thought, recalling Katanya in the attic.

"We had the advantage of seeing many photographs of you before dear Lily died. She brought you here when you were a baby. But of course you could not know this. We saw you only a dozen or so times. Your mother was very careful, very concerned to do the right thing. It was a difficult choice for her, but she and Adam had an agreement always that the marriage would be kept a private matter."

"Because he ... you ... " Lucinda stopped, fearful of giving offense.

"Because," Elise helped her, "my husband, your grandfather, was of mixed blood. And so, therefore, our children were also of mixed blood. To my family, in our country, this was not something extraordinary, as it is in America. Many people assumed that Guillaume and Adam were from the middle east—that they were Persian or Arabic or Syrian. Often, it was convenient to allow this assumption to remain uncorrected. Even so, it has not always been so easy for my children since we came here." She frowned, as if remembering specific hurts her children had suffered which she, in turn, had suffered on their behalf. "Quite often, we considered returning home." She gave a small shrug. "But in the end, we stayed—for many reasons, primarily because of Guillaume's business. He practiced international law for a very important company. The rewards, as you can see, were significant. But perhaps not so very great for our children. They had some—difficulties, as you might imagine." She paused, looking at Lucinda as if well aware of Lucinda's own difficulties. "The girls more strongly resembled me and so did not encounter very much cruelty. Anne, my eldest daughter preferred to be someone of no color. She chose a white husband, a white life. It was a great irony that in choosing Michael she married someone without prejudice, a kind and gentle man who insisted that their children must be close with all the family, including their cousins who are very dark. Adele, my youngest child, the one with much spirit, much *joie de vivre*, insisted always that she was a person of color and had great pride in this. Her husband, your cousin John, came from what was once the Belgian Congo. He is," Elise said approvingly, "very beautiful, as are their children. You will see this when you meet them. It was their son, Paul, who discovered your letter at his church. He was most excited when he telephoned to tell me." She paused, as if relocating her place in the narrative.

"So," she went on after a few moments. "I am French, as perhaps you have guessed. I grew up in Paris and after receiving my *baccalaureate* I attended a school in London for one year to improve my English. This is where I met Guillaume—William. Not at the school," she clarified quickly, "but in London, at the home of family friends where I stayed. He was the son of an English father and an Algerian mother. Guillaume's father was a diplomat—the British consul in

Algeria. Guillaume was the most wonderful man I had ever met, also very beautiful—as John is beautiful." She smiled and said, "Many wonderful-looking men in our family, as you will see. But Guillaume." She sighed. "I adored him instantly. And it was the same for him. My parents felt it was a good match; they approved, as did his parents. And he was beautiful, in every way, all of his life, until he died nine years ago."

"It's all so—exotic," Lucinda said, at a loss for a better word.

"Not really," Elise disagreed mildly. "At that time, it was quite commonplace for young men of the upper class to have foreign postings in the diplomatic service if they chose not to enter the upper echelons of the military. And it was not so very unusual for a young man like Guillaume's papa to lose his heart to someone so lovely as his mother was."

"When was this?" Lucinda asked.

"Wait, I must think," Elise said. "I am born in 1904. Guillaume was five years older than I. His papa would be in Algeria before the end of the last century."

Lucinda gazed at the woman, flabbergasted. She was ninety-two years old! In no way whatsoever did she seem that old.

As if reading her thoughts, Elise smiled rather impishly and said, "We live to a very great age in my family. My sister died only one year ago at ninety-eight. And my mother lived to one hundred and three. I am the *baby*." She laughed merrily. "A baby of *ninety-two* years."

"That's amazing!" Lucinda declared. "You certainly don't look anywhere near that old."

"My daughter Adele is seventy-two. Her sister Anne—the difficult one—is seventy-three." She shook her head briefly, ruefully, over her aged, troublesome daughter. "Had he lived, my Adam would have been seventy-five at the end of this year. It was quite usual for girls to marry young at that time," she elaborated. "I married at sixteen to Guillaume. We had a new baby each year for three years and we finished with babies when we were still very young. We had much fun with the children because we were not so far from being children ourselves."

"It makes good sense," Lucinda said. "Now that I think of it, Lily would have been seventy-one this year. I had the impression that he ... that my father was much older than she was."

"He had often an old way about him," Elise said. "He could be very serious sometimes, very determined. Also sometimes very silly. He and Lily were—like me and Guillaume—very young when they met and fell in love."

"Please," Lucinda begged, "tell me about them. How did they meet? Where?"

At that moment, Gwyn returned bearing a crystal vase with the roses which she placed on the table by the windows. The cook followed, wheeling in a two-tiered trolley laden with an ornately engraved silver tea service, plates, cutlery and serving dishes of crustless sandwiches and small iced cakes. It was far too much food for just the two of them.

"I am curious," Elise said while Gwyn poured the tea and the cook gave Lucinda and the old woman plates and small embroidered serviettes. "What gave you the idea to write to the church?"

"A little girl I met recently thought of it. I believed I'd exhausted every possible avenue, but that was one I'd never considered. I sent letters to several dozen churches in the area."

"A *clever* little girl," Elise said. "A child of color, perhaps?"

"Yes, and very clever—truly gifted. From Harlem. She was spending two weeks with a neighborhood family."

"Yes," Elise said thoughtfully. "A black child would think of this. It is very fortunate, is it not?"

"Very," Lucinda agreed, as her grandmother selected a pink *petit four* that was so perfectly iced—decorated with a tiny red rose—that it looked like artwork rather than a small cake. At the sight of it, Lucinda suddenly remembered a Hollywood birthday party she'd attended at the age of three or four. There had been a vast trayful of too-tempting *petits fours* on the dining table that all the children had found irresistible. En masse, they'd made a run at the cakes and gobbled them down in quantity, grunting like small animals as they pushed the sweet confections into their mouths. Then, in the throes of a collective sugar high, the twelve or fifteen of them had gone rocketing around the house like little deranged escapees from some esoteric asylum. Half an hour later, Lucinda (who'd eaten only one cake) was sitting at the white lacquered grand piano, picking out a tune while the rest of the children were sprawled on the floor and furniture, mouths agape, crashed from their high. Their outrageously expensive party outfits were stained and starchless, their fingers were glued together in odd configurations by the thick icing, fluffy white crumbs rimmed their mouths, and their eyes gazed vacantly into space. Two or three were asleep, snoring loudly, and one little girl had gone potty in a soup tureen she'd stood on tiptoe to lift down from the sideboard.

The incensed mother of the birthday girl stood in the living room doorway, gazing in disgust at the limp-bodied, lethargic children, declaring, "Those were for the *adults*, you dismal little shits!" Then, while still within range of Lucinda's hearing, the woman had stated, "I need ten or twelve stiff drinks! What a goddamned fiasco! We won't get one inch of print from this. Total bloody waste of time and money."

Resisting the temptation of the delectable cakes, Lucinda now took one triangle sandwich and set it on her plate, knowing she'd be unable to eat it.

"Milk, sugar?" Gwyn asked her.

"Just milk, please."

The cook positioned the trolley within easy reach, then she and the assistant left the room.

Neither woman touched their teacups but sat in silence for a time, assessing each other and their personal reactions to the situation. Then, setting aside her plate, Elise said, "He and Lily were introduced at a party by one of Adam's friends. It was on a weekend when Adam was home on leave. He was a pilot. Did you know this?"

"Eddie, my mother's friend, thought he was."

"My son was mad for airplanes, always. *Mad* for them. He would have nothing but to be a pilot. And so he did it. If they had believed him to be an American man of color, it could never have happened. But he had a French passport—all of the children did—and his father used much influence. You understand?"

Lucinda nodded.

"Even so, there were things that happened during his training ... not nice things. Incidents of the sort that moved Anne to separate from the family and live only in the white world where she believed she could not be hurt in the way that her brother and sister were. It was Michael who returned her to us for awkward visits; he brought the children who were always sad when it came time to go home. But now that Michael is gone too soon—six years now—and her children are grown and continue to be very close with the family in a way they are not close with her, Anne has discovered she wishes to be a part of the family again. She is the one, I think, you will find not so agreeable. She has a mistrusting nature, I am sorry to say. The others, all, including Anne's children and grandchildren, are mad with excitement to meet you. You will like them. And they will like you. You are most ... sympathetic. Not precisely the same meaning as *sympathique* but you know the word, I think."

"Yes, I do. Thank you," Lucinda said quietly. "You are, too."

"Yes," Elise agreed. "It is true. I think we have many feelings, many behaviors in common. I had a strong sense of you when I saw how you came to the door—fearful but determined, like your father. He would not permit himself to be bothered by what he called casual cruelty. Nothing could be allowed to stand in the way of his dream to fly. When he brought Lily here for the first time, I saw at once why they had such an immediate bond as they did. Because to each, the career was *everything*. They loved their work first and each other second. It was an understanding they had. And it was very real. Not something pretended, as people will do sometimes, to get what they want. You know? No, this was completely real. I have never *seen* such a pair as these two. Truly. Both so very dedicated to their work, and yet loving each other so much. Quite remarkable. Very much the reverse of most couples, where for the man, it is the career first and love second; and for the woman, it is love first and career perhaps third, or fourth.

"Lily went to California and Adam was abroad during the war, but they would travel great distances to meet when they could, where they could. The war ended and Adam was safe; he didn't suffer injuries or die as so many of his friends did. He grieved at the loss of those men and felt guilt for a long time that he was undamaged. I have come to learn that it is not so uncommon to feel as he did. But at the time, we were concerned for him. Lily came hurrying to be with him in the house he bought—the house where you now live."

"You've known all along I was there?" This information landed like a blow to Lucinda's chest. Twenty-seven years of believing herself to be entirely orphaned when, only half an hour away, she'd had a large family who knew all about her.

"Ah, yes. Always."

They looked at each other for a time, and Lucinda had to marvel at just how effectively Lily had "protected" her. Yet her actions were, as they always had been, not only understandable, but forgivable. But still ... "Please go on," she said finally.

"It has been difficult for you," Elise said with understanding. "For us, also. To know you are there, but to be obliged to honor old promises. Many, *many* times I decided I must make contact with you. I would even ring for the driver to fetch the car. Then I would think of how Lily had made me vow never to do that. If you were to come to us, that would be permissible. But if you did not, we had to agree to remain unknown to you, to keep silent. We hoped and hoped that you would come. It did not happen, and with time you became almost—what is the word? A legend, perhaps. You were someone spoken of at family dinners when everyone gathered, as if you were not quite real. A fairy tale or a dream we shared from long ago. The children and grandchildren have grown up hearing about you."

"I wish I'd known. All this time ... "

"I feel as you do: that it has been a loss for everyone. But it is ended now. No more legend or fairy tale, but here you are, very real. You have found your way home. Now you will come to know everyone, and they will come to know you. May we agree to put aside our regrets and not lose more time in considering what might have been?"

Lucinda nodded. She had no alternative but to agree.

"Good. We may look to the past—I think it is often necessary to assist us in comprehending our lives—but we must remain in the present. It is for the best."

"Yes," Lucinda whispered, knowing it was the truth. Attempting to rethink the past in terms of what hadn't been done merely left one frustrated and dissatisfied, unable to take pleasure in anything that happened in the here and now.

"So," Elise picked up again, "they would have a week or two here or there; once they had several months together and we saw them often. It was a happy time. Lily was a great success; she had fame. Adam was a captain. And then, the great surprise. They were to have a baby." Elise paused and reached for her tea.

Lucinda waited respectfully, her brain starting to feel swollen from the intake of so much information.

"It was wonderful but very serious, too," Elise went on. "Many arrangements had to be made—entirely for you, because Lily feared what might come about, should people learn that her husband, the father of the child that was to be, was one quarter black. I am sure you see the implications. And she was truly more concerned for your future than she was for any possible negative effect on her career. She had accomplished what she set out to do—to become a film star—and she was not a selfish woman, as I am certain you know. She and Adam *wanted* you. But, above all, they wished you to be spared any pain because of your father's background. At that time, they were not wrong in their thinking.

Adam had many unpleasant experiences in his life, as did his father. Even when they were thought to be Arabic, or merely foreign. It was unavoidable. No matter where you go, there are always people of prejudice, people who have been taught to hate those who are different. Compared to what we had known in France, we found it more so here. And Adam was determined that his child, who would be only one-eighth black and perhaps pale like Lily, would never endure a moment's misery because of being different.

"So, much planning was done and William again used his influence; arrangements were made. There could be no documents that might be discovered by those who would search, no proof of the connection, of the marriage. Yet they were happy. Extraordinary!" Elise smiled over at Lucinda. "They were madly happy. They traveled separately to France and stayed together, hidden away, until you were born. I think it was a time of rare joy for them. They were together, far from people who would judge them, who would do them harm; living quietly and waiting for you to arrive. Lily said to me the last time I saw her—it was perhaps one year before she died—she said it was the happiest time of her life. And I know it was true. Because after Adam was killed, she was not the same, ever again. One could see it so clearly afterward. It was as if one came to enter a familiar room that had once been very bright, but someone had stolen in and secretly removed most of the lights. Lily never again had the radiance she'd had while Adam was alive."

"I was too young to be aware of it," Lucinda said quietly.

"Yes, I know this." The old woman looked off into space as if measuring the depth of the chasm that existed between herself and people she'd once loved who were gone forever; the cherished ones who lived on in the vast resource of her memory. "Everything is here," she said mysteriously.

"I beg your pardon?"

"All of the documents, photographs, *everything*. Lily wished for the family to have these things, for you, should you come to us; for us, too, so that we could know of you. If you did not come to us, arrangements were made a very long time ago that all of it would come to you ... in time. It is a part of my will."

Lucinda had to think about that for several moments, reaching for her tea and sipping some to ease her throat. Then, surprising herself and her grandmother, she smiled suddenly and said, "I might have had to wait for another twenty or thirty years."

Elise laughed—a delightful sound. "This is quite true," she said. "I have told you we do live to a great age in my family."

"Exactly. So it's a good thing Katanya pointed me in the right direction when she did."

"This Katanya is your child of color?"

"My child of color," Lucinda repeated, feeling a small shock of gratification at the notion of Katanya's being the child in her life. For a few seconds, thinking back to her visit to that tidy apartment on One hundred and Twenty-third Street, she was moved once again by the graciousness Loranne and Jeneva had shown in their willingness not only to acknowledge Katanya's feelings for Lucinda but also to bear no resentment toward her—as many other women might have done. "She's very special, and so is her family."

"Indeed," said Elise. "It would seem so. And I am grateful for her cleverness. Perhaps you will bring her sometime to visit? Her family, too, if they would care to come."

"I think we'd all like that very much."

"I will not eat," Elise said, looking at her plate on the table next to her chair. "We are alike in this, I see. Too much excitement and food is not possible."

Relieved, Lucinda set her plate aside, too. "You're right. I couldn't possibly eat anything right now. May I ask a question?"

"But of course. I think you will ask many, many questions. It is to be expected."

Lucinda smiled. "I have so many," she admitted, "that my mind is tripping all over itself. But I am curious about one thing in particular. It may seem peculiar, but I was wondering if anyone in the family suffers from headaches."

"Ah, no!" Elise exclaimed softly, her tone dismayed. "You have the migraines?" She pronounced it "me-grens." Lucinda liked that. It gave the word a less proprietary sound than "my-grains" which had always struck her as an inadequate name for the ugly reality of the condition. "I was told by my first neurologist in Los Angeles that they're hereditary. Since Lily never got them, I couldn't help wondering if they'd come from my father's family."

"Indeed!" Elise said. "My Adele must take to her bed, she becomes so ill. Also her children and grandchildren and one of the great-grandchildren. Guillaume and his mother both had the headaches, Adam, too. They are very terrible," she said sympathetically. "Even with medication, Adele suffers very much. She is too thin, like you. It is because of the migraines, as she cannot eat and if she tries, she loses the food. Not a pleasant legacy, I'm afraid."

"No," Lucinda agreed. "But now at least I know that it really is hereditary."

They sat gazing at each other for a time. Then Elise asked, "What is it that you do now? You have a career?"

"Not really. I've done Internet work for the past few years, just to have something to do." Somewhat ashamedly, she admitted, "Until Katanya came along a few weeks ago, I almost never left the house."

"And why is this?" the old woman asked with concern.

"I was afraid," Lucinda confessed, seeing nothing to be gained in misrepresenting herself. "I found that photograph of my father after Lily died and suddenly I no longer knew who or what I was. I felt as if I'd been playing a role that had been assigned to me, that I wasn't the person I'd believed myself to be. I wasn't white. I wasn't black. I didn't know who to be, or *how* to be. And slowly I became more and more afraid to leave the house, feeling perhaps that people might suddenly see that I wasn't one thing or the other, that I was a complete fraud."

"I feared perhaps this was the case," Elise said. "You were distressed to be considered black?"

"No, that didn't bother me. Not knowing the truth of who I was scared me; it paralyzed me."

"A terrible pity you were so sad."

Sad? Lucinda thought about that. She'd applied any number of adjectives to her condition but sad hadn't been one of them. But now it was so obvious. Of course she'd been sad. It was incredible how hearing someone put words to a situation or condition made it become clearer, more real. "I was beyond sad," she said. "But it's over now. It's very hard for me to take this in."

"For me, as well. You were my first grandchild, and such a good baby, a happy baby, not at all fearful of strangers as some infants can be."

"Really?"

"Oh, yes. We passed you all around, and you laughed and put your fingers in our noses and our mouths. You liked to chew on your grandfather's hand."

"I did?" Lucinda grinned.

"And you would pull on Anne's hair, which made her very cross. Of course, you pulled on everyone's hair, but Anne would take it personally. That is the sort of person she is: disagreeable, egocentric. Adele found it very amusing; she'd let you pull on her hair while she laughed and laughed. Which, naturally, made Anne even more cross."

These offered images of herself as a baby took Lucinda off guard. She loved hearing about herself as an amiable, hand-chewing, hair-pulling baby. She burst out laughing gleefully; then, without warning, the laughter turned to sobbing. Mortified, she pulled a tissue from her pocket and lowered her head as she wiped her face. But caught in the grip of emotions too long in the making and too large to contain, the sobs continued on, and all she could do was gulp them down, trying to regain control of herself.

After what felt like a very long time but was likely no more than a minute or two, she risked looking over at her grandmother to see that her lovely features were sorrowful.

"Later," Elise said softly, "when I am alone, I will go to my room and I, too, will weep. I know you are embarrassed, but there is no need. This is a momentous occasion, with much emotion. And I see that we are alike in this regard, also. I very much dislike revealing myself in moments of weakness."

"It makes me feel stupid," Lucinda confided, managing a shaky smile.

"I feel the same," Elise said. "Sometimes, though, it is not such a good thing to have too much control of the emotions, to be intellectual rather than emotional. Others mistake it for coldness. My Anne, for one, has always accused me of being cold. To her mind, I am responsible for her many deficits of character."

"But you're not at all cold," Lucinda declared.

"No," Elise agreed. "I am like you, with much hidden, and with too much heart. We display our intelligence, we think our way through situations, to protect ourselves."

"Yes! That's it exactly," Lucinda said, her embarrassment dissolving in the face of this mutual understanding.

"You have the qualities of both your parents, and of your grandparents, as well. I see it more and more clearly. Anne, however, is a woman approaching old age who wishes to blame others, always, for her own failings. It is tiresome. I have always believed that once one is past childhood, one must take responsibility for one's own actions. To blame others is to show true weakness. And while I love my daughter, I am not able to like her. I have grown weary of her refusal to become an adult. She is"—Elise offered a wicked little smile—"a large, wrinkled *child*."

At this, both women laughed. Then Lucinda said, "She doesn't sound like someone who ever has any fun."

"She has no humor. People without humor make life tedious. Adele, now, has great humor. And I admire her very much, for if she is moved, she will weep without shame. I think it is a great gift, to be able to reveal one's self in that way."

"I think so, too. Lily was like that, even with all the secrets she kept. She let everything show, in private, that is."

"Lily was, always, very close to my heart—like my own child. I loved her deeply. She had goodness. I think in her occupation that is a rare quality."

"Very," Lucinda confirmed. "Most of the people we knew in California were like Anne—as you've described her."

"Most unpleasant. Have you friends, Lucinda?"

"I have one very close friend. Do you like movies? If you do, you may know who she is."

"I adore films. I am always sending Gwyn to rent videos, or I get her to take me to see an early film, when the theaters are not so crowded and no one will sit nearby and distract me with their talking. Who is your friend?"

"Gin Holder."

"Ah, yes. I know of her. Lily adored her. And I like very much her films. She is bold. That is also something I admire."

"She's very bold, and very fragile, too. Enormously talented."

"You also are enormously talented," Elise said. "I have seen the films you wrote. You no longer write?"

Lucinda shook her head, then said, "Not for many years. But I've just agreed to write one for Gin."

"Ah! This is wonderful! You will work together again, as you did when you were young?"

"Yes. She's even talking about moving east."

"That will make you very happy, yes?"

"Yes, very." Lucinda was silent for a time, aware of a layer of happiness beginning to blanket all the old sorrows. "Finding *you* is making me very happy."

"And me, as well," Elise said. "I thought that you might not find us in time." Smiling sweetly now, she said, "But you did. You *did*. And you will come again, often now, won't you? You will take up your place in the family, will you not?"

"Yes, absolutely," Lucinda promised. "I will. I will."

The sun had gone down but it wasn't yet dark. The heavy mid-August air was lifted by an intermittent breeze that made it comfortable on the porch. Soupboy had fallen asleep in Katanya's lap and she sat in one of the wicker chairs with one arm cradling his head, absently stroking his hair. Renee and Loranne were sitting on the settee, talking quietly. And Lucinda and Jeneva had pulled their chairs forward so they could prop their feet on the porch railing. A CD of the greatest hits of the fifties was playing quietly on the little Sony boombox Lucinda had bought online for Kat. Ben E. King was halfway through "Stand By Me," and Jeneva was humming along. In a few minutes, they'd all go inside to eat the massive meal Jeneva and Loranne had prepared earlier. But for the moment, as the darkness came on, they were content to remain where they were.

"I wish you weren't leaving tomorrow," Lucinda said softly, in a state of ongoing wonder at how much had happened in just over a month.

"I wish we weren't, too," Jeneva replied. "But it's not as if we're never coming back, is it?"

Lucinda turned and smiled at her friend. "No," she said. "It most certainly isn't."

About the Author

New York Times bestselling author Charlotte Vale Allen worked (among other things) as a sales person, a waitress, a secretary, an insurance broker, and as an actress and singer before turning to writing full-time with the publication of her first novel *Love Life* in 1976. Born in Toronto, Canada, Allen moved to the U.S. in 1966 and has lived in Connecticut since 1970. Her award-winning autobiography (and only non-fiction work) *Daddy's Girl* is in its third edition, after more than 30 printings. *Fresh Air* is her 37th novel. She is currently at work on a sequel to *Fresh Air*.

Please visit the author's website at:
www.charlottevaleallen.com

TELL THE AUTHOR

Dear Charlotte Vale Allen,
I just finished reading Fresh Air *and wanted to tell you what I*
thought of the book.

Sincerely,

*name*_____

*address*_____

city, state, zip
*code*_____

(*please print*)

If you are reading a library book, please copy this page and leave it for the next reader.

Charlotte Vale Allen
c/o INP
144 Rowayton Woods Drive
Norwalk, CT 06854
U.S.A.

TELL A FRIEND

Dear_____ ,

I just finished reading Fresh Air by Charlotte Vale Allen and wanted to tell you about it because I think it's a book you'll enjoy.

Sincerely,

_____

Fresh Air is published by MIRA Books
If your local bookstore or library doesn't have it, please ask them to order it for you.